MONUMENT HILL

We almost made it. Snow was still coming down hard when we reached the infamous Monument Hill, and I'd picked up another eighteen-wheeler behind me. I refused to believe it was the same rig that had followed us from Trinidad. Stop it, I scolded myself. Why do you always have to be so melodramatic?

Rosalie didn't seem to have any qualms about being melodramatic. "It's the same truck," she said, her voice rising in pitch. "We should have called the police."

The truck behind me was going faster than I was, and I prayed I'd get over the top before he ran us down. I tried to make the Hyundai move, but it had a mind of its own and very little traction. The truck kept right on coming. I put my foot down on the accelerator and gunned the engine. Big mistake. The car spun out toward the side of the road.

"Hold on," I said as calmly as I could. "We're going over the side. . . ."

Dell Books by Dolores Johnson

TAKEN TO THE CLEANERS
HUNG UP TO DIE
A DRESS TO DIE FOR
WASH, FOLD, AND DIE

WASH, FOLD, AND DIE

A Mandy Dyer Mystery

DOLORES JOHNSON

A DELL BOOK

Published by
Dell Publishing
a division of
Random House, Inc.
1540 Broadway
New York, New York 10036

ISBN: 0-440-23523-5

Printed in the United States of America

Published simultaneously in Canada

October 1999

10 9 8 7 6 5 4 3 2 1

OPM

In memory of my parents,
Egbert and Edna Dyer,
for whom I gave Mandy the family name

ACKNOWLEDGMENTS

I wish to thank Michelle D. Weiss-Samaras, chief deputy coroner, Office of the Medical Examiner for the city and county of Denver; Marc A. Chandler, personal banker, Norwest Banks, Buckingham Square branch, Aurora, Colorado; and Rahhmid Alahhdin, plant manager, Independent Cleaners and Laundry, Aurora, Colorado, for answering my questions in their various fields of expertise. Any errors in this book are mine and not the fault of the people mentioned above.

Thanks also to Joe and Kaye Cannata of Belaire Cleaners, Denver, for reading part of this book; to William Parenteau, retired Denver dry cleaner, for letting me use one of his old business slogans; and to Virginia Murphy for our memories of growing up together in Bend, Oregon.

A special thanks for their help to members of my two critique groups—Lee Karr, Kay Bergstrom, Carol Caverly, Diane Davidson, Christine Jorgensen, Leslie O'Kane, and Peggy Swager; and to Rebecca Bates, Thora Chinnery, Diane Coffelt, Cindy Goff, Donna Schaper, and Barbara Snook. And finally, a debt of gratitude to my agent, Ruth Kagle, and to Dell's editorial director, Maggie Crawford.

CHAPTER 1

Who would think the police would come to me, Mandy Dyer, a dry cleaner, for help in a murder investigation? And even if they did, who would think the person seeking my help would be my onetime boyfriend, Detective Stan Foster?

I looked up from the counter of Dyer's Cleaners one Monday morning in March as I was shoving clothes in a laundry bag, and there he was. Still tall, blond, and handsome but looking decidedly ill at ease. No wonder. We'd dated for a while last year, but I hadn't seen him since June.

My first thought was that he'd come to tell me he still lusted for me. After all, he wasn't carrying any clothes, and I knew he didn't have a dry-cleaning order on our conveyor. So what else could he want? To my credit, I had the good sense not to blurt out anything about my overly optimistic hopes for why he was here.

"Hi, Stan," I said. "What can I do for you?" I hoped he couldn't see my heart pounding through the yellow blouse I'd recently adopted as part of the uniform for our counter personnel.

He cleared his throat, then motioned over to the end of the counter. "I was wondering if I could talk to you for a minute."

I made a quick analysis of the situation. If he was here to talk about us getting back together, wouldn't he have wanted to hold the conversation in the privacy of my office?

"What do you want—a dry-cleaning tip?" That sounded more sarcastic than I intended, but after all, hadn't I given him a tip on how to get ink out of his shirt pockets the first time we'd met?

"No, it's nothing like that," he said. "I'm here for your professional help."

So what did he think my hints about stain removal had been? I brushed a strand of dark hair back from my forehead but resisted the impulse to smooth back the sides. It would seem too much like primping, and I'd be damned if I'd do that.

"We need some help on a homicide," he continued.

Until now my help in police matters had been totally unsolicited, and where Stan was concerned, unappreciated. In fact one of the reasons we'd decided to break up was that Stan thought I spent entirely too much time sticking my nose into things that were none of my business. He said he couldn't deal with me putting myself in danger all the time. That's a switch, huh? The homicide detective worrying about a dry cleaner who leads too dangerous a life. But Stan's former fiancée had been a police officer who was killed in the line of duty, and apparently Stan still had a lot of guilt about it. Until he resolved those feelings, I didn't think we'd have much of a future together whether I got in trouble or not.

"The police need my help?" I asked, my voice filled with disbelief.

He nodded.

"Really, *you* need *my* help?" I was beginning to sound cocky about the situation, so I tried for a more mature attitude. "Sure, anything I can do, just ask me."

And it wasn't as far-fetched as it sounds. After all, my uncle had once been called to testify at the trial of an air force lieutenant charged with the murder of a fellow officer. A button off a uniform had been found at the scene of the crime, and Uncle Chet's testimony about replacing a missing button on the suspect's uniform helped convict the man.

That was back when Uncle Chet owned a wholesale shirt laundry as an adjunct to his first dry cleaners—long before he built this new dry-cleaning plant near Cherry Creek Shopping Center here in Denver. I'd inherited the new cleaners when Uncle Chet died, but until now the police had never voluntarily come to me for help of any kind.

Stan took a small notebook out of the pocket of his tweed jacket. "I'm looking for information about a laundry mark we found on the shirt of a man who was killed over the weekend."

Stan had come to the right place, and I felt flattered. I knew all about laundry marks. Currently we used a tag in the collar with a corresponding numbered tag we put on the ticket. Other dry cleaners used different methods, including permanent laundry marks and even bar codes, as a means of identifying and reassembling the shirts of their customers.

"I talked to a couple of other cleaners," Stan said, "and one of them thought the mark looked like something your uncle used at a shirt laundry he had years ago."

Okay, so I hadn't been Stan's first choice when it came to seeking expert advice. He'd already sought help from other cleaners. I tried to swallow my pride as I waited for him to continue.

He consulted his notebook again. "There's a piece of cloth made of some washable fabric that was stuck inside the collar. It had some numbers on it."

I nodded. "That would be a tape with an adhesive backing that adheres to the shirt during washing, but I'm afraid it won't tell you who the owner is."

Stan didn't seem to appreciate my negative attitude. "Anyway, there was also a laundry mark on the tail of the shirt."

"We don't use laundry marks like that, anymore, but I suppose it could be one of the shirts from my uncle's shirt laundry," I admitted. "But isn't that a little weird that the shirt would show up after all this time? Uncle Chet sold the shirt laundry five years ago when he was raising money to build this new plant."

Stan frowned, and I could see he was losing patience with my editorial comments. "If you don't mind . . ."

"All right." I threw up my hands to indicate I was ready to dispense with the speculations. "Uncle Chet was a fanatic about keeping track of the shirts, so he used a stamping machine to put the first few letters of the customer's last name or else the first letter and the last four digits of his phone number on the tail of each shirt."

Stan studied whatever was written in his notebook, but he didn't yet seem willing to share the information with me.

"Was there a number at the end of the laundry mark?" I continued. "Uncle Chet did shirts on a wholesale basis for a number of other cleaners as well as for his own store, and he always assigned a number to each customer."

"There's an *A*, followed by the numbers zero-five-eight-six-one," Stan said finally.

I didn't have to consult any long-forgotten records to know what that final number represented. Uncle Chet had always used a "1" for work he did for his own plant, Dyer's Cleaners and Dyers, which had originally been in downtown Denver.

I wasn't sure if this revelation was good or bad. On the one hand, there was the possibility that the murder victim was someone I had known. On the other hand, it meant I would have an opportunity to talk to Stan again.

"That would have been one of our customers," I said, "but I'm afraid all the shirt-laundry records are in a storage locker out on Leetsdale Drive. It's going to take me a while to find the name of the person who went with the laundry mark."

Stan motioned toward our computer. "Can't you look in there?"

"That'll take a while too, but I doubt if it's there. Most of our customer base is new since we moved here to Cherry Creek."

Stan gave me one of his lopsided smiles. He probably thought I couldn't resist it. "Do you think you could get away for a while this morning to check on it? I'd be glad to take you over to the locker and help you look for the information."

I hesitated while I tried to decide whether I wanted to cooperate or make him wait. "Okay," I said finally, "I guess I could spare the time if the police really *need* me."

What I needed was to quit gloating about this unusual turn of events and do my civic duty. Besides, maybe I could seduce him while we were closed up together inside the storage locker and then he would forget all about our many problems. Problems or not, Stan still exuded an amazing amount of sex appeal for me.

I found myself wishing I hadn't switched all the counter

people, myself included, to uniforms—brown skirts or slacks and yellow cotton-blend blouses with our names and the Dyer's Cleaners' logo embroidered on the pocket. I needed a crushed-silk blouse that clung to my body and emphasized the five pounds I'd lost by swimming every few days in lieu of a social life since Stan and I quit dating. Eat your heart out, Stan.

I went back to my office and grabbed my purse so that I'd have keys to the storage locker. I took a detour to the rest room and glanced at myself in the mirror. I wished I'd taken more care with my makeup this morning, but there wasn't time for that now. I ran a comb through my hair, reapplied my lipstick, and joined Stan in his car.

"So how have you been, Stan?" I asked as I hooked myself into the seat belt. I figured he wouldn't tell me if he'd found another girlfriend—perhaps a librarian with a less exciting life than mine—so I didn't even try.

"Fine," he said, "and you?"

"Great. Just great."

I toyed with the idea of telling him about my exciting life since I'd seen him last. Maybe make up a story about how I'd gone to South Dakota on the back of my buddy Nat's Harley for the big motorcycle rally in Sturgis. I decided against it because Stan wasn't that fond of Nat, a police reporter, and besides, he would know I was lying. I tended to itch when I fibbed, and it hadn't taken him long to catch on to this unfortunate habit of mine.

"You're looking good," he said.

"You too."

After this sparkling bit of repartee, an uneasy silence settled inside the car, and I couldn't stand it. I considered discussing the weather since it was a beautiful March day, but that seemed worse than no conversation at all. If he wouldn't talk about personal things, then I had no choice but to inquire about the case. "What makes you think the body you found is the man who owned the shirt?"

Stan shrugged as he pulled out on First Avenue. "I don't know that it is, but it's the only thing we have to go on. There was no ID on the victim."

I gave him the address of the storage locker and then fidgeted in my seat. "So what happened to him?"

"He was shot Friday night in a downtown alley." Stan gave the location, but I couldn't picture it.

I did remember seeing a brief article by Nat in the Sunday paper. Nat had said the police received an anonymous phone call late Friday night, and when officers responded, they found a man with a bullet wound in the chest and no ID on the body. "Maybe he was a homeless person who found the shirt at a Goodwill store or something," I said.

"Probably, but he was wearing an expensive-looking suit for a street person."

"What kind of suit?"

Stan frowned at me. "I appreciate your help on this, Mandy, but I don't want you to start analyzing clothes again."

I ignored him. "Was the suit new?"

"It wasn't shiny from being worn too much, if that's what you mean. The jacket had a couple of slits in the back."

"Aha," I said. "That means the suit wasn't a recent purchase. Manufacturers don't use double vents anymore."

Stan fell silent, and I couldn't tell if he was irritated or awestruck by what I personally thought was a brilliant bit of deduction considering the fact that he'd given me so little material to go on. He drove down Cherry Creek North, across Colorado Boulevard, and took Leetsdale, which cuts southeast to a little enclave called Glendale that's squeezed in between Denver and suburban Aurora. All without saying anything.

In desperation I tried the subject of the weather, which I'd discarded earlier. "Some of the trees look as if they're almost ready to leaf out. Maybe it's going to be an early spring." I motioned to a few cottonwoods, but unfortunately they looked as if no one had told them about it.

Stan nodded but didn't offer an opinion. The silence lengthened, and I decided to wait him out and see if he might yet confess his love for me. Wasn't that a trick the police used to get a suspect to admit his guilt? And for a minute I thought it was going to work.

"Uh . . ." he said, giving me a sidelong glance before looking back at the road. "I was wondering if maybe . . ." A car pulled out in the road ahead of us, and Stan had to slam on his brakes to keep from hitting it.

"What?" I asked. "You were wondering if maybe— what?"

He shook his head, either at the other driver or because he'd thought better of what he was going to say. "Nothing. It can wait till later."

Okay, if that's the way he wanted to be about it. "The storage place is just a few blocks from here." I pointed to a street sign up ahead and told him to turn right at the corner. Then I went back to the subject of the clothes. "Was the laundry mark faded as if the shirt had been laundered a number of times?"

Stan pulled into the driveway of the storage company, and I directed him to the locker that held a lot of our old records from before we got computerized.

Apparently, he'd decided it couldn't do any harm to tell me one thing that puzzled him. "No," he said, "the mark wasn't faded. And the strange part about the shirt was that it had creases in it, as if the victim had just taken it out of a box and put it on."

That didn't sound like a homeless man's shirt. Even if he'd just acquired it at a thrift shop or been given the shirt at a shelter, it probably would have been stored on a hanger or been in a pile of clothes. I didn't share this information with Stan because he was already out of the car.

If he wasn't going to wait for me, I had no alternative but to save my professional opinion for later when I had him trapped inside the locker. I climbed out of the car, unlocked the storage locker, and rolled up its garage-type door.

"See what I mean?" I motioned to the stacks of cardboard boxes. "This is going to take a while."

Actually it didn't take as long as I expected. Stan took off his jacket, rolled up his sleeves, and started moving boxes around as if it were no effort at all. It was a joy to see his muscles ripple under his shirt, but as long as it wasn't going to lead to anything, who needed it?

"Here's a box marked shirt laundry," he said.

Good, it would give me something to do other than fantasizing about what could have been. I really didn't want to get hung up on him again. I'd spent enough time while we were dating wondering why he always drew back from any real intimacy. That's when he'd told me about his fiancée who had died.

I moved over beside him and began to open the shirt-laundry boxes as he located them. By the time I was half-way through them, I was covered with dirt and grime. Instead of wishing that I'd worn a sexy blouse, I began to regret that I hadn't changed into an old pair of jeans and a sweatshirt. That way I could have sat cross-legged on the floor instead of being forced to get down on my knees in what had to be the most uncomfortable position known to womankind.

I wiped my hands on my skirt and rubbed my palm across the end of my itchy nose. This wasn't because of any lies; it was because of all the dust.

"I think I found it," I said, and began to sneeze, not once or twice but half a dozen times.

"Gesundheit," Stan said, and he finally grinned. "If I didn't know better, I'd think you'd just told a fib and were having a guilt attack."

I gave him a dirty look and brushed back my hair, probably leaving a trail of dirt across my forehead. "Here it is." I pulled out a folder and ran my finger down the list of our shirt customers from five years ago. I didn't find anyone whose name started with A and had the right four-digit phone number until I went back several more years. I ran my finger down the list of phone numbers. There it was— 0586. It had been crossed out, and I ran my finger across the paper to the name that went with it. That's when I launched myself up from the floor, the folder clasped to my chest. I couldn't believe it.

"What's the matter?" Stan was watching me with concern. "Does the laundry mark belong to someone you know?"

I threw the folder into the box as if it were a red-hot iron that had just burned my hands.

Stan came over to me and grabbed my arm. "Who is it—a friend of yours?"

"The name is Jeremiah Atkins." My voice was shaking, and I wasn't about to add that he'd been a struggling artist and that I'd had a gigantic crush on him when I was a teenager. After all, I'd wanted to be an artist myself, and I used to dream that he would fall madly in love with me on one of his trips to the cleaners and decide to leave his wife.

Then the two of us would fly away to Paris, where, after a brief poverty-stricken time in a garret, we'd find fame and fortune and become the darlings of the Left Bank art world.

"Are you all right?" Stan asked. "You look like you've seen a ghost."

"It—it's just that he's dead."

Stan put his arm around my shoulders. "But we don't know that for sure. Maybe it's someone else."

I drew back from Stan. "No, you don't understand. It can't be Jeremiah Atkins because he's *already* dead."

Stan was trying hard to comprehend. "Then you're probably right," he said. "It has to be someone else in the shirt. Some street person must have found it at Goodwill and was wearing it the night he was shot."

"No, that's not it either." I grabbed the folder from the box and found the correct page again. I ran my finger down to Jeremiah's name. Yep, he had always wanted his shirts folded and boxed. "It *could* be Jeremiah," I said. "He disappeared seven years ago, but they never found his body. He wasn't declared legally dead until a few months ago."

CHAPTER 2

Stan was suddenly the cool, professional homicide detective, and he gave me a suspicious look. "How do you know all this—I mean about him being declared legally dead?"

"His wife, Rosalie—I guess you'd call her his widow now—told me. She's still one of our customers."

No need to get into the surprising things customers share with their dry cleaners. Uncle Chet used to say that, next to a doctor, a dry cleaner knows his customers better than almost anyone. And I guess the customers figure that as long as we clean their dirty clothes, they might as well share their dirty laundry with us too.

"Okay," Stan said, "you can give me Rosalie Atkins's address when we get back to the store." He grabbed one of the boxes and started to put it back where it had been stacked. "This shouldn't take long."

"Don't bother. I need to get out here sometime and clean the place up." I put the folder back in the box where it had been stored all these years, glad now that I hadn't destroyed the old records.

"So tell me what you know about Atkins," Stan said once we were back in his car.

"Like I said, he disappeared seven years ago. They found his car at their cabin up in the mountains, but that was it. At the time, his wife said she thought he'd been on his way to the funeral of a relative, and she didn't know why he'd gone to the cabin." I'd wondered if he'd been depressed, partially about his work as a painter and sculptor, and I'd secretly blamed Rosalie for not understanding the fragile personality of the true *artiste*. "Anyway the search teams never found his body, so this year his wife went to court to have him declared legally dead."

"Did anyone ever suspect the wife of killing her husband?" he asked.

"I think they probably did."

Well, at least I had. I wasn't about to volunteer that to Stan because, as I'd come to realize later, Jeremiah was not the sweet, sensitive man I'd first thought. In fact he was a real scoundrel, but his widow could tell Stan about him better than I could.

"Why did an artist bring his shirts to the cleaners anyway?" Stan asked. "I'd have thought he'd have worn paint-covered jeans and sandals."

I glared over at him. "I consider myself an artist, and I don't wear paint-covered jeans except at home."

Stan looked satisfyingly chastened. "I'm sorry."

I grinned at him despite myself. "Besides, Jeremiah was a real estate agent part-time—except I think he was pretty bad at it, according to what his wife said. She was the real breadwinner in the family."

Stan looked over at me. "So what does she do?"

"She's a draftsman—or maybe it's a draftsperson now—at an architectural firm downtown. She wanted to be an architect but gave up her studies so that he could pursue his art."

"How do you find out these things?"

"Simple," I said. "I'm a good listener." Of course that only applied to people who were willing to let me help them with their problems, and apparently Stan still wasn't one of those.

He pulled into the parking lot at the side of the cleaners, parked the car, and came inside with me. I looked up Rosalie's name in the computer and gave him her addresses and phone numbers, both at home and at work.

"By the way," I said, "Jeremiah always wore shirts with French cuffs, if that's any help."

"Do you keep that kind of stuff in your computer?" Stan asked, still puzzled by my encyclopedic memory.

"No, I just remember." When I was a teenager, I'd thought it was cosmopolitan and exciting of Jeremiah to wear shirts with French cuffs.

Stan didn't seem convinced that an artist could afford shirts with French cuffs. "I thought you said his wife supported him."

"She did, but ask her about it." I wanted Stan to realize that I was staying completely out of this.

"Okay, and thanks, Mandy." He started to leave.

"Stan . . ." I motioned him back to the counter. "In the car on the way to the storage locker, you started to say something. Then you said we'd talk about it later. What was it?"

He looked around at Theresa, my front-counter manager, who was waiting on a customer nearby. "It wasn't important." He seemed awfully uncomfortable for it not to have been important, but I let it go.

At the moment I needed to think about poor Rosalie. I wondered if I should call her, but that was the very kind of thing that Stan objected to—my sticking my nose in where it didn't belong.

Instead I went looking for McKenzie Rivers, my plant manager. Everyone calls him Mack, and despite the fact that he's black and I'm white, he's always been kind of like a father to me, not to mention that he's my sounding board when things are bothering me. He'd worked for my uncle for years, and when I'd inherited the cleaners, he'd not only helped me get through Uncle Chet's death but persuaded me that I could run the business as well.

"Got time for a cup of coffee?" I asked when I wended my way through the finishing equipment and freshly pressed clothes to the dry-cleaning machines, which were Mack's domain.

"Sure." He put his steam gun down on the spotting board and followed me to the break room. "What's up?"

I poured two cups of coffee and brought them to the table. "The strangest thing happened today. Remember Jeremiah Atkins?"

"The guy who painted the sets for some of our plays?" Mack asked.

I nodded because I knew Mack would remember that. In addition to being the best dry cleaner in the state, Mack was a part-time actor in amateur theatrical productions around Denver.

Obviously Mack also remembered Jeremiah's disappearance. "Don't tell me his body has finally turned up after all these years?"

"Maybe. Someone wearing his shirt was found dead in an alley downtown the other night."

"No kidding." Mack's deep voice echoed through the empty break room as if he were playing to an auditorium full of theatergoers.

I told him the whole story about Stan showing up and

asking for information about a laundry mark from Uncle Chet's old shirt laundry. Mack didn't even stop to ask me about Stan; he knew it was a sore spot with me.

"So we went to the storage locker, and when I found the list of our shirt customers, the laundry mark belonged to Jeremiah Atkins. Can you believe it?"

Mack shrugged. "You said the body was found in an alley downtown. You mean a construction crew was doing an excavation and found it?"

"No, that's the weird part. The police found this man who had just been shot, and he didn't have any ID on him except for the laundry mark on his shirt? Do you think it could really be Jeremiah after all these years?"

Mack ran his hands through his salt-and-pepper hair, which was getting to be a lot more salt than pepper these days. "Damned if I know. Where exactly was the body?"

"Stan said it was in an alley right downtown." Unfortunately I added the cross-streets to pinpoint the location.

"I know that alley." The voice came from behind me, and Mack and I both jumped.

It was Betty, a bag lady whom I was hopefully in the process of rehabilitating. I'd given her a job in our laundry back in June—not without a lot of protest from Mack, I might add. But actually she was working out better than anyone could have expected. Even Mack said so—all except for her habit of sneaking up on people. It was apparently a practice she'd found useful in her former life on the streets. However, back then she'd had a squeaky shopping cart that announced her arrival at our back door for handouts despite her stealthy approach.

"You have to quit sneaking up on people," I said.

"I wasn't sneaking up on nobody. I was just getting myself a drink out of the pop machine."

"Okay, go ahead. I'm sorry."

She fumbled in the pocket of her brown polyester pants suit, as if hoping I'd get tired of watching her and give her the money for a soda just to get rid of her.

I didn't offer and finally she came up with the change. Once she collected a can of lemon-lime, she popped the tab on top and sat down at the table between Mack and me. "I heard what you said about the cops finding a body in that alley downtown."

"I know you did," I said, remembering how she'd once told me that I had a bad habit of finding bodies. "But please don't say anything to anyone else and don't worry about it. I'm not going to get involved in another murder investigation."

She moved the can across her forehead just below her close-cropped gray hair, apparently to cool herself off. "I'm not worried," she said. "I just think it's interesting."

I started to get up from the table. "I guess I'd better go back to work."

Mack took a final sip of coffee before joining me.

"You know, I bet Honest Abe mighta seen the killer," Betty said.

Mack almost choked on his coffee. Never totally convinced of Betty's mental stability, I suppose he thought that she'd finally gone around the bend.

I sat back down, deciding to do a little reality check on her. "You're not talking about Honest Abe, the president, are you?"

" 'Course not. I'm talking about Honest Abe, a guy I knew when I was on the streets. Most folks called him Harpo for short."

I wasn't even going to touch that. "So why do you think he might have seen the man get shot in the alley?"

"That was Honest Abe's alley. He always slept there at night."

I started to get up again, now that I'd cleared up the sanity issue.

"Maybe Artie and I could go down and talk to him about it."

I dropped into the chair again. "No, don't you dare take Arthur downtown looking for this—this Honest Abe."

Arthur was a sweet old fellow who ran a doll-repair business in southeast Denver, and against all odds, he'd become smitten with Betty last summer, and they'd been keeping company ever since. I tried not to inquire about the relationship too much because I thought it was doomed for failure, and it was all my fault. I'd introduced them to each other in a failed attempt to hook him up with someone far more suitable for him.

Betty shrugged at my order to keep poor Arthur out of this. "Okay, then you can go with me."

I could already see Mack shaking his head. He was very conservative about such things, even though he'd once dressed up as a homeless person himself to help me find Betty when she was in danger.

"No," I said firmly. "I'll tell the police about this—uh— Honest Abe, and they can handle it."

Betty took a swig of her lemon-lime drink and shook her head. "He won't talk to them. He won't talk to hardly nobody. Why the heck do you think folks call him Harpo?"

I wasn't about to play games with Betty. Hell, I didn't even care why they called him Honest Abe.

Betty laughed, a cackle that was almost as loud as Mack's deep voice. "Knew I'd get you on that one."

Mack took a shot. "Because he's like Harpo, the Marx brother who never talked."

Betty looked pleased, her faith in the intellectual prowess of at least one of us confirmed.

"You got it, Mack," Betty said. "We figure that's where he got the name Honest Abe. You can't lie if you don't talk."

I wondered if that would work for me. If I didn't talk so much, I wouldn't be forced into falsehoods and then maybe my nose wouldn't itch so much. "So how do you propose that you could get anything out of Honest Abe?"

"Most folks thinks he's a deaf mute who don't know nothin', but him and me used to talk all the time. You'd be surprised what you can find out from a person who shakes his head."

Tempting as it was to accompany Betty to the alleys of downtown Denver and have a stimulating conversation with a head-shaker, I nixed the idea. "It's out of the question, Betty. The police will have to handle this."

"Suit yourself." Betty finished off her pop and announced that she was going back to the laundry to get a load of shirts out of one of our washing machines.

I wasn't completely convinced that she would heed my advice to stay away from Honest Abe, but I couldn't be responsible for her—any more than Mack could be for me.

"Don't even think about it," Mack said as he started to head back to the cleaning department.

And why should I think about it? Logic said that this newly dead body couldn't be Jeremiah Atkins. After all, he'd died seven years ago.

For all I knew, the victim in the alley could be poor Honest Abe himself, all spiffed up in a new set of clothes and unable to yell out for help when he was shot.

CHAPTER 3

I went to my office, but instead of working on the weekly reports or returning phone calls, I couldn't help thinking of poor Rosalie. What if the shooting victim really was Jeremiah? How would it affect her? Would it reopen all the old wounds? When she'd told me, about six weeks ago, that her husband was finally *legally* dead, she'd said she could at last get on with the rest of her life. She finally had some sort of closure.

I'd become acquainted with Rosalie two years earlier when she'd come into the call office, which is what we call the customer area of the cleaners, and asked if we could have lunch together sometime. We wound up going over to Tico Taco's, a Mexican restaurant nearby, that same day.

Rosalie is probably about ten years older than I am—maybe in her early forties. Her skin had the tanned look of a person who spent a lot of time outdoors. There were a few wrinkles around her eyes, but she was still attractive in an athletic sort of way with freckles sprinkled across her nose like cinnamon. Still, she had never seemed like the type of woman Jeremiah would have chosen for his partner. The sensitive aesthete and the woman with a yen for the mountains. I say that because, as I learned later, she spent most of her weekends outside, either skiing in the winter or hiking in the summer.

But the reason for Rosalie's sudden urge to have lunch puzzled me. Surely not to confess to the murder of her husband—even though I'd always harbored that as a possibility. Either that or he'd fled to Paris and forgotten to take me along.

"I'm getting ready to move to a new place," she'd said after Manuel, the owner and host of Tico Taco's, had taken our orders. "And I was wondering if you'd like to have Jeremiah's old art supplies."

I was surprised she would offer them to me. "How'd you even know I was an artist?" I thought maybe Jeremiah had told her.

"Your uncle used to brag about you," Rosalie said. "He said you'd painted the mural and those landscapes in the cleaners. They're very good."

"Thanks." I was pleased, especially that Uncle Chet had thought enough of my artwork to tell his customers about it.

The mural was a history of fashion from the early 1900s to the present that Uncle Chet had "commissioned" me to do. The paintings were of golden wheat fields out in eastern Colorado with the jagged outlines of the Rockies in the background. They went with the "yellow" sunshine decor of the call office.

"Jeremiah had a lot of canvases, brushes, oil paints, and acrylics, not to mention sculpting supplies," Rosalie said. "Some of the paints may have dried up, but a lot of the tubes have never even been opened. So would you like them?"

"Well, sure, I guess. How much do you think they're worth? I'd be glad to pay you for them."

Rosalie shook her head, which made a length of her short brown hair fall across her face. "No, I don't want money for them." She tossed the stray hair back with a careless jerk of her head. "I just want them out of my sight."

"But art supplies are very expensive," I protested.

"Tell me about it," she said. "I had a small inheritance when Jeremiah and I got married—enough, I thought, for him to work at his art and for me to finish college, but poof, it evaporated into thin air—just the way Jeremiah did. Anyway, that's the same thing he always told me: 'Art supplies are very expensive.'" She gave the quote a sarcastic inflection, then shrugged. "But so were his tastes for everything in life, including women."

I didn't know what to say, but it kind of proves my point about what customers will tell their dry cleaners. I wasn't sure if I wanted to have my bubble burst about the object of my teenage crush.

"He had a wandering eye," Rosalie continued, and of course I knew she wasn't referring to a problem with a lazy retina, because Jeremiah's eyes had been a dark brown under a thatch of black wavy hair, and they'd seemed to have a way of boring directly into your soul while carefully masking his own. He also had the most perfect profile I'd ever seen, but apparently that was the only thing that was perfect about him.

Rosalie went on to tell me about the time she'd come home and found him in bed with one of his models. "And wasn't that convenient? She didn't even have to get undressed because of course she was one of the nude models he always used so that he could sculpt the beauty of the female form." Her round, freckled face contorted in anger for a moment. "Still, I kept supporting the jerk and taking him back because I really thought he was a genius. I must have been nuts."

Who knows, maybe she still was? But I decided to give her the benefit of the doubt. After all, I'd been a little crazy myself when my ex-husband, Larry Landry, dumped me. "I—I thought Jeremiah sold real estate to support his art," I said, hoping to get her off the memories of his love affairs.

"Ha," she said. "What he made in real estate wouldn't have paid for his canvases for a year."

It was what she said later that really swung me over to her side. "I wanted to be an architect, but I dropped out of school because I believed in him."

Did this part remind me of someone? Darned right it did. I'd worked in a variety of office jobs, as well as holding down a second job at the cleaners, to get my ex-husband through law school, and then Larry the Lustful Law Student, as I called him, had dumped me just after he passed the bar. Unfortunately he'd already passed a singles' bar and stopped awhile. That's where he'd met a lady lawyer, who was the reason for the dumping.

"At least you have a divorce to give you closure," Rosalie said.

How had she known about my divorce? And then I remembered that she'd asked me once if I still used my maiden name of Dyer or if I used my married name. She'd explained that my uncle had told her I was married, so I responded with some facetious remark about being in the throes of a divorce because I'd gotten tired of having a name like Mandy Landry. When she didn't seem to think that was funny, I admitted that he'd found someone else. That had been more than I usually revealed to customers, but maybe it's why she decided to bare her heart to me over lunch that day.

"That's what I want—some kind of closure," she said.

"Jeremiah just ups and disappears, and I'll bet anything he's out there someplace laughing at everyone for pulling off the great escape."

She told me he'd cleared out their checking account of everything except five dollars and eighty-nine cents and left her with a pile of debts. "Five friggin' dollars and eighty-nine cents" is how she put it, and I said maybe he'd left the account open because he would have needed her signature to close it out.

If I hadn't already gotten over my teenage crush on Jeremiah, I'm sure what she told me next would have done the trick. On the day he disappeared, she said, she'd packed his suitcase so that he could drive down to Trinidad to attend his uncle's funeral. To people in Colorado, Trinidad is not only an island in the Caribbean but a town in the southern part of the state, near the New Mexico border.

But his car had turned up abandoned miles away from Trinidad at their cabin—*her* cabin, she said, because she'd inherited it from her parents—with a spot of blood on the seat. She'd been sure the police had suspected her of foul play. They hadn't seemed to buy her story that he'd cut himself shaving that morning, and were even more dubious when she said she didn't even know the name of his uncle who had just died. For that matter, she told me she didn't know any of his relatives and wasn't even sure that Jeremiah Atkins was his real name.

I especially remember her final remark that day. "Besides, he's still alive," she said. "I feel it in my bones, and if the bastard ever does show up, I'll kill him myself. Just to make sure he's really dead."

After I collected the art supplies, which I insisted on paying her for, we continued to see each other occasionally for dinner or a movie. However, we never talked about

Jeremiah again. Not until she made the special trip to the cleaners six weeks ago to tell me he'd been declared legally dead. She said she finally had closure, but now . . .

I was brought back from my thoughts about Rosalie when Theresa, my front-counter manager, knocked on my door. I swung my chair around from where I'd been staring out the window above my desk. All I'd been able to see when I started my musings was blue sky, but now a dark cloud had moved across my line of vision.

"That detective is here to see you again," Theresa said.

I got up and followed her to the front counter. Was he back to discuss that matter he'd brought up in the car? I'd always seemed to make bad choices in men—starting with my teenage crush on Jeremiah and continuing on through my disastrous marriage to Larry. Stan was no different. Maybe it was about time I got some closure from him, and I intended to tell him so.

But when I reached the counter, I realized he must not be here for personal reasons. He was standing by my mural, talking to another man who was short, slightly overweight, and balding.

"Oh, Mandy," he said when I came around the counter to meet them. "This is Phil Carlisle. He's an investigator with the medical examiner's office. I was just showing him your artwork."

Carlisle shook my hand. "Stan says you have a good memory for faces, Ms. Dyer."

Never mind that the first time we met, Stan had said my figures in the mural didn't look like real people.

"We were wondering," Carlisle continued, "if you could do us a favor and take a look at the victim."

I moved away from them in a reflex action that must have said volumes about what I thought of that idea. I felt a little foolish when I realized he was holding a photograph in his hand, but the idea of looking at a picture didn't appeal to me much either. It had to have been taken in the morgue.

"Look," Stan said. "We would have had Rosalie Atkins do it, but we can't find her, and no one seems to know where she is."

That stopped me in my backward flight. Had something happened to her too?

Finally I grabbed the picture and looked at it. It was a Polaroid and not very clear, but after all, it hadn't exactly been taken under studio conditions. I squinted my eyes to bring the face into focus. The man on the slab had a bushy mustache and a heavy dark beard. Jeremiah hadn't worn either when I'd known him, but what about Betty's friend, Honest Abe? After all, he'd acquired his nickname from a man who'd been famous for his beard. The photo looked a little like Jeremiah, but it could just as easily have been a homeless man like Honest Abe.

I handed the photograph back to Carlisle. "I'm sorry. I can't be sure whether it's Jeremiah Atkins." I figured I'd done my civic duty, and I started to leave.

Carlisle was undeterred. "I know the picture isn't very good, but maybe you could get a better idea if you came down to the morgue and took a look." What a dirty trick.

I tried to tell myself that now not only the police but the medical examiner's investigator *needed* me. Okay, I would go to the morgue with them. I could at least satisfy myself that the body wasn't Jeremiah's, that it was probably some transient, perhaps even Betty's friend. And that way I could spare Rosalie from the trauma of having to go there herself. She wouldn't have to pry open all the old wounds, the way she had when she'd cleared out her house and moved to an apartment. Except nothing I said to myself seemed to help. I didn't want to go to the morgue. I didn't like seeing dead bodies, and I was afraid I would get sick and embarrass myself by throwing up on either Stan or his friend, Carlisle, or maybe even both.

I hardly noticed the trip up Speer Boulevard in Carlisle's car, and when I did, it was from a now-cheerless perspective. The leaves on the trees no longer seemed to be ready to burst forth into spring. Their bare limbs, still dormant from the snow and cold of winter, cast skeletal shadows across the roadway. But at least trees shed their leaves, and then there's a rebirth in the spring. Not so with people. Except maybe with Jeremiah, if he'd died twice.

I knew we were headed toward Denver General Hospital. Most people still call it that, but the official name is now Denver Health Medical Center. It's one of the changes that the powers-that-be are always making to change their image. Kind of like the Denver Broncos changing their logo and their uniforms in their quest to create a new image and win the Super Bowl. Hey, it worked for the Broncos, plus it made the merchants happy since they were able to sell a whole new set of caps, T-shirts, and jackets with orange-maned horseheads galloping across the front.

So if it worked for hospitals and football teams, why not for people? I wondered if Jeremiah could have done the same thing, changed his image and gotten himself a whole new identity, become a famous artist—albeit under a different name—and come back to strut his newfound success, only to be shot down in an alley in the heart of Denver. It seemed unlikely.

"Could you give us a description of Mr. Atkins?" Carlisle asked, turning around to me in the backseat.

I closed my eyes and tried to summon up a memory of him. "About six feet tall, one hundred and eighty pounds. A high forehead. Dark hair and eyes." My own eyes shot open. "And I just remembered—he had a tiny scar at the corner of his eye. On the right side, I think it was." I felt a great sense of relief. "Maybe that will help you, and I won't have to look at the body after all."

Carlisle ignored my suggestion and drove on toward Denver General, but instead of going into the hospital compound, he parked in a lot beside a five-story building on Bannock Street that was identified as the Denver Health Administration Building.

When we got out of the car, Stan led the way to the north end of the building and up a few steps to a door that said OFFICE OF THE MEDICAL EXAMINER. He set such a pace that both Carlisle and I were puffing by the time we got there.

Inside, there was a reception desk that looked like a teller's cage and to the right was a door to a conference room. Carlisle motioned both Stan and me inside the room and said to have a seat. Then he disappeared into the back of the building.

I took that opportunity to ask Stan about Rosalie. He said she had apparently taken the week off from work, but none of her coworkers knew where she'd gone.

"I bet she went skiing," I said.

"Maybe, but she sure didn't tell anyone about it."

I could tell he thought that was peculiar, but I could identify with Rosalie. Sometimes I yearned to go off by myself, away from the telephone and endless customers, and not tell anyone where I was. In fact I wouldn't mind doing it right now.

"But couldn't you have found someone else to take a look at the body?" I asked finally.

"None of her neighbors or coworkers seem to have known her husband," Stan said. "She'd changed addresses and jobs since he disappeared."

I thought Stan sounded suspicious of that, and I wanted

to set the record straight. "It was her attempt to forget the past and start a new life. There's nothing wrong with that."

"Hey, I didn't say there was." Stan sounded so defensive that I decided he must think I was criticizing him.

But I wasn't. I just wanted to get the viewing over with. The body probably wouldn't even be Jeremiah. I remembered the suitcase that Rosalie had said she packed for him. If she'd thought he was going to a funeral seven years ago, she would have undoubtedly packed a suit and tie, plus a couple of shirts that we'd folded and boxed for him the way he always liked them.

What if he'd put the suitcase in a storage locker like the one that I rented for Dyer's Cleaners? Maybe the company had finally gotten around to clearing out stuff that had been abandoned years ago. That could explain how a shirt, all neatly pressed and folded, had gotten into the hands of a homeless person. It would also explain how the laundry mark hadn't washed off or faded in all these years.

I started to say something to Stan, but just then Carlisle came back in the room. He sat down and asked me to describe Jeremiah again. He explained that this wasn't a mortuary and that the body I was about to see wouldn't be fixed up for a public viewing the way it would be for a funeral.

I nodded, and he asked me to sign a statement that I understood. Then he escorted Stan and me down a very ordinary-looking hallway with a bathroom at the side and a door at the other end.

"Our morgue is in the basement," he explained, "and the body has been lifted up on an elevator and is already in place behind a window in our viewing room. Please come in."

I could see the window to the left and a sofa to the right

with a lamp beside it that gave off a subdued glow. Unfortunately I could still see the body.

Carlisle had his hand on a switch. "If you're ready, I'll turn on this light."

I didn't want to do this, but never let them see you sweat. That should be the motto for us dry cleaners. I took a deep breath and said to go ahead.

The window lit up like a big-screen TV. The body on the other side was covered with a white sheet, all except for the head, which rested on a block that resembled a pillow.

I went over to the window to get a closer look. I could see now that the man's dark beard was laced with gray. More gray at the temples of the curly dark hair, but his mustache, which looked like something Pancho Villa would have worn, was almost black. I bent down to look at his profile. A perfect profile. It was Jeremiah, all right. He had grown a beard and a mustache since he'd disappeared, and he was seven years older, but I knew it was him. And besides, I could see the scar by his right eye.

I didn't realize I'd been holding my breath until I started to speak. A puff of air came out before my voice did. I nodded and started to walk away. "It's Jeremiah."

"Are you sure?"

"I'm sure." I didn't wait to be excused. I turned, opened the door, and walked down the hallway to the conference room before anyone could stop me.

Surprisingly I wasn't thinking of Jeremiah. I was thinking of Rosalie. Could she have done what she'd threatened to do on that long-ago day at Tico Taco's—kill Jeremiah herself if he ever came back—just to make sure, once and for all, that he was really dead?

CHAPTER

4

No, Rosalie could never have killed her husband, I decided by the time I reached the conference room.

I sat down and waited for Stan and Carlisle to join me. When they did, Carlisle had me sign more papers attesting to the fact that I had identified the body as Jeremiah Atkins. He asked me for any family history I might know about the "decedent." I wasn't about to get into Jeremiah's mysterious past, and I said he'd have to ask Jeremiah's widow about that.

"Can I go now?" I asked when Carlisle appeared to be through. He nodded, and I headed for the door with no clear idea of what I was going to do after that.

"Why don't you wait outside," Stan said. "I'll be out in a minute, and I'll take you back to work."

I nodded and hurried out to the sidewalk, as far away from the death room as possible, where I continued to think about Rosalie. She was a gentle person, I'd come to realize from our infrequent dinners together. She loved nature and was a strong advocate for the protection of the environment, but she deplored the tactics of some of the ecology groups. She didn't even fish, she'd told me, because she couldn't stand killing the trout. Was this the profile of a person who could kill her own husband, scoundrel though he was? I didn't think so.

Stan came through the front door and down the steps. "Want to go have a cup of coffee in the hospital cafeteria?"

I shook my head. The cafeteria brought back memories of when I'd kept a vigil over Betty the time she'd been stabbed. Stan had been there, too, waiting for her to get out of surgery to see if she could identify her assailant. We'd shared a cup of coffee in the cafeteria, which was the first time we'd really connected. I didn't want to think about that now either.

"Okay," Stan said, "but I wondered if you could tell me some more about the victim's wife."

"She didn't do it," I said, and headed down the street, the thought of getting as far away from the morgue as possible still uppermost in my mind.

Stan pointed out his car parked at a meter on the street and was silent until we got to it. When we were seat-belted inside, he turned to me. "Strong as your opinions are about her, I need a little more than 'she didn't do it.'"

"Okay," I said. "She frequently went up to the mountains on backpacking and skiing trips. It's not unusual. That's just in case you think she killed Jeremiah and went up to the mountains to hide." Then I had a terrible thought. "But what if she was planning a vacation, and before she could go anyplace, Jeremiah showed up and killed her? Have you looked inside her apartment?"

Stan shook his head. "Let me review this. What you're saying is that you think Jeremiah killed his wife and then himself?"

"Maybe." I shuddered at the thought.

"Problem," Stan said. "Then where's the gun? No, someone else shot him and took the gun when they fled the scene."

That's when I thought of Betty's friend. "Well, maybe Honest Abe saw something—or stole the gun, for that matter."

Stan had started the car and was pulling out of the parking space by then. He slammed on the brakes. "Who the hell is Honest Abe?"

I guess I'd been deliberately vague because I was more angry at Stan than I realized. "He's a homeless man who apparently sleeps in the alley where Jeremiah was shot. I guess he thinks of it as *his* alley."

"And how do you know that?" Stan stepped on the gas and the car darted forward. "Oh," he said, answering his own question, "you got it from Betty the Bag Lady, right?"

I nodded, and since he already knew that she worked for me, I said, "She prefers just to be called Betty now."

Stan seldom breaks the law, but he made an illegal U-turn to Sixth Avenue, where he took a left and then a right on Speer heading back toward the cleaners. "And how did you happen to be discussing this with—uh— Betty so soon after our trip to the storage locker?"

I immediately dug myself into a deeper hole. "She overheard a conversation I was having with someone else."

"And who, for God's sake, might that be?"

"I was talking to Mack about it."

I was relieved when Stan decided to drop that line of questioning. "Okay," he said finally. "We'll check out Honest Abe."

"Betty says he won't talk."

"Well, it's worth a try," Stan continued as he passed several of the local television stations, which would be after the story as soon as their news departments found out. "Maybe he was the guy who called in the report."

I had to take my satisfactions where I found them. "I doubt it," I said. "When I said he wouldn't talk, I meant he doesn't talk, period, although he will respond to questions by nodding or shaking his head."

"Great."

And speaking of talking or not talking, I spent a few minutes wondering if it would be out of line for me to call Nat, my police reporter buddy at the *Denver Tribune,* and tip him off about Jeremiah's death. I needed him to keep an eye out about Rosalie's so-called disappearance.

Then I continued. "Betty says Honest Abe won't even do that with most people."

"Well, thanks for the lead anyway." I could detect only the slightest hint of sarcasm in Stan's voice. "It sounds like Honest Abe is going to be a real help."

"Anytime."

We drove past the Denver Country Club with the old stately mansions of Denver on the other side of Speer, across University Boulevard, and were immediately in the midst of the traffic congestion created by shoppers heading to and from the Cherry Creek Mall. But at least the conversation about Honest Abe had helped lessen my black mood, which had been half angst about Stan and my failed relationship and half sorrow about the discovery that Jeremiah was dead, not just legally but physically as well.

I didn't bring up the subject Stan had wanted to discuss with me earlier. If it wasn't important to him, then it sure wasn't important to me. Well, okay, maybe I was curious about it, but I'd be darned if I'd ask him about it a second time.

I was proud of myself for minding my own business. Not only had I been able to resist showing any curiosity about what Stan had wanted to talk to me about, but I didn't actually discuss the case with anyone. Well, I did tell Mack that the victim was Jeremiah, and I got a lecture about not getting involved. And to relieve Betty's mind, I told her that the body wasn't Honest Abe's. However, much as I was tempted, I didn't call Nat, but somehow the news had gotten out that the body had been identified as Jeremiah Atkins, who had disappeared seven years ago under mysterious circumstances. Nat wrote an article about it without any reference to me. Thank God, I hadn't contacted him. I kept trying to reach Rosalie but without success.

By Friday afternoon I was so frustrated about her whereabouts that I decided to take a break. Even though I had to be back at the front counter for the after-work rush when customers pick up clothes for the big weekends they have planned, I needed a little R and R myself, and a trip to a few art galleries in the area would be just the ticket. After all, art was food for the soul, and it had been far too long since I'd fed my artistic side. Maybe it would inspire me to get out my easel and work on one of my paintings on Sunday. Strictly as a secondary goal, I thought I could see if any of Jeremiah's paintings were on the market now that he was in the headlines again. I'd heard that his work had escalated in price after he disappeared, and I wondered if that could have brought him back to Denver.

I whipped through two of the galleries in Cherry Creek North. They netted me nothing. I finally had to admit that I was less interested in feeding my soul than I was in satisfying my curiosity. The owner of the second gallery said it was interesting I should ask about Jeremiah's work. He thought he'd seen one of his paintings at the Deverell Gallery, which was a couple of blocks west across the street.

"The owner was a friend of the artist and used to sell a lot of his work before he disappeared," the man said.

I hurried out to the sidewalk, intent on visiting the third

gallery before I had to get back to work. Unfortunately it had never been my plan to go gallery-hopping in the company of Betty, whose appreciation of art, as far as I knew, had always been confined to a casual interest in graffiti.

"Where you goin', boss lady?" she yelled at me from a bench where she was apparently waiting for a bus to take her home. Her apartment was a place I'd deliberately found for her in South Denver so that it was far enough from my own apartment on Capitol Hill that she wasn't a regular drop-in visitor.

"Uh—you're off early," I said, pulling up the sleeve of my long tan coat to look at my watch. It was three thirty, and she usually finished work at four.

Betty bounced up from the bench, shoving the hood of a forest-green jacket off her head. Between the jacket and a pair of red polyester slacks underneath, she looked as if she were a couple of months late for Christmas. "I got caught up on the laundry, and Mack told me I could leave early," she said.

"Good. I'll see you Monday."

I started to head on down the street, but she stepped in front of me. "Did *that* cop fellow ever talk to Honest Abe?"

It seemed like a moot point since Honest Abe never talked back, but I shrugged. "I haven't heard."

"Honest Abe'll prob'ly be mad at me for siccin' the cops on him. I doubt if he'll ever speak to me again."

I let that one go rather than argue that he had apparently never spoken to her anyway. Still, to make her feel better, I said, "Stan would never tell Honest Abe where he heard about him." I started to move past her.

Betty followed me.

"Look, Betty, I have to get back to work in half an hour, and I want to visit that art gallery across the street before I do." Big mistake.

"An art gallery, huh? Maybe I'll just tag along." She hurried so that she could fall in step with me. "I been trying to think of what to do until Artie picks me up at seven for a movie."

How could I have been so wrong about Arthur, the doll doctor whom I'd planned to fix up with a motherly neighbor of Betty's? Now even Betty had something to do on a Friday night, while I, the failed matchmaker, couldn't even get myself a date. Somehow that was so unnerving, I was unable to think of a single reason why she shouldn't accompany me to the Deverell Gallery. One good reason, I realized as soon as we were inside, was that she was very vocal in her disdain of modern art.

But on the way to the gallery she managed to distract me by recalling how she had once been a regular visitor to various museums around the country, including the Metropolitan.

"The Metropolitan Museum of Art?" I asked.

"Of course the Metropolitan Museum of Art. It was a good place to sit for a while when you wanted to get out of the cold." So much for her appreciation of the finer things in life.

We had barely crossed the threshold of the gallery when she proclaimed in a loud voice, "Well, isn't that the dumbest painting you've ever seen." It was a huge canvas of orange and yellow swirls, entitled *Sunset*. "It looks like somebody puked on the wall and they framed it."

I hustled her by the painting, which I might have liked under other circumstances. Now it was spoiled for me forever.

"Get a load of that." She chuckled as she pointed her finger at a wire sculpture of a unicorn. "It looks like somebody stole some hangers out of our recycling bin and made themselves a statue." She bent down to take a look at the price tag. "Well, if that doesn't bake the cake. They want five thousand bucks for that piece of junk."

"Shhh," I said, putting a finger to my lips.

"What's the matter? This ain't no library, is it?" She paused for a minute. "That was another good place to get out of the weather, but they were always shushin' you up."

I hurried on, realizing there was no way she was going to keep her art criticism to herself.

"I think you're missing the boat, boss lady," she continued as she trailed after me. "You should make something out of all those old hangers at the cleaners instead of paintin' pictures." I gathered she'd noticed my canvases during her two rather unnerving—for me, at least—stays at my apartment. "Five thousand bucks for bent hangers. Wooee."

Suddenly I was sweating. I think it was less from the temperature in the gallery than because I'd hoped not to call attention to myself. Being with Betty made that impossible, but maybe I could shake her. I stopped to take off my coat, then feigned interest in a seascape that was too realistic to hold her interest. She trotted on past me into a back room. I was hoping she would find something to occupy her interest up ahead so that I could sneak into one of the alcoves and lose her for a while.

"Hey," she said, missing me almost immediately. "Come here. This is kind of a kick."

I tried to ignore her, tipping my head as if I were analyzing the significance of waves crashing on rocks.

"Back here, boss lady," she yelled. "You gotta see this."

A woman who'd just walked in the main door must have thought Betty was calling to her. She looked nervously around and then retreated to the sidewalk. I headed in Betty's direction just to shut her up.

"Will you look at this?" she asked more quietly. "Reminds me of one of those kiddie books: 'Find ten forest friends in this picture.' "

Darned if she wasn't right, and what's more, she'd zoomed in on a genuine Jeremiah Atkins canvas. I know because his work had always been a rip-off of Beverly Doolittle, although imitative of her style might be a kinder description.

Whereas Doolittle did mountain scenes with bears and Indians camouflaged behind the firs and birch trees and were rather spiritual, Jeremiah favored primeval forests with dinosaurs hidden amid ferns and giant redwoods and seemed to have no deeper meaning.

"That's a real hoot," Betty said as she reached down to see the price tag. She bounced right back up again. "Well, if that ain't the frostin' on the cake. They want fifty thousand smackeroos for this one."

I have to admit I was surprised too. I bent down to double check the price. Betty was right.

"I got to tell you," she said, "if I want to find 'some forest friends,' I think I'll just buy me a picture book."

"May I help you?" A silken voice came from behind my right shoulder, and I swung around guiltily as if I'd been planning to spray-paint the canvas.

The woman's appearance matched her silken voice. Anywhere from thirty to fifty years of age, she was tall and slender, her hair the color of gold as it glimmered under the track lighting. It was smoothed back in a chignon with only a few wispy tendrils at her temples. They hadn't escaped accidentally, I was sure; they had been arranged that way.

She was wearing a silk pants suit that went with her silken voice, but its hot-pink color made it look as if it might more correctly be called lounging pajamas. She also had on a lot of gold jewelry and a pair of open-toed heels to match.

"I'm Laura Deverell," she said, smiling pleasantly. "Isn't this a wonderful painting?" She touched the frame with one of her beautifully manicured fingers, her long square-tipped nails the same shade of pink as the pajamas.

"Isn't it by Jeremiah Atkins—the man who was just murdered over the weekend?" I tried to look wide-eyed and innocent as I posed the question.

"Yes, wasn't that a tragedy?"

I became aware that I was in my front-counter skirt and blouse with the Dyer's Cleaners' logo on the pocket. Since I didn't particularly want to announce who I was, I pulled on my coat as if I'd had a sudden chill.

"Is this a new painting?" I asked.

"Oh no." She looked shocked that I would even suggest such a thing. "The artist disappeared some years back under a shroud of mystery, in case you didn't know, and there were never any more paintings."

I should have dropped it, but I couldn't let it go. "But he wasn't dead—well, not until last weekend. He probably continued to paint, don't you think?"

She shook her head. "Not as far as I know."

"So this painting is from before he disappeared?"

Betty stuck her face up close to the painting to get a better look, but she suddenly jumped back. "God, I didn't see that dinosaur hiding behind the bush."

I completely lost my train of thought, but luckily Laura Deverell didn't.

"Yes," she said, "a private collector decided to put it back on the market." Before I could ask who the owner was, she added, "Of course he wishes to remain anonymous."

Of course.

"Boy, the guy's really good—the way he hides the critters back in the forest," Betty said, giving her seal of approval to the painting.

I tried to ignore Betty as she moved back in for another look. "Did you happen to know the artist before he disappeared?"

"I met him a few times." Laura's smile now seemed forced, as if it were pasted on as part of a paper collage. "But why did you want to know?"

I grappled for a reason that would sound as if I were just making casual conversation. Unfortunately I came up with the one I shouldn't have used. "I just wondered if he came into the gallery when he got back to town just now." Laura eyed me suspiciously, which only made me more compulsive in my need to explain. "It just seems as if that's why he might have come back to Denver—to visit some of the local galleries to see how much his paintings had increased in value since he disappeared."

"I never saw him, if that's what you're asking." Laura's smile suddenly disappeared.

Betty chose that moment to give out with a loud guffaw, totally inappropriate to the occasion unless she was laughing at my discomfort.

She could have cared less about Laura and me, as it turned out. "You gotta see this, Mandy." Oh, swell, now she calls me Mandy instead of "boss lady" to further identify me to the gallery owner. "There's a little horse down here that's hiding under some leaves." She started to poke her finger at the lower right-hand corner of the painting.

Laura grabbed her arm at once. "Please, do not touch any of the artwork." With that the gallery owner started to whisk Betty away in the general direction of the front door.

Suddenly a blond young man who looked like a transplanted California surfer came out of a back room.

"I think you'd better handle this," he said nervously. "There's a woman at the back door who says she has to see you right away, and she won't take no for an answer."

Laura looked only slightly irritated, but maybe that was because she'd had a few face-lifts and couldn't frown. "Can't you tell her to wait?"

"No, I don't think so."

"Did you find her?" The voice from the back room sounded angry. "Tell her I want my money or I'm going to raise hell."

Laura was still escorting us toward the front of the gallery. What a dilemma—whether to get rid of us first or handle the person in the back?

Finally she made up her mind. "Will you please take care of these customers for me?" She looked from the young man to us and said imperiously, "Kevin will be glad to show you something that might be more in your price range."

Well, there's one thing I've learned in the dry-cleaning business, and it's that you can't necessarily tell the wealth of people by the clothes they wear.

Armed with that knowledge, I pulled my faux camel's hair coat around me, grabbed Betty by the other arm of her hooded green jacket, and said just as imperiously, "Don't bother, Ms. Deverell, my aunt and I will be going. We're already late for our bridge game at the Club."

CHAPTER 5

"**B**oy, that lady's as jumpy as a rabbit in heat," Betty said when we were outside the gallery. "What'd she think I was going to do, steal one of her stupid paintings?"

"No, she probably thought you were going to punch a hole in one," I answered, and I have to admit I'd been a little nervous myself when Betty started jabbing at a fifty-thousand-dollar work of art.

I couldn't believe it would actually fetch that price, but who's to say how much all the media coverage about the artist had added to its value? Anyone foolish enough to buy it would probably feel ripped off as soon as the publicity died down. But everything in the gallery seemed over-priced, which may have accounted for the disgruntled woman at the back door.

"I still wish you could have seen that mean little horse looking out from under all those red leaves," Betty said, reflecting on what had started our ignominious departure from the gallery in the first place.

"It was probably an ancient ancestor of the modern horse," I said, although why I wanted to try to impress

Betty with my knowledge was beyond me. "I believe it was called *eohippus,* or the dawn horse."

Betty gave me a who-cares look, which I probably deserved.

"Well, I'll see you Monday, Betty." We were approaching the bus bench, which is the same thing I'd said just before I'd picked up Betty as a tag-along to the gallery. I was hoping we really could part company now.

"Hey, boss lady," she said before I could make my escape. "Do you suppose you could give that cop fella a call about Honest Abe?" Somehow Betty couldn't seem to bring herself to call the cop fellow Stan or even Foster.

"I'd really rather not bother him over the weekend."

"I thought you and him were *friends.*"

"Not anymore."

"That's too bad." Betty's distrust of the police was so deep-seated that her reaction surprised me. "Maybe you could pretend you still like him just long enough to find out about Honest Abe for me."

I was unjustifiably pleased that Betty assumed I'd been the one to dump Stan. But despite her faith in me, I didn't call him. Unfortunately that didn't mean Betty didn't call me, not just once but repeatedly throughout the weekend.

And I have to admit that I broke down and called Nat, my friend at the *Denver Tribune*. Since Jeremiah's murder was all over the papers and TV, I thought it was safe to ask a few questions.

"I was wondering if you've heard any news about Jeremiah's widow, Rosalie." I didn't want to give away my part in identifying the body to the newshound from hell, so I added, "She's a customer of ours, and I've been trying to reach her all weekend."

"Oh, yeah, that's right." I could hear the excitement

rising in his voice. "I'd forgotten about that. Didn't I meet her once when we ran into each other at Tico Taco's."

"When you tracked me down at Tico Taco's is more like it," I said. "You wanted me to fix you up with one of my employees, as I recall."

"Sure. I remember. It was that tall, sexy woman who worked at the front counter for a while."

Despite the fact that Nat thinks he bears an uncanny resemblance to John Lennon, let's face it, he's only five-eight, and he's always attracted to women who are six feet tall and don't particularly want to wear flats and slouch when they go out on a date. I guess the results of the date I arranged for him with my employee were understandably disastrous; I like to think it didn't have anything to do with her departure from the cleaners shortly thereafter.

"I should have known better than to ask you for help in the romance department." Nat began to chuckle. "Aren't you the same woman who fixed up a poor, unsuspecting doll doctor with *Betty*?"

Unfortunately I'd admitted to Nat that Cupid's arrow had badly misfired on that one, and I wanted to get off the subject. "Back to Rosalie," I said, "all I get is her answering machine, and she hasn't returned my call yet."

"Well, I hate to be the bearer of bad tidings," Nat said, which was a lie if I'd ever heard of one. Nat thrived on bad news; he was a police reporter, after all, and he wallowed in the dirt he dug up about Denver's seamy side. "No one can find her. She's been missing ever since the body was discovered."

"Oh, God," I said, which was what I already knew but couldn't admit. "I hope the police don't think she did it."

"I wouldn't count on it."

"Do you suppose you could let me know as soon as you hear anything about her?"

"Sure," he said, "but wait a—"

"Thanks, Nat, I'll talk to you later."

Now that he was on the scent of something that might be newsworthy, he wouldn't let me go. Well, I could have hung up, but I was sure he'd show up at my door within the hour.

"What do you know about her?" he asked. "Maybe you can give me some background stuff."

I finally managed to get off the phone without revealing anything damaging. I'd also extracted a promise from him that he'd call me when he heard something.

That's why I pounced on the phone when it rang in the early hours of Monday morning. I'd finally fallen asleep after turning and tossing since ten o'clock.

"Nat," I said when I picked up the receiver, "Did you find out something?" After all, who else could it be in the middle of the night.

"No, I'm—maybe I have the wrong number." The voice on the other end of the line sounded confused and female.

Surely it wasn't Betty at this hour, but I wouldn't put it past her.

In my groggy state I guessed again. "Is this Betty?"

There was silence on the line, and I realized I'd once again jumped to conclusions about the caller. It was a bad habit of mine, and I probably should get Caller ID so I could tell who was calling before I answered the phone.

"Mandy?" the woman asked finally. When I said it was, she continued. "Do you suppose I could come over and talk to you if it's not too late?"

Well, it was too late, but I felt an immediate sense of relief mixed with apprehension. "Rosalie, is that you?"

She ignored my question, but I knew I was right.

"It's just that I can't believe what happened," she said. "I just got back from the mountains this evening, and the police were waiting for me. They told me they identified the b-body"—she paused for a moment, and then went on—"from a laundry mark on his shirt. How can that be?"

I wished Stan were here so I could say "I told you so." See, Stan, Rosalie didn't know anything about the murder. She'd been up in the mountains on an innocent vacation, just the way I'd told him, and now she was seeking me out so she could try to make some sense of what had happened.

"Look, I'll come and get you, Rosalie, and I'll tell you all about it. Where are you?"

Actually she sounded as if she might be on a cell phone in her car in the middle of a traffic jam.

"I don't even know what I'm doing," she said. "I'm numb, and I've just been driving around ever since the police talked to me. . . ." It sounded as if a semi was rumbling past her, and for a minute I couldn't hear her. "I feel like I'm in some surrealist dream, and I keep hoping I'll wake up."

"Where are you?" I repeated.

"I don't know." She stopped as if she might be looking around to try to figure out the location. "I'm at a phone booth outside a convenience store on West Colfax someplace. . . ." Her voice trailed off.

"Okay, why don't I come over there and get you?"

She didn't sound as if she was in any condition to drive; she sounded as if she was in a state of shock. So when she agreed, I told her to find out the exact location from the clerk inside the store. She left the phone off the hook and returned in a few minutes with the address.

"I'll be there in twenty minutes. Wait in your car for me, okay?"

I went to my walk-in closet to get some jeans and a sweatshirt. My cat, Spot, who's actually more the color of a ripe pumpkin, gave me a dirty look because he'd already settled down for the night in my laundry hamper.

"I'll be back soon," I said to him as I stripped off the pajama bottoms and slipped into some underwear and the jeans.

Spot didn't care. If there was some sort of automatic scoop to provide him with food and clean out his litter box, he'd probably be just as happy if he never saw me again. Some people have cats that will curl up on their laps and purr, but I have one who hardly tolerates me.

I slipped on a sweatshirt over my pajama top, turned out the light in the closet so as not to further irritate the cat, God forbid, and grabbed my purse before I left.

When I reached the convenience store, I saw Rosalie's car, but no one appeared to be inside. I ran over to the driver's window and found her huddled down on the seat as if she had retreated to the womb. I tapped on the window, and she jumped.

"Mandy, I'm so glad you're here," she said as she tumbled out of the car and grabbed me in a bone-crushing bear hug. It was as if I were her only means of support. Never mind that she was taller, stronger, and in a whole lot better condition than I.

Once I managed to get out of her grip, I reminded her to lock her car and said we'd go someplace where we could have a cup of coffee. She was like a robot in a ski jacket and jeans, obeying my every order.

I found a Denny's a few miles west on Colfax, and once we had a couple of mugs of coffee in our hands, I tried to explain about the laundry mark and how I'd gone to the morgue and identified the body.

She shook her head helplessly. "I feel as if I'm having a flashback like one of those Vietnam veterans you hear about. How can it be happening a second time?"

"I don't know, but we need to figure out why Jeremiah might have come back to Denver after all this time. That must have had something to do with why he was killed."

"Are you really sure it was him?" Her face was sunburned so that the freckles across her nose seemed to have disappeared, but her eyes were rimmed in white from the goggles she'd obviously worn during her week in the mountains. It gave her eyes a sunken look. I would have liked to make her feel better, but all I could do was nod.

"But why would he be wearing a shirt from seven years ago?"

I shrugged. "I was hoping you might have some idea."

She had her elbows on the table, and she rested her chin on the palms of her hands, as if she couldn't keep her head up otherwise. Finally she said, "All I can think of is that I packed his good suit and put a shirt in a suitcase because he was supposedly on his way to his uncle's funeral when he disappeared."

That's what I had speculated. "So were the police ever able to find out anything about the uncle and the funeral?"

Rosalie dropped her hands and gripped the table. "No, and I'm sure they thought I'd been lying about it."

"What about his friends? Someone must know where he was all these years and why he came back."

She shook her head. "I didn't know any of them either—just a few of the other realtors where he worked, and they said they were only casual acquaintances."

I was unwilling to give up. "But he must have had some artist friends?"

"I suppose so, but I never met them. He'd go off sometimes because he said he needed to be alone, and I accepted that. I thought he was a genius who needed his space, but he must have had a whole other life and maybe even another name out there someplace that I didn't know about." She could apparently see the skepticism in my eyes. "Let's face it, Mandy. He married me for my money, and when it ran out, he didn't want anything else to do with me."

I didn't know what to say—I'm sorry, maybe, but that seemed inadequate. "What about the nude model that you thought he was having an affair with? Maybe she knows something. Do you know what happened to her?"

She shook her head. "I've spent the last seven years trying to forget the whole thing, but I think the police talked to her at the time."

I picked up my coffee to have a sip. "So what was her name? Maybe she still works for some modeling agency around town."

Rosalie laughed, but it was a hollow sound that went with her sunken eyes. "Her name was Bambi—are you ready for this?—Deere, like the farm equipment."

I almost choked on my coffee. "Bambi Deere. She sounds like a stripper."

"You got it," she said. "The police may have found out her real name, but I don't know what it was."

Rosalie hadn't touched her coffee, and I finally suggested that we order something to eat. She said she wasn't hungry, but when I asked her how long it had been since her last meal, she shrugged as if she couldn't remember.

"Look, maybe we'd both be able to think more clearly if we had some food." I hailed down a waiter, and Rosalie finally ordered a hamburger.

I ordered the same, but with cheese, even though I'd had a Lean Cuisine dinner earlier in the evening on the theory that inspiration would come to me in my painting if I fed my stomach. I'd tried to feed my soul earlier at the art gallery, but that hadn't worked.

If having another meal would encourage Rosalie to eat,

then I'd sacrifice. Besides, maybe the low-cal food I'd eaten earlier hadn't been enough to nourish the muse.

"What did he l-look like?" she asked while we waited for the order.

I didn't really want to describe the corpse. "Aren't they going to let you see him?"

She nodded. "I didn't think I could handle it tonight, so I have to go there tomorrow morning. I just wanted to try to prepare myself for it."

"He hadn't changed much." I hated to say that. He was dead, for Christ's sake, but I wanted to comfort her if I could. "A little older, of course, with a beard and a mustache."

She was in denial the way I'd been before I got to the morgue. "He never had a beard and a mustache."

"He does now, and that little scar by his right eye."

She began to tremble. "They're going to arrest me this time. I'm sure of it, Mandy. I don't even have an alibi."

"But you were up in the mountains," I protested.

"Yes, but the police said he was shot Friday night. I didn't get up there until Saturday afternoon. They'll think I killed him before I left and then took off. No one saw me that night because I was busy getting ready for the trip."

"Where'd you go—to your cabin?" I was really wondering why she hadn't heard about Jeremiah's death, since it had been all over the news.

"No, it's not near the place where I like to go cross-country skiing, so I rented another cabin for the week." She must have realized what I was getting at. "There's no electricity, and the radio in my car doesn't work."

Our order arrived, and I urged her to eat, saying it would make her feel better if she did. She began to nibble at her food. I, on the other hand, ate every bite on my plate. That's what I do when I'm upset, but it does help me think better.

"I was wondering," I said when we were nearing the end of the meal, "did you find out anything about him when you were cleaning out your house to move a couple of years ago? You know, when you gave me all his art supplies?"

She shook her head. "I appreciate your trying to help, Mandy, but it's hopeless. Believe me, I would have taken any information to the police if I'd found it."

I pushed my plate away as Rosalie picked up the second half of her hamburger. "I have an idea," I said. "It's really remote, but it's worth a try."

She looked up at me as she took a bite of the hamburger. There was the slightest glimmer of hope in her eyes.

"I remember that Jeremiah was a charge customer at the cleaners when I was a teenager," I said. "I worked there after school and on Saturdays, and he'd come in."

The hope flickered and went out; she must have expected something more.

"Well, back in those days," I continued, "my uncle had an application form that a person had to fill out in order to become a charge customer. We didn't accept Visa and MasterCard in those days, so the application asked for a lot of history, including references from friends and relatives who could vouch for the customer."

"Yes, go on," Rosalie urged, probably wishing I'd get to the point.

"So I was thinking that maybe I could go through all those old application forms and see if I could come up with the name of a friend or relative that he used as a reference. Uncle Chet never threw anything away, and all the paperwork is stored in a locker we have out in Glendale."

"Really?" Rosalie still didn't sound hopeful.

I didn't blame her. It was probably dumb to even suggest it. What made me think a man with a phony ID would slip and give the name of a real relative? But maybe he'd changed his name for his art, just as a writer might use a pen name. Couldn't he have kept some of his old ties for a while until he gradually became the character he'd created? It seemed unlikely, and I probably should have looked into it on my own before I told her about it.

"Do you suppose you could do it soon? I could help," I heard Rosalie saying from across the table.

"Sure." I needed to clean out the locker anyway, and it wouldn't hurt to reacquaint myself with what was there. Hadn't I already thought about that when Stan and I were there? "We can get at it first thing tomorrow," I said. "So maybe we should get out of here right now and try to get some sleep."

Rosalie got up reluctantly. "I can't do it tomorrow morning. I have to go to the—" She swallowed and continued. "That's when I'm going to the morgue."

"I'll start without you, but I'll give you the address of the storage locker. You can join me later." I figured she'd need to talk to someone after she went to the morgue anyway. I was always grateful that I had Mack to talk to, despite his inevitable words of advice.

"Do you want to spend the night with me?" I asked after I paid the bill and we headed to my car.

Rosalie said, no, she needed to be by herself. I could relate to that. Sometimes a person needs to cry alone.

When I dropped her off at her car at the convenience store, I said I'd follow her home. She seemed more capable of driving now, but I still wanted to make sure that she got there safely.

On the way, alone in my car, thoughts churned around in my head haphazardly. I couldn't quite believe Rosalie didn't know a single thing about Jeremiah's past. But what did I know about the people around me, come to think of it?

I'd always had a live-and-let-live philosophy. But if something happened to Betty, for instance, what did I know about her? Nothing. I wouldn't even be able to tell anyone whom to contact in case she died. And what did I know about my own father, when it came right down to it? Mom never wanted to talk about him, preferring to live in the present with whatever husband she happened to have at the moment. It was too late to ask Uncle Chet, so Mack was the only one left, and although I'd thought about discussing the subject with him at one point, I never had. Maybe I was afraid I'd find out something I didn't want to know.

That's what had happened with Stan. I'd insisted on knowing about his frequent out-of-town trips to Fort Collins, and he'd finally told me he was trying to help the son of his former fiancée, a woman who'd also been a police officer and who'd died in the line of duty. *His* duty. He'd taken off for a few days, and she'd pulled his shift—only to be killed by a robber. Instead of making things better, that news had created a wider breach between us. I was left with the impression that what he'd wanted to explain to me the other day was that he couldn't quite make a place for me in his life because he'd never been able to get over his old love.

So maybe it was better to let sleeping dogs lie, which is another story. His damned dog, Sidearm, hated me, not to mention what might happen if Sidearm and Spot, the cat with the disposition of a coiled rattlesnake, ever got together.

I'd have to give the whole thing some more thought—just as soon as I got through poking and probing into Jeremiah's past.

CHAPTER 6

I didn't get to the storage locker as early as I intended. One of the steam lines in the plant had sprung a leak, and Mack and I had to work on it before I could leave work. Also Patty, the full-time inspector I'd hired recently to check the clean clothes, found some black streaks on a couple of dresses. I finally tracked down the cause, a touch-up iron at one of the stations on the press line. Now there's a real detective job.

There was starch on the bottom of the iron, and I managed to remove it by running the iron over a sheet of wax paper. There are other methods, such as running the iron over a flat piece of cedarwood. But who has a slab of cedarwood?

Once I cleaned the iron, I had to answer questions from Betty and Mack, as if I were holding a press conference. No, I hadn't found out anything about Honest Abe, but I promised Betty I'd call Stan right away. And yes, I told Mack, Rosalie had surfaced over the weekend and was devastated by the news that her long-missing ex-husband had been murdered.

"You mean she was still carrying a torch for him after he ran off and left her?" Mack asked.

"No, but it was a shock anyway, and now she's sure the police are going to arrest her for his murder. After all, she just got through having him declared legally dead."

I tried to call Stan when I finally got to my office, but I only reached his voice mail. I asked him to call me about whether or not he'd found Honest Abe. Betty was worried about him, and I said I'd appreciate it if Stan would call me at home and leave a message on my answering machine. I didn't particularly want people at the front counter to get the message if someone took it here. I'd already told my front-counter manager that I'd be gone for a while and to pull in Lucille from mark-in if she needed help on the counter. Lucille, a middle-aged woman who doesn't like her routine disrupted, wasn't happy about it, but what else was new?

Then, still wearing the jeans and sweatshirt I'd had on while Mack and I worked on the steam line, I prepared to leave. I even dragged out the purple and green down jacket that I seldom wore around the Cherry Creek area anymore. I'd decided it didn't look good if I ran into a customer while wearing such a disreputable outfit, but it was just the thing to wear in the chilly storage locker.

Again I had to answer questions from Mack. I told him I was going to the locker to clean it up after the mess Stan and I had made there the week before. I left quickly before Mack asked any other questions about my trip.

Wind swept across the parking lot between the cleaners and the strip shopping center behind it as a cold front moved into Denver. Today spring seemed far away, but that's how the weather is in Colorado. There would probably be snow by morning.

As I drove, I kept wishing I hadn't told Rosalie about the

applications for charge accounts. Not only was it a long shot that I'd find any pertinent information, but I wasn't even sure if I'd saved the applications. As I said, Uncle Chet never threw anything away. I remembered sorting out papers and throwing things away when I first took over the cleaners, but it was such a daunting job that I finally gave up and moved everything to the storage locker. Still, it was arrogant of me to think I'd saved the applications. I could just as easily have thrown them away.

When I reached the locker, I opened the roll-up door, entered, and pulled it down again as soon as I was inside. Unfortunately there wasn't enough light from the single bulb hanging down from the ceiling to see what I was doing. It was a toss-up whether I wanted to be marginally warm or be able to see what I was doing. I finally settled for rolling the door up a quarter of the way. This wasn't going to be fun. The wind swept under the door like a minihurricane and sent papers sailing across the room as soon as I started digging through one of the boxes.

Forty-five minutes later I'd eliminated a dozen boxes as repositories of the old charge applications. I was sitting cross-legged on the floor, pleased that I hadn't been stupid enough to wear a skirt this trip. I had just opened another box when I noticed someone standing on the other side of the door. Well, actually what I noticed was a pair of black shoes and legs covered in gray pants. It startled me, but it also reminded me of a shot in those old cowboy movies that zoomed in on the lower half of the gunfighter's body, his legs spread apart, ready for a showdown with the bad guy. The theme song from *High Noon* would have been appropriate if I could think of how it went.

Somehow the shoes looked too big for Rosalie. I decided it was probably the operator of the storage locker, come to inquire about the partially open door. But would he be wearing dress shoes and good trousers? An uneasy feeling settled over me, like a too-tight dress you couldn't quite get into, causing you to have a panic attack and think you were going to suffocate with it wrapped around your head.

Get a grip, Mandy. This wasn't like one of those other murder cases I'd had the misfortune to be involved in—where someone had actually tried to do me bodily harm. The imaginary dress disappeared from around my neck. I bent down to take a better look at the person on the other side of the door, my face almost touching the floor in a contortion I was pleased to know I could still accomplish. Just as I did, Stan Foster bent down to take a look inside. I scrambled to disentangle myself from my Buddha-on-floor position.

"Just push up the door," I said. By the time he did, I was trying to get to my feet. "What are you doing here?"

"I got your message, and I called the cleaners." That was not what I had told him to do when I left word on his voice mail, but oh well. "They said you were out here, and I happened to be in the neighborhood."

Like I was going to believe that. Glendale wasn't even in his jurisdiction, much less his neighborhood.

"What are you up to?" he asked, lowering the door to its previous position.

"Oh," I said smartly. I hoped I didn't look shifty-eyed and suspicious as I glanced around at the mess and wondered if he'd buy my explanation. "I decided I needed to clean up the place." Unfortunately the locker looked worse than it had when we'd been here before.

"Need some help?" he asked. "I could give you a hand for a few minutes."

I rubbed my dirty hands on my jeans. I could hardly feel my fingers because they were numb from the cold.

"No, that's okay. I need to find out what's in all the boxes." Maybe he'd buy that.

"Okay," he said. He then went over and sat down on one of the as-yet-unopened boxes, apparently with the intention of watching me work.

Damn. I really needed to get him out of here. Rosalie might show up at any minute, and I thought it would be wise if he didn't get the idea that I was meddling again.

"So what did you find out from Honest Abe?" I went over and rolled up the door, hoping he'd get the hint that I was much too busy to spend a lot of time on this.

"We can't find him. None of the other street people know where he is."

My stomach sank to a lower level than it had already been. It had started its descent when Stan showed up just as I'd been expecting Rosalie.

"Do you think something happened to him too?" I asked.

"I doubt it. These street people have a habit of taking off all the time."

"But what if the person who shot Jeremiah killed him too?"

"We haven't had any other reports of unidentified bodies."

I was relieved about that, but I wasn't sure that Betty would accept that explanation. She was going to be upset to find out her friend was missing, at least if all the calls she'd made to me were any indication.

"Well," I said, "thanks for letting me know about him, but you really didn't have to come way out here to tell me."

He made no indication that he planned to leave.

"I don't want to keep you," I continued, "and I guess I'd better get back to work anyway."

Sometimes Stan's blue eyes could look hard and icy.

Right now they seemed to be filled with a vulnerability that was very appealing. I wanted to go over to the packing box where he was sitting and ask him to forgive me for every past transgression I'd ever committed. All of them, as far as I could remember, had to do with my snooping around in things that were none of my business. Just what I was doing now, as a matter of fact.

He ducked his head. "I was wondering if maybe we could talk about something else while I'm here. It's something I've never told anyone before, and I need to tell you about it."

I glanced at the open door, praying that Rosalie wouldn't show up just yet. "Sure, go ahead."

"This is going to be really hard," he said, and I'd never seen him quite so upset before. Well, maybe when he'd told me about the death of his fiancée, but this time he seemed to be having an even harder time. I dragged another packing box over beside him and sat down. I was filled with both sympathy and apprehension, not sure I wanted to hear what he felt he needed to tell me.

"Okay." He took a deep breath and plunged ahead. "I wanted to tell you how it was with Erin. Remember I already told you about—"

A shadow fell across the room from the open door. It might have been a metaphor for the way I felt just then with the shroudlike dress once again descending over my head. But the metaphor wasn't even close to what the shadow really was.

When I looked up, Rosalie was in the doorway. She had already started to talk before she saw Stan. "I'm so glad that's over, Mandy. Oh, Detective—" She floundered around for his name.

"Detective Foster," I supplied, wishing I could crawl into one of the already opened boxes and close the lid.

"I didn't know anyone else was here." You wouldn't think a face as sunburned as hers could blush, but it did. "Should I leave and come back later?"

"No." Stan rose to his feet. "I was just getting ready to leave." I thought for a minute that he didn't recognize her, which would have been a lucky break for me. Unfortunately it just wasn't my day. "I trust Investigator Carlisle met you at the morgue on time, Ms. Atkins. I'm sorry we had to put you through all that."

Rosalie didn't seem to know what to say; she looked from Stan to me in confusion.

"I'd better get going," Stan said. "Walk me to the car, will you, Mandy?"

I was sure the conversation that had been so painful for him was over, but I tagged along.

"What is she doing here?" he practically hissed as we reached his standard-issue Ford.

I'd been trying to think of a suitable explanation as we went. "Rosalie called me last night because someone told her about the laundry mark. When she said she was going to the morgue this morning, I thought she might need a friend when she was through. I told her I'd be working here and suggested she come over if she needed to talk."

Apparently Stan accepted that.

"I'm sorry about her timing. I could sit in your car for a minute if you still want to tell me about . . . Erin."

I was assuming Erin was the fiancée, and maybe he thought what I said sounded sarcastic. He gave me another look, half irritated and half relieved. "No, we'll talk about it some other time. I'll call you later."

"Want to set up a date right now?"

He shook his head. "I'll give you a call." He got in his car and slammed the door, which, as I knew from past experience, was a sign of suppressed anger. Yep, I was in the doghouse again, and it had nothing to do with his dog, Sidearm.

"I'm sorry," Rosalie said as soon as I returned to the locker. "I didn't know he was here. What'd he want? Was he talking about me?"

I realized Rosalie didn't know anything about my relationship with Stan, and right now I didn't feel like discussing it. "No, he was telling me that they couldn't find a man who might have been a witness to the shooting. It was someone that one of my employees knew who—uh—lived in that area."

"Wouldn't it be wonderful if someone had witnessed the shooting and came forward to exonerate me?" Rosalie went over and collapsed on the same packing box where Stan had been sitting. She ducked her head just like Stan had done, and after a few minutes, she said, "God, it was horrible, Mandy, seeing Jeremiah that way." Her voice sounded choked. "I know I said I hated him, but I loved him too. At least I had at one time, and it's hard to see someone you've once loved lying there dead." She started to cry.

I went over and sat on the box I'd scooted up to be near Stan and put my arms around her. I didn't say anything. Just waited until she finished crying.

Finally she rubbed her eyes and sniffed. "Thanks, Mandy, for putting up with all this. I went home last night, and I thought I'd have myself a little crying jag." She sniffed again. "But I couldn't do it. I was too mad at him for putting me through all this again. I guess when I saw him, the reality finally set in. Even though the police may suspect that I killed him, he's the one who's dead."

"It's okay." I patted her on the shoulder. "You needed to get it out."

"To top everything off, all these reporters have been calling and leaving messages, and if that isn't bad enough, the medical examiner's office is ready to release the body, and I don't know what to do about it. I guess some families refuse to claim the body, but I c-can't do that."

She started to cry again, but finally she pulled a Kleenex out of her ski jacket pocket and blew her nose. "I need to think about something else." She stood up. "So, have you found the charge applications yet?"

I rose from the other box. "Not yet—so why don't we get to work?"

Suddenly I had a delayed reaction to not telling Stan what I was really doing here. I began to sweat, which brought on an itching episode. I had to remove my jacket and scratch for a while. "I must be allergic to all the dust in here," I explained. Another lie, but who cared? I was already itching.

It took us another hour before Rosalie and I found the box with the old application forms in it. Thank God, I hadn't thrown them away. It took me another half hour to go back through the years to the early ones, and I still wasn't finding Jeremiah's name.

As soon as I'd mentioned it to Rosalie last night, I'd begun to wonder why I even thought there might be something revealing on the credit application. If he'd lied about his real name, wouldn't he also have lied about his references? The only thing that gave me any hope was that Uncle Chet had been a stickler about checking out references in those days. He'd always said that doing business with deadbeats could be the death knell for your business. And even if Jeremiah hadn't given the name of a relative, he might have given the name of a friend who knew more about him than Rosalie did

Just then I found it. *Atkins, Jeremiah.* Back twenty years ago when he'd first become a customer of Dyer's Cleaners, long before he married Rosalie. I skimmed down past the bank accounts. He'd had one at a downtown bank.

Rosalie was looking over my shoulder. "There it is." She pointed to the bottom of the page. "He does list a reference."

For a guy who could paint so well, he sure didn't have good handwriting, or maybe it was deliberately sloppy. I squinted to make out the name. It said Maxine Perez, listed her as his aunt, and gave an address and phone number in Trinidad, Colorado.

"Hallelujah," Rosalie said. "You were right. I could kiss you." And she did—on the cheek, which only made it begin to itch again. "Bless you, Mandy."

I removed the sheet from the rest of the applications I was holding. "Don't get too excited, Rosalie. Didn't you say he told you he was going to an uncle's funeral the day he disappeared? This could be the deceased uncle's wife, and she may have died too or moved away."

"No, no, I refuse to believe that." She shook her head so fiercely that her hair came loose from behind her ears. "Even if it is, some of her neighbors in Trinidad will surely remember her."

Not very likely, it seemed to me.

I didn't voice my doubts, and Rosalie continued. "And they should be able to direct us to other relatives."

Us. What was this "us" stuff? My itching had begun to fade away with the thought that we would have something to deliver to the police that might be helpful to the case. I wasn't sure I wanted to call Stan myself. Best to let Rosalie do it. Maybe not even say where she got the information.

"We'll go back to the cleaners and I'll make a copy of this," I said. "Then you can take it to the police." Of course that would reveal exactly where it came from. Dyer's Cleaners and Dyers was printed plainly on the top of the application, and then Stan would be able to figure out what I had been doing in the storage locker this morning. Well, I'd simply have to bear the brunt of his wrath in the name of justice.

"No," I heard Rosalie saying. "You have to help me on this. I need to go down to Trinidad and talk to the aunt myself. I don't want the police to get there first. I need to know something about this man I was married to for all those years."

I was shaking my head, but my short hair wasn't swinging. It was probably plastered to my head from a combination of the dust, the sweating episode that went with my itching, and the knit cap I'd plunked on my head and then removed while we argued about what to do. I was itching again, too, at the thought of what Rosalie had in mind.

"Please, please please," she said. "I need it for my peace of mind. For closure."

Well, yes, there was always closure. I could use some of that myself with Stan.

"I'll be forever in your debt. I'll start wearing more wool suits at work instead of just bringing in my ski clothes to be waterproofed every winter."

"No," I said firmly.

Rosalie started out of the storage locker. "Okay, I'll go by myself. Promise me you won't tell the police until I get back." She paused and gave me a pitiful look that was enhanced by the white around her eyes where her ski goggles had been. "I just hope I'm not too shook up to drive all that way by myself."

Talk about somebody knowing how to push the right buttons. I followed her out of the locker, which was now in far worse shape than it had been before. Oh, well, I'd save the housecleaning for another day. I slammed down the door and locked it, thinking about how I'd gone and picked her up, then followed her home because I didn't think she was in any condition to drive. "You really shouldn't go alone."

She looked back at me hopefully. "We could go right now. It's only like maybe a four-hour trip. We can be home by ten o'clock tonight at the latest. And then maybe I'll have some real information to give to the police to get them off my back."

I guess I'm a marshmallow when it comes to helping a friend. I finally said I'd go with her, but I was reminded of the slogan Uncle Chet had used at his old cleaners downtown: "Give us the *shirt* off your back, and we'll take the *wrap* for you."

I hoped it didn't turn out to be true.

CHAPTER 7

I should have known it wasn't a good sign when it started to snow on Monument Hill. The hill's a geologic bump on Interstate 25 between Denver and Colorado Springs that you hardly notice in the summer. However, at the first hint of snow, it is infamous for causing monumental traffic problems and road closures. We'd be lucky to get back by tomorrow morning, much less by ten o'clock tonight.

We were in my car, which was probably another mistake. As long as I was going along, I volunteered to drive. Unfortunately the tires on my Hyundai were almost as bald as Michael Jordan's head.

But the snow tapered off as we got closer to Colorado Springs, and I breathed a sigh of relief. It had stopped completely as we passed the Air Force Academy and hit the Springs, but the storm clouds hung low and choked off the view of Pike's Peak. You wouldn't even have known we were paralleling the mountains because the cloud cover was so dense that we appeared to be out on the Kansas plains.

We stopped to eat at Pueblo, and I finally called the cleaners to let someone know I wouldn't be back today. I'd waited until we reached what I considered the point of no return. Once I'd committed myself to the trip, I didn't want to be tempted to go back to the plant just because there was a problem that no one else wanted to handle. Theresa, my front-counter manager, assured me that everything was under control. I'd deliberately called her because she didn't ask me questions, which is the complete opposite of what Mack would have done.

Before we left Denver, I'd tried to call the aunt's number in Trinidad, but there was no longer a phone in that name. Rosalie had wanted to make the trip anyway to see if anyone remembered the woman. I thought the whole thing was an exercise in futility, but at least Stan couldn't get mad at me for meddling in a police matter if the whole thing turned out to be a flop. So I'd go to Trinidad with Rosalie, and when she didn't find anything, the whole matter would be closed. No harm done.

We continued on south, bypassing the town of Walsenberg on the interstate. A few snowflakes began to fall again as we hit the city limits of Trinidad. Raton Pass, dividing Colorado from New Mexico, was just on the other side of town.

"So what are you going to say if we find this Maxine Perez?" I asked Rosalie.

She'd been elated at first about the possibility of actually locating a relative of Jeremiah's, then pessimistic about our chances of tracking down the woman. "I don't know—that I'm her nephew's widow and does she know where the hell he was for the last seven years?"

"Don't forget to ask why she thinks he might have come back after all this time."

"Yeah, that too."

When we got to downtown Trinidad, I saw a sign that pointed off the interstate to the Colorado Visitors Center. It was three in the afternoon by then, but the office should still be open. I decided it was as good a place as any to start. I asked a man at the information desk how to get to the last-known address for the mythical Maxine.

He wasn't used to answering questions about anything except the local museums. Trinidad had once been a coal-mining town and a stop on the Santa Fe Trail, but it's not known as a vacation destination. In fact a few years back there'd been a proposal on the state ballot to allow small-stakes gambling in Trinidad as a way of boosting the local economy. That was after voters had approved gambling in several mountain communities. The ensuing boom in those old mining towns destroyed a lot of historic sites to make way for casinos. Voters had had enough and turned down the amendment to expand gambling to Trinidad and nearby Walsenberg.

Trinidad was left with the rather dubious distinction of being one of the sex-change centers of the United States. It was known that a lot of transsexuals who didn't want to go to Europe for operations came to Trinidad for their sex changes. In fact I'd wondered about that earlier when Rosalie mentioned the Trinidad connection. After all, that would have been a really good reason for his disappearance. Jeremiah to Geraldine. However, I'd seen him at the morgue, and it was obvious from his beard and mustache that he hadn't undergone any estrogen treatments.

The volunteer at the tourist center didn't know where the street was that we were looking for, but to his credit, he called someone who gave him the directions. He relayed them to us, and I wrote them down.

In appreciation I asked him something he was prepared to answer: What was the weather prediction for the rest of the day?

"Flurries changing to heavy snow by night," he said.

It wasn't what I wanted to hear, but I thanked him anyway.

Rosalie read off the directions as I drove. The instructions led us to an area of town that was definitely in need of an urban renewal program. We found the right street, but we had more trouble with the address. That was because there were no numbers visible on some of the houses, or else they were hidden behind the weeds and untrimmed bushes that had overgrown the yards. I finally went up to one of the houses and inquired.

"What you want?" asked a guy with a potbelly protruding from between his T-shirt and jeans.

"I'm looking for Maxine Perez." I held my breath. This was the moment of truth. Either he had never heard of her or he'd recognize the name and tell me she'd died years ago. Another possibility was that he would say she'd moved away sometime in the intervening twenty years since Jeremiah had filled out the credit application. That's what I would have done if I'd lived in this neighborhood.

There was of course one final option, and I was almost afraid to believe him when he answered. "Two houses down." He pointed with an unopened can of beer to the south. "It's the white house, but she has to be at work at five, so she may be gone by now."

"Thanks." I started to retrace my steps along the cracked, uneven sidewalk, then turned back to him. "Do you know where she works—just in case we miss her?"

He almost had the door closed, but I'd caught him in time. He poked his head back outside and popped the top on the can of beer simultaneously. "She works at that truck stop out on the north end of town." He slammed the door.

"Okay," I said to Rosalie when I returned to the car. "The next one's up to you. She lives in the white house two doors from here."

White was just a figure of speech. The house was peeling so much that there was hardly any paint left, and what there was had yellowed with age like an old pair of drapes.

Rosalie's face had turned pale at the realization that we'd actually found the woman, and she seemed nervous when she climbed out of the car. "You'll go with me, won't you?"

"Of course I will." As long as I'd come this far, jeopardizing all my best intentions to stay out of things, I wasn't about to miss the ending. "You'd better hurry. The guy"—I motioned toward the house where I'd just made my inquiry—"said she goes to work at five."

Rosalie came to an abrupt stop. "I thought she'd be old and feeble if she was alive at all."

I grabbed her by the arm. "So did I, but we'd still better hustle."

Our image of Maxine Perez couldn't have been farther from the truth. The woman who answered the door was not only younger than we expected, she didn't look Hispanic. She had fire-red hair that was obviously dyed and pale skin that was wrinkled from too many cigarettes—one of which was between her heavily painted red lips. She was wearing a short silk wraparound robe with a gap at the top that showed her bra.

"Yeah, what d'ya want?" she asked.

Rosalie seemed to be dumbstruck.

"Are you Maxine Perez?" I asked.

She looked at us suspiciously, as if we might be bill collectors. I guess we passed the test. She finally nodded.

"We're here to inquire about your nephew, Jeremiah Atkins."

"He's dead," she said, and started to slam the door.

I put my foot between the door and the frame the way I was always reading about in detective novels. She nearly amputated my toes. The snow was only one reason that I should have worn something sturdier than a pair of canvas tennis shoes.

"Please, we have to talk to you."

"Look, all I know is what I heard on TV."

I motioned my head toward Rosalie. "But this is Jeremiah's widow, and she needs to find out something about him."

"His widow, huh?" Maxine pulled the door away from my mangled foot and looked Rosalie up and down. "You're not the kind of gal I would have figured him to marry."

Rosalie paled, even through her sunburn, and she still couldn't seem to find her voice. I couldn't say I blamed her.

"Could we come in for a minute?" I asked. "We really need to talk to you."

I was afraid the woman would refuse, but she opened the door wider and motioned us inside. "You'll have to give me a few seconds. I got to get dressed for work."

"That's fine. We'll wait."

Maxine disappeared down a hallway, and I looked around the room. It was littered with old newspapers, overflowing ashtrays, and a scattering of empty beer cans. Rosalie and I cleared a space for ourselves on a sofa and sat down.

"She's sure not what I expected," Rosalie whispered.

I nodded as Maxine came back in the living room in a short red skirt and a white blouse with red trim on the collar. Her name was monogrammed on the blouse, just like our new uniforms at work, and she had a red-and-white candy-striped cap on the top of her henna-enhanced hair.

"So what do you want to know about the bastard?" she asked as she slipped into shoes that looked like the ones nurses wear. They were in sharp contrast to her skimpy uniform.

"I can't take being on my feet anymore unless I wear these clodhoppers," she said, sounding embarrassed. "So I have to save my dancin' shoes for later at night." She held up a bag where I could see some spike heels poking through the plastic, apparently filled with her dress-up clothes for a late date.

"Can you tell us something about Jeremiah?" Rosalie finally asked, but her voice came out in a squeak.

"I got about ten minutes, so what d'ya want to know? That he was too good to use his daddy's name or that he corrupted my kid, Joey?" Maxine plopped down in an overstuffed chair, not even bothering to remove the papers we'd tossed there.

I'd meant to keep quiet, but I couldn't stay out of it. "For starters, what was his real name?"

"Luis Perez, but that wasn't good enough for him, not by a long shot." She practically spat out the words.

"You must have heard about it when he disappeared seven years ago," Rosalie said, her voice barely above a whisper. "Why didn't you tell the police who he really was?"

"Hey, I mighta been pissed at him, but I don't go squealing to the cops. Besides, Joey said the two of them were working on some sort of scam that was going to put me on easy street in my old age."

"What kind of scam?" It was me again, unable to keep my mouth shut.

Maxine opened a gold purse that she'd brought out of the bedroom, pulled out a cigarette, and lit it. "Sorry, kids, I don't know." She inhaled and blew out a trail of smoke. "Just something about Luis—pardon me if I don't call him Jeremiah—going to Mexico and pullin' off the scam from there. I figured it was drugs, and frankly I didn't want to know."

Rosalie didn't say anything, and I kept quiet on the theory that Maxine would go on if we just waited.

The silence lengthened while I considered asking her for one of her cigarettes, which, as a recovering smoker, I always want, especially in times of stress.

"Fine lot of good it did me too," she said, the old silent treatment working once again. "Joey gets sent to the slammer and I'll probably still be working when I'm old and gray."

Actually she might be gray already under all that flaming-red hair. I'd pegged her for somewhere in her late fifties.

When Rosalie didn't ask the obvious question, I did. "So what was your son sent to prison for—selling drugs?"

Maxine took another puff. "No, for pulling off some sort of dumb break-in in Denver five years ago." Smoke came out of her nose as she spoke and exhaled at the same time. "And you're never going to make me believe that Luis wasn't behind it, even though he was supposedly lolling on some beach South of the Border."

"What did your son say about the break-in?"

"He said he pulled the job all by himself—but I didn't believe him for a minute. And for that he got five-to-ten at Canon City."

That's where the Colorado State Penitentiary is, and I wondered if he was out by now, since she'd said the heist took place five years ago.

When I asked her about it, she shook her head. "Wouldn't that have been nice?" For the first time her hazel eyes, which looked hard mainly because of the heavy eyeliner she used, teared up. "But no, he got stabbed to death by another inmate a couple of years ago."

"I'm sorry," Rosalie and I both said in unison.

She shrugged, trying to regain her hard edge. "Poor Joey never did have much luck. And for that I hold his precious cuz responsible."

What I really wanted to ask right then was if I could have one of her cigarettes, but I didn't want to get her sidetracked. "Why do you say that about Jeremiah—I mean, Luis?"

"Because those two kids were thick as thieves when they were growing up." She laughed, which came out as a half snort because she took another puff on her cigarette right then. "And look where it got Joey—sent to jail for a burglary that Luis probably put him up to."

"Were they the same age?" Rosalie asked the question, and she'd been so quiet, it surprised me.

"Nope, Joey was younger, and he worshiped Luis. His mother was my older sister, and we made the mistake of marrying brothers when we were still kids ourselves. Then they up and die in a car accident when the kids were small."

I was remembering what Rosalie had told me about him saying that he was going to the funeral of an uncle when he disappeared. "Did he have another uncle besides your husband?"

Maxine looked puzzled.

"Jeremiah told me he was coming to his uncle's funeral when he disappeared seven years ago," Rosalie explained.

"Nope, there was no other uncle. Just me and my sister, and if you want my opinion, I think little Luis was the death of her, the way he kept getting into trouble in high school. He always wanted to be a big shot, and the rest of the family was never good enough for him. Then some art teacher decided he had talent, and I guess he figured that was his ticket out of town."

I saw Rosalie moving her head up and down beside me in understanding. I jumped in. "Did you hear from him after he came back just now?"

She had a deadpan expression on her face as she shook her head. "All I heard was that he was dead."

"Are there any other family members or friends who might know something about why he came back to Colorado?"

"Not that I know of. He never had any contact with his sister after he left here, and Joey was my only kid."

"Could we get the sister's name and address?"

"I don't see why not. She lives in Denver." Maxine got up and left the room, returning with an address that was jotted down on an order blank, apparently from the truck stop where she worked. "I wouldn't mind knowing why he came back myself," she said as she handed me the piece of paper. "Maybe there'd be something in it for me. You know what I mean?"

I glanced down at the address. "But there's no name or phone number."

"Oh, that's where Joey was living when he got arrested. I don't have the phone number for Juanita—that was Luis's sister—here at home. It must be in my other purse at work. If you want to stop by, I'll give it to you." She gave us the name of the truck stop, which I'd remembered seeing on the way into town.

"So why'd you give us your son's old address?" Rosalie asked. "Do you think anyone there would still remember him after all this time?"

Maxine shrugged. "I thought maybe the bimbo he was shacked up with back then still lived there."

Oh, good, a bimbo. "Does she have a name?" I asked.

Maxine picked up the cigarette from one of the over-flowing ashtrays, knocked off the long ash, and took one final puff before she snuffed it out. "I don't know. Suzy Q is what Joey always called her—my sweet little Suzy Q, but she looked like a bimbo to me. You know the type. Blond hair, big bazooms, and a totally blank look on her face."

Maxine didn't have such small bazooms herself, although they sagged a little from age, and I could almost picture someone calling her a bimbo, too, in her younger days. But she was actually too brassy and street-smart to be what I considered a genuine bimbo.

I figured the possibility wasn't very good that Joey's bimbo was still at the same address, but I asked if Maxine had a phone number anyway.

"Nope," she said. "Joey always told me he didn't have a phone, but I have a feeling he just didn't want me to bug him all the time. And what's funny about it is that the bimbo probably would have dumped him by now anyway, so I would have wound up supporting him in my old age."

Again I thought I saw the hint of a tear in her eyes, but she sniffed hard and shrugged it off. "Well, kids, this has been fun, but I gotta go."

With that she popped out of the chair with a whole lot more agility than I had when I attempted to get up from the sofa. I attributed this to the broken springs that had sent me almost to the floor when I first sat down.

She was one tough lady, I decided, and she'd probably go kicking and fighting to her grave in the middle of her shift at the truck stop. The oldest living waitress in Trinidad.

"Okay," I said. "We'll stop by the restaurant on the way out of town to get Juanita Perez's address." She hurried back into the recesses of the house as we let ourselves out the front door.

Rosalie remained quiet until we were in the car. "Maybe I could help her out some way," she said. "I can't believe all the things she said about Jeremiah. He was the worst kind of creep, wasn't he?"

"Seems like it." I started the engine and waited a few minutes for it to warm up before I turned the heater over to defrost to keep the snow from sticking to the windshield. I'd already spent about five minutes clearing off the windows while Rosalie sat in the car, apparently in shock.

Then we waited for Maxine to come out of the house so that we could follow her.

"Once we get the address," Rosalie said as the woman came out the front door and climbed into a beat-up old Chevy, "I guess the next thing we should do is talk to the sister and try to find the bimbo, huh?"

No way. I wasn't buying into this "we" stuff again.

CHAPTER 8

I've always loved truck stops. Don't ask me why. Maybe it's because I've always had a fantasy about being a long-haul truck driver. Hitting the open road. Sleeping in the back of my cab. Leaving my troubles behind me. Talk about escapism.

I especially liked these new truck stops out in the wide-open spaces of the West, often miles from the nearest population center. They're like minitowns, open twenty-four hours a day for the truckers and tourists who pass that way.

What particularly intrigued me about them were the telephones at every booth, including the special section set aside for the truckers. It seemed almost as classy as having a phone at your seat on an airplane. As if you have something so important to communicate that you can't possibly wait to call until you reach your destination.

As soon as Rosalie and I were seated in a booth at the truck stop where Maxine worked, I had this urge to call someone. I probably would have, too, except that I wanted to keep a low profile as to my whereabouts.

I looked around for Maxine, but I didn't see her anywhere. I'd tried to follow her from her house, but she apparently had a far more cavalier attitude than I did about driving in snow—or else she had a better set of tires. She'd lost me in the blowing snow before we were even out of her neighborhood.

And in fact the storm raging around outside somewhat dampened my usual desire to be a long-haul trucker, although I still had an overwhelming urge to escape my problems. Okay, they were really Rosalie's problems, but it seemed as if they were slowly but surely becoming mine.

"About this 'we' stuff," I said to her after we ordered coffee so we'd have something to do while we waited for Maxine to appear. "Now that we know something about Jeremiah's family, you need to take the information to Detective Foster and let him handle things."

Rosalie nodded, which I took as a sign of agreement, even though her mind appeared to be elsewhere.

"And I'd appreciate it if you didn't tell him about the charge application and my coming here to Trinidad with you. Okay?"

"Okay," she said, still distracted. "I can't believe Jeremiah was really Luis Perez and had a sister and a cousin in Denver that I never even knew about."

The waitress returned with our coffee while I was scanning the restaurant for signs of Maxine. I couldn't help wondering if Jeremiah might have inherited his disappearing gene from his aunt. What if she'd deliberately ditched us and wasn't going to show up at work tonight?

Luckily she appeared in her short waitress uniform and orthopedic shoes just about the time another waitress delivered our coffee. "The boss is pissed I'm late," she said. "I'll be with you as soon as I catch up on some of the orders." She hurried toward the truckers' station, which was like an island in the middle of the restaurant.

After a while I noticed her laughing with one of the men, a burly guy with a bald head and bushy eyebrows, who looked like a sumo wrestler. He was just finishing his meal, and Maxine bent down and whispered something in his ear. He looked over at us. I wondered what she'd said to him, but I tried to take the nonparanoid approach. It was probably just some innocent remark about her needing to talk to us—or maybe she was discussing her newfound niece-in-law.

I'd finished my coffee, but Rosalie's was still untouched by the time Maxine finally got around to coming over to our booth. She handed me a piece of paper, torn from another order blank. It had a name, address, and phone number scrawled on it.

"Here's the info on Luis's sister," she said. "What'd you say your name was, by the way?"

"Mandy Dyer." I don't know why I felt I needed to add anything, but I did. "I'm just a friend."

Maxine turned to Rosalie. "What about you? Got an address and phone number where I can reach you if I ever think of anything about Jeremiah?"

Rosalie pulled a business card out of her purse and began to write on the back. "This is for the architectural firm where I work, but I'll put my home address and phone number on it. Maybe we could have lunch together if you ever get up to Denver."

"Yeah, sure," Maxine said as if that would be a cold day in hell, which of course was exactly what kind of day it was right now. "But you gals better get going before they close the road." With that she pocketed the card and started toward the kitchen to place her orders.

"Hey, Maxine," I yelled before she disappeared. "What's your phone number if we want to reach you?"

She turned for just a second. "Don't have one. Ma Bell shut it off a couple of years ago."

So that explained the lack of listing in the phone book and her don't-call-me-I'll-call-you attitude. I wouldn't hold my breath for her to call if I were Rosalie.

I handed Rosalie the sister's address and motioned toward the window. "She's right that we should be leaving, so why don't you drink your coffee and we'll get going."

"I don't think I want it. I'm feeling a little queasy."

That made me feel queasy too. It would be hard enough to fight the storm without a carsick passenger.

The snow wasn't coming down too hard when we moved the car over to one of the gas pumps to fill up for the trip home. It wasn't until we reached the interstate that the wind started to blow, whipping the snow that had already fallen across the open highway like a giant whirlwind. These ground blizzards are the worst kind of storm in Colorado. They reduce the visibility to zero and pile up high and unpredictable snowdrifts that shut roads and stop traffic for days.

The highway patrol hadn't set up a roadblock yet, so I plunged ahead into the near-whiteout. It was slow going, and in order to even know where the road was, I had to follow the tracks another car had made earlier, but they were disappearing fast. The car itself was nowhere in sight, and I had the feeling that we were all alone in a sea of white.

After a while headlights appeared behind me. I could see their reflection in my rearview mirror, and it was a comfort to know that Rosalie and I weren't the only travelers dumb enough to be out on a night like this. The other car gradually overtook us, and I decided it was a truck because of the placement of the headlights. They were on the high beam and pierced through the snow like two giant cat's eyes, reflecting in the mirror so that I could hardly see. I finally had to adjust the mirror so the lights would appear dimmer. I remembered that the car's operating manual warned that the lights would appear farther away than they actually were when you changed the position of the mirror. That was scary because the lights appeared to be riding on the trunk of my car as it was.

Rosalie was oblivious to the lights. "Mrs. Luis Perez," she said. "Rosalie Perez. Can you imagine that? I've been using a fictitious name all these years."

I slowed, hoping the driver would pass. Then I could follow his taillights instead of having to duck my head to keep from seeing the two laser beams burning into my rearview mirror. But the driver must be doing the same thing I wanted to do. He was letting me lead the way through the storm. Unfortunately the tracks of the earlier car that had passed this way had now been obliterated as the wind-driven snow swirled across the highway.

"And why, if he were going to change his name, didn't he change it to something other than Jeremiah?" Rosalie said. "To tell you the truth, I never liked the name very much."

I gave her a few possibilities. Maybe he'd picked the name off the tombstone of someone who was about his age so that he could apply for a Social Security card in that name, or maybe he'd gotten a set of fake IDs from the same source that provides illegal aliens with phony green cards.

"I suppose," she said, and went on talking about Jeremiah.

I have to admit I tuned her out for a while. I was too busy thinking about the truck behind us. Where had it come from? Had it pulled out of the truck stop's parking lot just behind me? It didn't really matter, but I wanted it to pass. I slowed, and the truck slowed behind me. I speeded up, and it did too.

Rosalie didn't seem to notice the headlights, even though their glow lit up the inside of the car as if we were being trailed by a giant spaceship.

She was too busy discussing what we'd learned from Maxine. "So Jeremiah was in Mexico all these years while I was struggling to pay his debts with that lousy five bucks he left in our bank account. I bet the police will be interested in what he was doing down there, don't you think?"

"I'm sure they will," I said to make her feel better, but I didn't think it was going to get her off the hook as the prime suspect.

"And I'm sure they'll want to talk to Maxine," Rosalie continued. "She seemed to hate his guts."

I nodded and continued to fight the storm up ahead and the lights behind me.

It wasn't until we reached Walsenberg that Rosalie seemed to notice the truck. "Maybe you should slow down so that car back there can pass us," she suggested.

Oh, good idea. I was already going so slow that the driver would probably run over us if I decelerated any more. Now I really wanted one of Maxine's cigarettes. Something to relieve the wild thoughts I kept having.

I was remembering Steven Spielberg's first TV movie, *Duel,* where Dennis Weaver was pursued by a huge tractor-trailer with tinted glass on the windows and a crazed driver behind the wheel. Soon it was just man against machine as the truck took on a life of its own.

Or could it be that this truck was being driven by the bald-headed guy that Maxine had been talking to? Had she sicced him on us and asked him to follow us to see what we were really up to? That's why the man could have glanced over at us in the restaurant. It was a possibility that was worth considering, more logical than the *Duel* scenario but no less scary. She had been open about hating Jeremiah, but that didn't mean she was ignorant of what he and her son had been up to.

"Why doesn't that car pass?" Rosalie asked, straining in her seat belt to look around at the other vehicle.

I didn't want her getting hysterical on me. "It's a truck, and the driver's probably just using us to guide him. Are you feeling better, by the way?"

"Yes, once I got outside in the cold, I think the nausea went away."

Speaking of which, the car was like the inside of a refrigerator. All the energy was going to defrost the windows. I blew on my hands to get the circulation going.

"Do you think Maxine was right—that Jeremiah and his cousin were smuggling drugs?" Rosalie asked.

"You tell me. Did he do drugs?"

"I didn't think so. Well, maybe a little marijuana, but who knows? I don't seem to have known anything about him."

We drove through Pueblo, mostly on an elevated roadway that cuts through the middle of town. It seemed as if the truck fell back as we went through the heart of the city. I kept hoping the driver had pulled off at one of the exit ramps, but then it would reappear and overtake me when we were on the open highway again. Of course I didn't know that it was the same truck, but the fact that it never tried to pass made me suspicious.

"I wonder if that's the same truck back there," Rosalie said, interrupting her recounting of our visit with Maxine. "Why don't you pull off the road and let him get by us?"

Because he might stop too. That's what I wanted to say, but I didn't. "Because I might not have the traction to get started again," I said instead.

Rosalie was quiet for a few minutes. "Do you suppose Maxine could have had someone follow us from the truck stop and he's planning to do something to us?"

I looked over at her and could see in the light coming in our back window that her eyes were wide with fear. "If he was planning to run us down, I figure he would have done it by now."

"What if he's trying to frighten us so that we won't do any more checking into Jeremiah's background?"

I tried to smile. "Then I would say he's doing a pretty good job of it, wouldn't you? So maybe we should stop in the Springs for something to eat and see if he goes on or not. I have a hunch it's just what I said—that he's using us to guide him." I wasn't sure if she bought that last remark, but my suggestion to stop was probably a good idea.

It was already eleven o'clock when we reached Colorado Springs—an hour after Rosalie had predicted we'd be home. There were a few other cars on the road now, and the truck had pulled back just as it had when we went through Pueblo. Still I didn't put on my turn signal as I turned off the interstate. I actually would have preferred to continue on to Denver, as I've always found it complicated to get off the interstate and wind my way to the row of fast-food restaurants north of the Springs. The car began to slide on the snow-packed pavement as I tried to stop at a red light at the end of the ramp. It hadn't been so bad when I kept going slowly on the highway, but now I realized how really treacherous the roads were.

We found a Village Inn Pancake House, and I took note that the truck hadn't appeared to follow us. There were two big tractor-trailer rigs already parked at the back of the lot, and if another one showed up, I would call the police and have them check it out.

When we got inside the restaurant, we grabbed a booth.

I wasn't really hungry, but I ordered breakfast anyway because, at this rate, we'd be lucky to get home before I had to be at work the next morning. Besides, maybe it was low blood sugar that had caused me to get carried away about the *Duel*-like truck that had pursued us all the way from Trinidad. I ordered a glass of orange juice to boost my sugar level.

Once the waitress left, I asked Rosalie something I'd wondered about in the odd moments when I hadn't been fixating on the truck. "You were talking about drug smuggling," I said, "but I was wondering if maybe the scam was something else. For instance maybe he was still painting and sending the canvases up to Joey to sell as if they were some of his earlier work. I'm sure his painting increased in value after he disappeared."

"I don't know. I tried never to go near art galleries after he disappeared. They all reminded me of him."

"If you saw one of his paintings, could you tell if it was one he did before he disappeared?" I was thinking of the one Betty and I had seen at the Deverell Gallery.

"I doubt it. They were all pretty similar—except the ones of the nude models. . . ." Her voice faded away.

"Did he put a date on them by any chance, or make a list of the various titles? Maybe take color slides of them?"

"No, nothing." She shook her head helplessly.

By then we had our coffee—two full mugs and a thermos for the table so that we could get refills without having to wave down a waitress. I wanted to stay in the safety of this place forever.

I was holding the mug in an attempt to warm my hands, which were cold partly from gripping the steering wheel so hard and partly from the lack of heat in the car. I drank the coffee as we talked, but I couldn't see that it was doing much to bring me back to rational thinking. I wondered why I'd even asked if Jeremiah had dated his paintings. Obviously if he were still turning them out in Mexico, he would have backdated them anyway.

I finally decided to tell her about the fifty-thousand-dollar price tag I'd seen on the painting in the gallery.

Rosalie was stunned. "That's impossible." She shook her head. "It simply can't be. He sold all his paintings before he left, and told me he got six hundred dollars for the lot."

"I'm only telling you what I saw."

"Where was it? I have to see this for myself."

"Not a good idea. I'll tell Detective Foster, and he can check into it." After all, he knew I was an artist, so he couldn't prove that I'd been snooping when I went to an art gallery.

"But fifty thousand dollars . . ." Rosalie shook her head.

"Well, think about all the publicity his disappearance and now his murder have generated. That's what undoubtedly sent the price soaring. Remember, there's no such thing as bad publicity when it comes to making money."

Rosalie didn't answer. We ate our breakfasts when they arrived, had a couple of refills on the coffee, and then set out in the storm, which had picked up again while we'd stopped. There was no *Duel*-like truck in the parking lot, only the same two trucks that had been parked at the back of the lot when we pulled in. Unless of course one truck had pulled out and another had taken its place to wait for us. Get a grip, Mandy, I told myself. Just be thankful that the danger had been a figment of our imagination with a dose of sleep deprivation thrown in.

There were a few other intrepid motorists on the road between the Springs and Denver, plus a truck and a few cars that had pulled off on the shoulder. I noticed the truck because I was still feeling skittish about anything with eighteen wheels. It was about a mile from the freeway entrance, and I saw a blurred image of a bird's head on the side of the cab as we drove by. And in one of those totally irrelevant thoughts I have sometimes, I wondered, Wouldn't that have been a more suitable logo for a fly-by-night airline than a trucking firm?

"I owe you big-time for this," Rosalie said. "You know that, don't you?"

"Darned right," I said. "And I'm going to think of some suitable repayment when we get back to Denver."

And we almost made it too. Snow was still coming down hard when we reached the infamous Monument Hill, and I'd picked up another eighteen-wheeler behind me. I refused to believe it was the same rig that had followed us from Trinidad. Unless it was the one that had been parked at the side of the road. Stop it, I scolded myself. Why do you always have to be so melodramatic?

Rosalie didn't seem to have any qualms about being melodramatic, though. "It's the same truck," she said, her voice rising in pitch. "We should have called the police from the restaurant and told them about it."

"You're probably right, but we can't do anything about it now."

"Well, can't you at least go any faster?"

Well, actually, no, I couldn't. We were creeping up to the crest of Monument Hill when it happened. Several stalled cars and another semi were off the road, but if I just kept moving, I thought, I could make it to the summit.

The truck behind me was going faster than I was, and I prayed I'd get over the top before he ran us down. That's when I finally made up my mind that, once and for all, if I could just reach the summit, I would pull over to the side of the road and get the truck's license number as it went by. If it went by. At least there were enough stranded motorists that there must be a highway patrolman around someplace to come to our rescue if we got stuck.

The eighteen-wheeler looked as if it was going to rear-end us if I didn't get out of its way. I tried to make the Hyundai move, but it had a mind of its own and very little traction. The truck kept right on coming. I put my foot down on the accelerator and gunned the engine. Big mistake. Just after we crested the top of the hill, the car spun out toward the side of the road.

"Hold on," I said as calmly as I could. "We're going over the side."

Actually that was better than the alternative. The huge semi could have slammed into the car and killed us both. But just as we hit the shoulder, it thundered by, its driver never even braking when he saw the Hyundai skid out of control. Worse yet, I was too busy plowing downhill through the snow to get its license plate number.

"Oh, my God," I heard Rosalie say as we headed down the incline. Then she started screaming, and she didn't stop until we reached the bottom.

CHAPTER 9

I looked over at Rosalie anxiously. "Are you all right?"

"I think so," she managed to get out once she quit screaming.

The descent had been a relatively gentle ride except for a bump along the way, where we'd apparently hit a rock that was jutting out of the snow.

I moved my head back and forth to make sure I didn't have whiplash, but I seemed to be okay. "Look," I said, "I'm going to see if I can drive the car back up on the highway. Do you want to get out while I do or stay inside?"

"I'll stay here."

The car was still running, and I tried to back out of the snowbank we'd created as we came to a stop. It didn't work. I made a few more attempts, but it was no use.

Rosalie had calmed down by then.

"I'm going to go up to the highway and see if I can get some help," I said, opening the door.

I climbed out into the ankle-deep snow in my totally inappropriate canvas shoes and scrambled up the bank to the highway. Rosalie followed me, and together we managed to hail down a passing motorist in a four-wheel-drive vehicle. Actually, it was a couple with a cell phone who called the highway patrol. We were informed that the patrol wouldn't respond tonight if it was a one-car accident, there were no injuries, and the vehicle wasn't in the roadway. I could file a report the next day.

I was disappointed. I wanted to tell someone that a crazed trucker had forced me off the road, but it would have to wait. I didn't know what good it would do anyway. I didn't even know the color of the truck, much less its license number.

Rosalie and I eventually made it back to Denver, even if my car didn't. The highway patrol would have a tow truck haul the Hyundai out of the ditch, hopefully the next day and without too much damage. Meanwhile Rosalie and I hitched a ride with the couple in the four-wheel-drive.

The man and his wife were kind enough to take us to Rosalie's car, which was still parked at the storage locker in Glendale. In one of those fickle flukes of Colorado weather, it hadn't even snowed in the Denver area, and I drove Rosalie home in her car since she said she was still shaking too much to drive. She lived in a secured condo development that required a gate card to get inside, and once I made sure she was safely in her apartment, I called a taxi to take me the rest of the way home. She wanted me to spend the night in her spare room, but I declined. After all, I had a serious need to be alone, plus a cat waiting to be fed.

"Don't forget to call Detective Foster first thing tomorrow and tell him what *you* learned," I said when the cab driver buzzed to be let into the parking lot.

"Thanks for everything," she said, "and I'll keep your name out of it."

It was already two thirty in the morning when the taxi dropped me at my less-than-secure apartment building. No one accosted me on my way up to my third-floor apartment, and once I was inside, I began to wonder if we'd imagined the threat from the truck. After all, it hadn't actually run me down. Skidding off the road had been my own doing. But then why hadn't it stopped when it saw us go over the side?

Spot had raised havoc in the place, having gotten into his dry food on the counter. That'll serve you right for leaving me alone for so long, he seemed to say as he eyed me from the sofa. He'd recently changed his sleeping habits, kind of like I imagined a lion did once in a while out in the wild. He was curled up on the sofa, where he seldom slept when I was home, and I hoped I could lure him off with food. Otherwise I might have to sleep in a chair all night or risk being clawed. I got ready for bed and then opened a can of his favorite food. Once he heard the can opener, he jumped to the floor. I hurried over, pulled the sofa out into a bed, and fell on it, exhausted.

I didn't even bother to check my answering machine. I'd have to find a way to get to work in a few hours, now that my car was out of commission, but I'd think about it and the "duel" with the truck when I woke up.

I was glad Mack had the assignment of opening up on Tuesday, a task we took turns doing on a weekly basis. It allowed me the luxury of sleeping in. It was eight o'clock when I woke up, not my usual six. I hadn't bothered to set my alarm clock.

First things first. I fed Spot again, took a shower, and changed into a freshly laundered uniform. Then I called Mack and told him I was on my way. I tried to ignore the blinking light on my answering machine as I dialed.

"Where'd you go yesterday? Why are you so late?" Mack demanded, always suspicious that his surrogate daughter had been up to no good. "I left a message on your machine last night to call me when you got home."

"Sorry. I didn't check the messages when I came in. I'll see you in half an hour." I hung up.

Mack was probably a little hurt, too, that I hadn't called him personally to let him know I wouldn't be in for the remainder of yesterday. I couldn't very well ask him to come and get me at this point. I didn't want to tell him my car was in a ditch somewhere between here and Colorado Springs.

Instead I called a taxi again, but I finally took the time to check the blinking light on the answering machine. Eight messages—the one Mack had told me about and a bunch from Betty after she got home from work last night. She still wanted to know if I'd found out anything about Honest Abe from *that cop*. A final message was from Nat. He'd called to let me know that Rosalie had shown up in Denver Sunday night and that she'd supposedly been on a ski vacation the previous week.

"But that doesn't give her an alibi for the time of the murder the previous Friday night," he added into the machine. "No one saw her that night because, she said, she'd been busy packing."

Of course I already knew all this. Tell me something I don't know, Nat, I said to the machine. He didn't, but that gave me an idea of something he could research for me. I'd have to think of a way to phrase it so as not to raise his reporter's antennae. Once I had a dream about him, and he had these "rabbit's ears," like the ones on old-time TVs. For some reason I knew in the dream that they weren't "Martian" ears, even though they came out of the top of his head. That's because they appeared only when he sensed that something you knew might be grist for one of his articles.

I'd been kind of hoping Stan would have called, but he hadn't. Having Rosalie show up at the storage locker had probably set back whatever was left of our relationship once again. Every time I did something that he didn't regard as a suitable task for a dry cleaner, it was a giant step backward for us. But get real, Stan—I'd have to tell him sometime, even a dry cleaner has to have a life outside of work. But was this the life I wanted—going around being furtive with my friends?

I wouldn't be able to tell him anything today. Work was waiting for me when I finally got to the cleaners. The taxi dropped me at the back door, and just my luck, Mack was standing outside when I arrived.

"What are you doing out here in the cold?" I asked after I paid the cabbie.

"Just taking a break," he said. He was probably worrying and waiting for me, but he wouldn't admit it. "Why the taxi?" he asked, coming back inside with me.

"My car wouldn't start this morning."

I knew he wouldn't drop it there. "So where'd you go yesterday?"

"Rosalie was upset and needed to talk to someone."

"I don't like to see you getting involved in this," he said, shaking his head. I guess he felt it wouldn't be right if he didn't give me a word of advice before he moved on to work-related issues.

He said Josalyn, a woman who worked at our shirt press, had given a two-week notice this morning. Harry, one of our pressers, had called in sick, and Betty had been bugging Mack about where I was and when I would be getting to work.

I sought out Betty, who was already in the lunchroom on her own morning break. After all, she came in at seven o'clock, and it was already past nine.

"So did you find out anything from that cop guy?" she asked the minute she saw me.

"That's what I wanted to talk to you about." I sat down at the table where she was having a cup of coffee from our bottomless pot. Bottomless providing anyone remembered to fix it, that is. I tried to assume a reassuring manner as I prepared to give her the bad news. "Stan said they couldn't locate Honest Abe, but they'll keep looking."

"Oh, damn, I was afraid of that. Somethin's happened to him for sure." Betty got up and started to pace.

"No, I bet he just found some other place to stay for a while. Who would want to stay in an alley where a murder took place? I'd be afraid the killer would come back." Wrong thing to say.

"That's what coulda happened. The killer prob'ly came back and shot poor ole Honest Abe, too, and dragged his body off to God-knows-where and threw it in a Dumpster."

"No, Betty, no." I tried to head her off before she worked herself into a real state. "Stan said there hadn't been any reports of other unidentified bodies."

Betty refused to be comforted. "Nope, ole Honest Abe wouldn'ta given up his alley that easy. There was this grille in the ground where the warm air came up from a building. You don't just give up a spot like that without a fight in this cold weather."

"How about the way you took off Christmas before last after we finally caught the person who tried to kill you? You said you went to Florida."

"Well, yeah, there's that," Betty admitted, "but old Honest Abe didn't like to travel much. He was a Colorado native, and far as I know, he'd never been out of the state."

I really couldn't spend all morning trying to comfort her, but I did give it one more try. "Look, it will be okay.

Stan said he'll let me know the minute they locate your friend."

"Poor old Abe," Betty said. "He'll prob'ly be scared to death if they come after him. Somebody ought to warn him, but I bet he's already dead in some dump somewheres."

There was something about that last remark that made me uneasy. I decided it was her certainty that he was dead. I should have concentrated on the first part of the sentence about somebody trying to warn him.

I glanced at my watch and knew I'd better start work. "I have to get going," I said. "I'll talk to you later."

She nodded and sat back down. Her break should have been over by then, but I decided to let it go. If Honest Abe were my friend, I might want to think about him for a while too.

I continued to the front of the building to check with Julia to see if everything was under control at the counter. She said it was. Then I flipped through the messages that had come in for me the day before. Someone had called about a dress they said we'd ruined, a high school music director called to see if we could clean the school's band uniforms, and a hotel manager wanted to know if we could clean a tapestry that hung in the hotel lobby. All messages that required a response.

I'd barely returned to my office when Julia rapped on the door. "I forgot," she said. "There was one weird call—someone asking if a person named Mandy worked here. When I told him that would be the owner and gave him your name, he hung up."

"Are you sure it was a man?" My first thought had been that it might be Maxine from Trinidad. After all, she'd specifically asked what my name was. But how would she know to call the cleaners? But what about the Deverell woman from the art gallery? Had she noticed I was from the cleaners and figured out who I was?

"It sounded like a man to me," Julia said.

"Well, thanks." I couldn't afford the time to worry about it right then when I had so many other things to do.

I spent the next two hours on the phone. I called the highway patrol and gave them the information for their accident report. I told them about the truck, but the woman taking down the information didn't think there was much they could do about it. After all, I didn't even have a license number. I decided not to tell her about the bird logo on the cab door of the truck I'd seen, lest she think I was, for lack of a better word, a birdbrain.

She told me that my car would be towed by Smitt Towing Company to Miller's Garage and that I could call about it later. I reported the accident to my insurance company and then tried to reach Rosalie. She wasn't home, and I left a message for her to call me when she finished talking to Stan.

Then I started returning the business calls. Yes, we'd be glad to clean the band uniforms; we'd need to inspect the tapestry and see if we could hand-clean it; and if the woman would bring in the dress that had been damaged, we'd be glad to take a look at it. In the name of good public relations, we'd pay for the dress, but since it sounded expensive, we'd need the price she'd paid for it, prorated for how long ago she'd purchased it. We wouldn't pay the full price if she'd had it for ten years.

I also called several people at Mack's request to say there were spots on their garments that we couldn't remove without possible damage to the fabric. If the customers wanted to give us the go-ahead to try further, knowing the risks, we would be glad to do it for them.

While I'd been talking, I doodled on a scratch pad. I

often do this, but this time I was trying to remember the logo on the side of the truck from the night before. When I was through with the phone, I studied the doodles. Every sketch looked like the head of a generic bird. Not an eagle, a blackbird, or even a sparrow. Just a generic bird.

I picked up the white pages of the phone book, which were the only pages I could find right then. Just for the heck of it, I looked up Bird Trucking and then *Byrd* Trucking. My long shot didn't pay off. There was nothing.

I tossed down the phone book and headed for the front counter to relieve Julia and Ann Marie for their lunch breaks. After that I took over on the press line for the ailing Harry and kept working until we were caught up.

It wasn't until three o'clock that I had a chance to get back to the phone. I called Nat at his extension at the *Tribune* and caught him on the way out.

"Thanks for the call about Rosalie," I said.

Nat brushed me off. "Sure, but I gotta go."

"This won't take but a second, Nat. There's a man named Joey Perez, who was sent to prison for a burglary here in Denver about five years ago. I wonder if you could look up any stories on it in the newspaper files and get back to me."

Nat asked me if his first name was Joseph, and I said I wasn't sure. I could almost picture the antennae rising from his head. "So why do you want to know?"

I began to itch, but Nat couldn't see me. "I'm trying to do a more thorough background check on people when they apply for jobs," I said. That was true, but of course it didn't have anything to do with my inquiry, and as soon as I said it, I realized he'd figure that out as soon as he saw the article about Joey's death in prison. Unfortunately it was too late to change my story.

*   *   *

I'd had a call from the garage in the late afternoon. The towing company had delivered my car, and the mechanic told me he would check out the Hyundai and let me know the damage the next day. I told them to put some new tires on it while they were at it.

I might have commandeered the company van in order to get home that night, but our route driver who picked up and delivered cleaning to businesses in the area was using it to get back and forth to work until his own car was fixed.

Mack and Betty had left long before our seven-o'clock closing time, so I prevailed on our afternoon counter manager, Theresa, to give me a lift home. It was only a short distance out of her way, and I wasn't planning any further outings for the night.

The only thing I had on my mind when I got home was to go to bed. Well, that and to feed Spot again of course. I'd already grabbed a late lunch at five thirty, which I ate at the mark-in counter behind the wall that divided the plant from the call office. Lucille, who's in charge of marking in the clothes, had already gone home for the day, or she would have had a fit at my using her space for my lunch table. She was already mad at me for making her help at the front counter while I was gone the day before.

I was asleep by eight thirty and had no idea what time it was when the phone rang. I bounced out of bed with a start and was at the phone before I knew it. That's the way I am when I'm exhausted but not quite into a deep-sleep cycle yet. When I'm really sound asleep, the phone can ring and I won't even hear it, or if I do, I wait for the answering machine to pick up and answer only if it's an emergency at the plant.

I looked at the clock and saw that it was nearly ten. At first I thought it was ten in the morning and that I'd slept around the clock. It took me a while to realize it couldn't be morning because it was dark outside.

If it was still night, it wasn't even late enough for me to be afraid that the call was bad news. I stared at the phone anyway, my heart pounding in my ears because it had scared me in my just-fallen-asleep mode. I finally decided the caller must be Rosalie or Nat, and I picked up the receiver just before the answering machine came on.

"Hello, this is Mandy." My voice sounded clear and alert. No one would have guessed I was still groggy, but I knew better than to trust what I might say under these circumstances. I'd once told a friend I'd enroll in a cooking class with her when she'd caught me in my vulnerable half-asleep stage; I'd had to call her back when I was fully awake and retract the promise.

"Ms. Dyer," a polite voice responded.

"Uh-huh." Nat never called me Ms. Dyer, but it was a male voice. I wondered if it was the man who'd called the plant earlier, but it wasn't.

"This is Arthur Goldman, Betty's friend."

Oh, swell, the doll doctor. Now she had him making calls for her.

Finally I was beginning to wake up. "How are you, Arthur?" I almost called him Artie, which was Betty's nickname for him, but he seemed too dignified in an Albert Einstein sort of way to be an Artie. I say that because of his short, slightly pudgy stature and electrified white hair.

He hesitated for a minute. "Ms. Dyer, I hate to bother you with this, but I'm really worried about Betty."

My heart had just settled down from the sharp jolt of the telephone, but now it started pounding again. "What about Betty? Is she sick?"

"No," Arthur said, "but I called her just now. We usually

talk for a while every evening, but she said she didn't have time tonight."

"Why not?"

"Uh—well, this may sound a little crazy. . . ."

Nothing sounded crazy if it came from Betty.

Arthur continued. "She said she was going out tonight to try to find someone named Abraham or Abner—something like that."

"Honest Abe?" I asked, but I knew I was right.

CHAPTER 10

"Yes, that's it—Abe," Arthur said.

I decided I'd been right to think the doll doctor wasn't a "nickname" type of guy, but it didn't give me any satisfaction.

Betty might already be searching the back alleys and underpasses of Denver looking for her friend, Honest Abe, and from there it might be only a short step for her to be back on the streets herself. A sip of wine from a bottle in a paper bag and she'd be gone.

"When I asked her if I could be of assistance, she said she didn't want to jeopardize my welfare," Arthur continued in his courtly manner. I'm sure it wasn't a literal translation of what Betty had said. "I tried to make her wait so I could go with her, but she refused."

"Did she say where she planned to go?"

"That's what really alarmed me. She said she was going downtown somewhere. I told her it wasn't safe this time of night, but she said she was going anyway."

Damn, I thought, but I didn't say it to Arthur.

"I was wondering if you might go with me to look for

her?" he continued. "I've tried calling her back at her apartment, but there's no answer."

"Look, why don't you keep trying to call her, and I'll go see if I can find her. I'm closer to downtown than you are, and we'd waste a lot of time if I waited for you to get here."

I was relieved when he agreed, and before I hung up the phone, I promised to call him as soon as I found out anything.

The last thing I needed if I was really going to go searching for Betty was a chubby sixty-year-old sidekick who was shorter than I am. He's a doll doctor, after all, and used to the gentler side of life.

Besides, what I needed was the big, husky black man who'd once disguised himself as a homeless person to help me search for Betty on another occasion. That man was Mack, and besides, I needed his pickup truck. Wouldn't you know I'd have an urgent need for wheels just when my car was out of commission?

I tried Betty first, just in case she'd chickened out at the last minute or had the good sense to return home. No answer. Then I tried Mack, but there was no answer there either. I wondered if he had a play he was rehearsing. I couldn't remember him mentioning anything to me at the moment, and I didn't know the number for the cell phone he'd recently purchased.

So far I'd rejected the idea of getting a cell phone myself because sometimes I liked to get out of the reach of everything and everyone. The trip to Trinidad was a good example. I'd even made fun of him for getting one, but now I could see its value.

I had no choice but to wait for his answering machine. I started to leave a message for him to call me if he returned within the next few minutes. He picked up before I was through, and I was relieved to hear his voice.

"I need your help, Mack."

"Shoot," he said.

"You know that homeless man, Honest Abe, that Betty was talking about who might have been a witness to Jeremiah's murder?"

"You mean the guy they call Harpo?" I could practically see him grinning over the phone, pleased that he'd been able to figure out why people called a guy named Honest Abe by a nickname.

I refused to engage in any more discussion about it. "Well, Betty's friend, Arthur—you remember him, don't you? He just called and said she has gone out looking for Abe."

"What the blazes possessed her to do that?"

"I don't know what possesses Betty to do anything, but Arthur's threatening to go out searching for her himself. I told him I'd give it a try if he'd sit home and wait in case she called."

"You know it's going to be like looking for a needle in a haystack, don't you?"

"Yes, but she said she was going to look downtown, and I thought maybe we could drive along the bus route from South Broadway and see if we can spot her."

Mack may have been wondering about this "we" stuff, the way I had with Rosalie, but all he said was "Okay, it's a long shot, but I don't have anything else to do tonight. I'll be over in a few minutes."

"Oh, and why don't you bring your cell phone, just in case?"

I didn't add what the "in case" was, but Mack gloated a little just the same. "See, I told you they could be useful sometimes, and that you should get one too." Then he hung up.

Fortunately he didn't live too far from me, and I was

dressed and waiting for him on the curb when he pulled up in front of the apartment in his truck.

"Where's your car?" He'd apparently already noticed that it wasn't parked along the street.

"It's at the garage being fixed."

Surprisingly Mack accepted that explanation and told me to hop in. He was in his old navy pea jacket and black knit hat that he'd worn when he dressed up as a homeless man that other time we were looking for Betty. I blended in well myself because I was wearing jeans and a black parka that I'd found at the bottom of my closet. The parka had cat hairs on it, but I hadn't taken the time to brush them off.

Mack shuddered a little at the blast of cold air coming in the door. "What makes you think Honest Abe won't have gone to a shelter for the night?"

"He probably did go to a shelter if he's smart," I said, "but I'm not as interested in finding him as I am in finding Betty."

Mack nodded, put the pickup in gear, and pulled away from the curb.

I had a bus-route brochure in my pocket, and I pulled it out. "See"—I pointed—"the bus from South Denver goes up Lincoln and then turns and circles around through the downtown area. It might take Betty a while to get there if she left just before Arthur called, so, if we're lucky, she might be getting off the bus just about the time we get downtown."

We drove along Fifteenth and circled back on Nineteenth along the route the bus took, then cruised the area again. No Betty. We even followed one of the buses I was assuming she would have taken to get downtown. It dropped off and picked up passengers along the way, but none of them was Betty.

I pointed to a cross-street. "This is the area where Jeremiah was killed. Maybe Betty came here to start her search. Why don't you drop me off and then come around the block and pick me up? I'll see if I can spot her."

"Nothing doing." Mack pulled around the corner and parked the pickup. "I'm coming with you."

I have to admit I was glad he decided to tag along. It was easy to identify the alley. There was still a piece of crime-scene tape attached to a wall. It was fluttering in the wind.

"Betty," I yelled into the alley that was like a narrow canyon with walls so high you could barely see the top and only a faint light at the other end.

"What are you going to do, just stand out here and holler?" Mack asked as he shuffled up to me, now into his role of a homeless person.

"I was hoping to get an answer." I yelled again, but I got only an echo.

"I'll go down to the other end of the alley and see what I can dig up," Mack said as he headed into the dark hole. "Wait here."

I was beginning to think this was a very bad idea, and I grabbed his arm and told him so.

He shook me off. "Look, there's still traffic going up and down both streets. What could happen?"

That's what I didn't like to think about. "Okay, I'm going with you."

To his credit Mack didn't try to stop me. Together we entered the alley, which seemed to swallow us up immediately with its darkness and dank smells. We couldn't see any chalk lines where Jeremiah's body had once been, so what chance did we have of finding a real live person? There could be a dozen people hiding in the shadows, for all we knew.

A quarter of the way through the alley we heard a noise, and I instinctively grabbed Mack's arm.

"Hey, what you doing in here? This is my alley!"

I squinted into the darkness, but I couldn't tell where the sounds were coming from.

"Get the hell out of here." The voice was hoarse from the ravages of alcohol.

"Honest Abe, is that you?" My own voice came out sounding almost as croaky as the person who was demanding that we leave. What's more, it was probably stupid of me to ask if the speaker was Honest Abe, who never spoke to anyone.

As my eyes adjusted to the dark, I could make out a cardboard lean-to but no person. "Please, Honest Abe, if it's you, we're looking for a woman called Betty. Has she been here?"

"It'll cost you," the voice said from inside the makeshift home.

Mack had some money handy. He leaned over, and a hand whisked out and grabbed it. A beam of light from a flashlight blinked on, and I could see a face through the opening. Apparently the man was satisfied with the amount, and he came halfway out from under the cardboard.

"You mean that old lady in the trash bag?"

"That's the one." Betty must have gone back to wearing the Hefty bag, which had been her trademark when she was on the streets. She wasn't called Bag Lady just because of her habit of carrying her possessions around in a paper sack.

"She was here a while ago looking for Honest Abe. He said I could sleep here while he was gone."

"Gone where? Betty probably went there, too, and she might be in danger."

"It'll cost you some more."

Mack supplied another bill. Again, the man inspected the money with his little flashlight.

"Abe went to that old warehouse down near the railroad tracks—the one that's about to be tore down."

"But where?" Mack asked.

"They had somethin' in the paper about it a week or so ago. That's all I know."

God, I wished Nat was here with us. He'd know about the warehouse for sure, but I thought I remembered reading about it. "I think I know where it is," I said to Mack. "The article said the police had been trying to clear the transients out before it was demolished."

And now I believed Betty really was in danger. From what I remembered, the building had been an ongoing problem. It would have been called a hobo jungle years ago, but that was a different time. Nowadays people went there to shoot up, sleep it off, and occasionally to stab each other in the back.

I felt as if I might throw up, and it wasn't just from the smells of urine and rotting food. I gasped a thank-you, then turned and ran out of the alley with Mack right behind me.

"You okay?" Mack asked.

I breathed in the exhaust fumes from the streets, and it had a mildly restorative effect. It was the odor I was used to in Denver's sometimes polluted winters.

"I don't know if I have the guts to go there," I said, still afraid I'd lose what guts I did have.

"Let me handle it."

"No." I'd never forgive myself if something happened to Mack. "We'd better call the police. They were looking for Honest Abe, and maybe they can find him now."

It was perhaps the only sensible suggestion I'd made in

the last few days. Mack agreed with me, but first we had to make sure I knew where the building was. Since Mack had the cell phone with him, we could call when we located it. Maybe we'd even get lucky and find Betty walking along the dark streets on the way.

We didn't find her, but I did a lot of soul-searching on the trip. What I'd been thinking about Sunday night came back to me: How little I knew about some of the people around me. Not much different than Rosalie's experience, really, except that Jeremiah had been Rosalie's husband whereas Betty was simply someone who worked for me. But what if something happened to her? I wouldn't even know how to notify her next of kin.

I'd had an opportunity to find out about Betty's real identity once when a woman showed up at my door asking if I knew a Florence Lorenzo. The woman claimed to have seen me with her at a flea market, and I'd suspected that Betty was the woman she was looking for. But I hadn't pushed it. I just dropped the subject, and when Betty finally came to work for me, she'd produced a dog-eared Social Security card with that name on it. But I hadn't asked who Florence Lorenzo had been in her other life. Did she have a husband? Children? Where was she from? Why had she hit bottom and wound up on the streets? I vowed to ask her some tough questions when we found her.

"Turn left up there," I said. "I think it's down there toward the tracks."

We bounced over deep potholes in the road, and Mack finally stopped where the road dead-ended at a huge dark building that rose two stories above the weed-choked parking lot around it. I didn't remember what the structure had once housed, but I recognized it from the picture in the newspaper. It had an archway over a gate that was no longer there and a gaping hole in the front that looked like the entrance to hell but had once been a loading dock. There were a few windows at odd spots above the doors, their glass long since broken. They looked like huge pock-marks on the surface of the building.

"This is it," I said. "I remember seeing a picture of the arch."

Mack dialed his cell phone and handed it to me. "You're better at this than I am."

I doubted that, but I waited for the 911 operator to come on the line and told her where we were. I explained about Honest Abe as well as Betty, figuring she would have more interest in finding a possible witness to a murder than in finding a crotchety former bag lady.

"Let's get out so that we can direct the police down here when they come," Mack said, popping his door open.

I followed him out of the truck and edged over toward the nonexistent fence. I didn't see any activity from the building, only the flickering of light from inside the double-wide doors. It was cold and I zipped up my down jacket to my chin, then shivered as I stood there wondering if the police would ever come. Maybe I hadn't given the right directions after all.

The noise of lower downtown was only a hum in the distance, carried by the wind that swept across the road we'd just come down. I strained to hear the first sounds of a siren or even the engine of a silent patrol car approaching. Nothing until suddenly a scream pierced the darkness.

I didn't have time to think. I took off toward the building at a run. I was afraid someone had attacked Betty. The noise had sounded like the high-pitched scream of a woman who needed help.

Damn the police. Why hadn't they arrived yet? I could hear Mack pounding along behind me. He didn't catch up with me until we were at the big gaping hole that had once been a roll-up door.

"What do you think you're doing?" he asked, grabbing my arm.

I yanked away. "I'm trying to help Betty."

"What makes you think that was Betty?"

"It sounded like her." Of course I didn't know how Betty sounded when she screamed, but as I looked ahead through the flickering light of a fire that someone had started on the bare cement floor, I saw the glint of her Hefty bag. I might not be sure of her scream, but I knew that was Betty's bag. Someone was trying to rip it off her.

I was gone before Mack could snatch me again.

"Stop that," I yelled when I finally reached a woman with scraggly hair who was pulling on the bag. "Let go of her."

The woman with the unkempt hair pulled away. "Who the hell are you?"

Worse yet, who was the woman in the Hefty bag? It wasn't Betty. Instead the person I'd been trying to defend was about a hundred pounds heavier than Betty and looked as if she could take care of me and the other woman combined.

"It's mine," she said, moving toward me menacingly. Apparently she assumed I was someone else who coveted the bag.

"I'm sorry. I thought you were Betty," I said in defense of my moment of attempted gallantry.

The woman moved back. "She gave me this here bag, and then she went thataway." She pointed toward a stair-well that looked as if it disappeared into the bowels of hell.

Mack had reached us by then. In fact he'd apparently been here for a while, waiting to jump in if needed. "Let's get out of here quick before we get into real trouble."

I looked back the way we'd come and noticed that several people had moved out of the shadows and were watching us. Mack grabbed my arm and started hauling me toward the door. I hadn't realized how far we'd come into the building, and I began to shake.

"Do you ever have the feeling you're not in Kansas anymore?" he said so quietly that only I could hear.

Our game of guessing movie quotes didn't help much right now, and unfortunately Mack wasn't the Wizard of Oz, or he could have given me some much-needed courage. I'd used whatever I had in my attempt to save Betty, and now my legs felt like they belonged on the Scarecrow.

We'd just about made it past the gauntlet of staring eyes when the police arrived. En masse. The invisible people in the nooks and crannies of the building began skittering off in all directions. Out of the corner of my eye I glimpsed someone in a top hat heading for the stairs. A top hat? More precisely a stovepipe hat. Honest Abe? Wasn't that what the real one had been famous for wearing?

I hesitated a split second, then took off after him. I might have caught him, too, if one of my feet hadn't slipped off a dilapidated board halfway down the flight of stairs. I caught myself momentarily, then bumped the rest of the way to the basement on my seat. Just as I struggled to my feet, someone grabbed me and slammed my hands behind my back.

CHAPTER
11

Strong arms yanked me around and hauled me back up the stairs. I strained to see who had grabbed me, but it wasn't until we emerged from the stairwell that I realized it was a cop.

"Okay, we're clearing all you people out," the man said. "You can't stay here. How many times do we have to warn you?"

I saw Mack, who was getting the bum's rush too. "Show him your cell phone," I yelled. "We're the ones who called you."

It didn't impress the cop. In a place that had become a natural breeding ground for rats and a sanctuary for homeless people, runaways, and junkies, I can only assume that some dealers who serviced the inhabitants had cell phones too.

Someone shuffled toward us out of the shadows. "It's okay. They're looking for me." It was Betty without her Hefty bag. "Let 'em go, and we'll get out of your hair."

I was delighted to see her but not necessarily to have her come to our aid. Betty as a guardian angel was not something I wanted to think about. She'd never let me live it down.

The police grabbed her too. Together we were rousted from the building, but it wasn't until we were nearly at the fence that I saw Stan. I assumed he'd gotten the report that this might be where Honest Abe was hiding and had rushed to the scene.

He looked at Mack and me as if he thought he might be hallucinating. "What are you two doing here?"

"I'm the one who called in the report that Honest Abe might be in there," I said, "and I think I saw him—a guy in a stovepipe hat."

I guess he hadn't been asking for an explanation. "You have no business being here."

"Get your hands off me. I ain't done nothin'," That was Betty, bringing up the rear, and beginning to lose her Good Samaritan persona.

"And what's *she* doing here?" Stan was staring at the former bag lady.

I guess Mack decided it was time to jump in. "That's why we're down here. We were looking for Betty."

"When *you* couldn't find her friend Honest Abe," I added, "she went looking for him herself."

"I don't know nothin'," Betty said, "and tell them to get their paws off me."

"Let them go," Stan said, "but I'll need to talk to this one." He pointed at Betty.

"I don't know nothin'," she repeated, glowering at me.

I have to admit I had doubts about her innocence, since she'd come from the same general direction where I'd first spotted the man in the stovepipe hat, but to appease her, I said, "Arthur was worried about you."

She ignored me. "I got nothin' to say."

"Did you find Honest Abe?" Stan asked.

"Look, Betty, talk to him," I said. "Tell him what you know. Mack and I will wait for you in his truck." That was assuming that we weren't under arrest.

She shrugged. "Okay, but I don't know squat."

Stan took her away to his car. Meanwhile people kept scurrying from the building like ants from a hole that some kids had set on fire. After about thirty minutes I saw Stan escorting Betty toward Mack's truck.

"Okay, you can go home now," Stan said as he delivered her to us. "You should be glad you have friends who were worried about you."

I wondered if that was meant as an apology to us, even though it was directed at Betty. Probably not, because what he said next was "I'll talk to you later, Mandy." The words had all the warmth of a teacher talking to a rebellious child who had just been told to report to the detention room after school.

"Look, you shouldn't have done something crazy like this," I said to Betty as Stan stalked away. "You scared Arthur to death, and he was going to come down here and look for you himself."

She looked contrite but only for a minute. "Yeah, but he never woulda found me. He doesn't have any street-smarts."

I took that as a compliment that Mack and I did, and I forged ahead. "So did you find Honest Abe?"

"I said I didn't." She folded her arms over her scrawny chest.

"But I saw someone in a stovepipe hat. I thought maybe that was him."

"I got nothin' to say." She gave me the silent treatment all the way back to her apartment.

She didn't want us to go inside, but I insisted. I said we had to call Arthur, but I could have done that from Mack's cell phone. It was just an excuse. Once she talked to Arthur, I was hoping she might feel guilty about the worry she'd caused him and tell us more about tonight, plus reveal something about her mysterious past. I punched in his number, told him she was okay, then handed her the phone and went to the bathroom.

When she hung up, I heard Mack talking to her. I couldn't hear what they were saying, but if he was getting her to open up, I decided to hang out in the bathroom for a while. I'd had the distinct impression on the ride to South Denver that she held me personally responsible for her altercation with the police.

Finally the talking ceased, and I decided it was time for me to make an appearance. I opened the door, but when I saw Mack and her sitting at either end of a tweed sofa covered with doilies, courtesy of her neighbor, Mrs. O'Neal, I was appalled.

The two of them were sitting there drinking red wine. Mack must be out of his mind to let a recovering alcoholic have wine.

I guess I went a little crazy at the sight. That's the only way I can explain what happened next. I ran over and tried to grab the glass out of Betty's hand. Betty held on to it.

"What the hell do you think you're doing?" Mack yelled.

"Betty shouldn't be drinking." I tugged at the wineglass and wrestled it out of her grip. Its contents spilled out and went cascading down the front of her blouse.

"It's grape juice," I heard Mack saying as the juice spread out as if it were paint that had been splattered on a canvas.

"Grape juice." I stopped and stared at him. "What the devil is it doing in a wineglass?" Then I grabbed a piece of paper from Betty's hand and tried to sop up the mess. She wasn't having any of that. She yanked the paper back and started to get up. Grape juice spilled out of her lap and dripped to the tan carpet. I ran to the kitchen and grabbed the materials to sponge the purple liquid from the rug. "Go change out of those clothes, Betty," I said from down on my hands and knees. "I'll get the stain out. I promise."

Betty gave me a dirty look and went into her bedroom to take off her blouse and a pair of corduroy pants. At least she had a bedroom, which was more than I had. It took me a while to sponge up all the grape juice from the floor. Mack didn't offer to help. He just sat there with an amused expression on his face.

"Oh, get that dumb look off your face," I grumbled.

It didn't do any good. Mack was still grinning when Betty came back out of her room wearing a bilious green pants suit that was one of her favorite outfits. If I'd spilled grape juice on that, I might have thought twice about cleaning it.

Betty handed me the stained clothing.

"Fooled you, didn't we?" she said, and I could tell that her rather warped sense of humor was returning. "Sometimes those wineglasses fool me, too, and I think I'm having a nip of the old grape. The good kind."

Okay, if grape juice kept her sober, fine, but if I ever saw her drinking from a wineglass again I would still want to smell the contents to make sure it wasn't fermented. You can never put too much trust in a former bag lady, and I was about to have that opinion confirmed.

"Betty was telling me that she did find Honest Abe," Mack said calmly.

I swung from him to Betty. "You did what?"

She had a satisfied look on her face. "Yep, and I had to let myself be caught to help him get away. They'da never caught me if I didn't want them to."

So her efforts to play Good Samaritan hadn't been totally altruistic on her part, and I was afraid of what the answer to my next question would be. "Did you tell Stan about talking to Honest Abe?"

"You kiddin'? I didn't give the cops spit."

"Oh, God, Betty, you lied?"

Betty shrugged. "Well, sure. I had to give old Honest Abe time to get out of there, and I have to tell you he lit out of there like the devil hisself was after him. That's what I should have done, too, if you hadn't got in the way."

"I guess we interrupted their conversation when we showed up and all hell broke loose," Mack said.

I sat down in a chair at the end of the sofa and shook my head, assuming she hadn't had time to find out anything from her friend. "I'm sorry, but Arthur and I really were afraid for your safety."

"That's okay," Mack said. "Honest Abe told her a couple of interesting things before he took off."

It had never occurred to me that Betty might actually have gotten anything out of a guy who didn't talk.

I glanced over at Mack. "Go ahead, Betty," he said. "Show her the drawings."

She went back in the bedroom and got the sheet of paper that she'd had before. Thanks to me it was now covered with grape-juice stains but still legible. She pointed at a poorly drawn sketch, but I could tell it was a pair of women's high-heeled shoes.

I looked up at Betty for interpretation. After all, she'd been so free with her art criticism at the museum the other day. "And so?"

"That's what he saw when he peeked out from under his cardboard box the night that guy was killed."

"A pair of high-heeled shoes?"

This was wonderful. Now at least we knew Jeremiah's killer had been a woman or else a guy in drag. Suspects went tearing through my mind like a herd of wild horses: Jeremiah's aunt with the high heels in the plastic bag; Laura Deverell from the gallery in her gold-colored shoes with the stiletto heels. And then there were all the people I'd never even met: Bambi, whom Jeremiah had been having an affair with before he left; his sister, whose name had been written on the piece of paper I'd passed along to Rosalie; and even Cousin Joey's girlfriend, the bimbo, Suzie Q. The bimbo must be bitter about her boyfriend being killed in prison if, as Jeremiah's aunt thought, Jeremiah was the one who'd planned the caper he was convicted of. And Bambi and the bimbo both sounded like the spiked-heel type, while all of them had plenty of reason to hate Jeremiah. Except maybe for the gallery owner, and with her I was sure I just hadn't found the connection yet.

The only person I didn't think it could have been was Rosalie, and I was relieved about that. I'd never even seen her in a pair of high heels. Almost like me, except that I did have a token pair of black pumps.

I let out a sigh of relief and asked the critical question: "So what else did he remember about the person besides the high heels?"

Betty seemed astonished at my naiveté. "You kidding? He wasn't about to look any farther when he hears the shot and sees the guy land right in front of him."

"What did he do?"

"Well, he plays dead of course until he hears the high heels run out of the alley, and he doesn't come out of his hiding place until he's sure they're gone." Betty peeked out from under what I gathered was an imaginary cardboard shack, the way Honest Abe must have described it to her in some sort of sign language. Then Betty moved over to me, still mimicking her friend, and grabbed my wrist. "And then he checks for a pulse to see if the guy is dead." Betty dropped my hand and shook her head sadly. "If the guy'd been alive, old Honest Abe woulda gone for help right then."

I wasn't too sure I had as much faith in her friend as Betty did, but why argue about it?

Betty had moved back from me, and she started pulling out the pockets on her bilious green jacket in an imitation of what Honest Abe must have pantomimed himself doing.

I was appalled. "He went through the dead man's pockets?"

"Well, how is he going to find out who the guy is otherwise?" Betty continued to turn her pockets inside out.

Yeah, right, I thought.

Betty gave a gigantic shrug. "Nothin'. The guy didn't have anything on him." She started stuffing her pockets back inside her jacket.

"What's this?" I had turned the paper over to the other side. Honest Abe had drawn a simple rectangle on it with the word *Tribune* at the top. That was the newspaper where Nat worked, so what was Honest Abe doing drawing a sketch of that? I could make out the misspelled word *Febuary* in smaller letters.

"That's the only thing the guy was carrying," Betty said.

I was confused. "I thought you said he didn't have anything on him."

Betty put up her hand to quiet me. "No, the guy was carrying this newspaper, so Honest Abe shows me how the dead guy was holding it"—she jammed the paper with the drawings on it under her arm—"and how it fell when he was shot."

With that Betty grabbed her chest as she took a few steps backward. The paper fluttered to the floor; then Betty spun around and collapsed.

I was so startled that I tried to grab her. Maybe she was

having a heart attack. Fine help I'd be if she were. She toppled to the floor facedown through my outstretched arms and on top of the piece of paper.

"Oh, God, are you all right?" I bent down with the idea of checking her pulse or whatever Honest Abe had said he did.

"Like that," she said, getting back up to her knees. "That's what Honest Abe said happened."

"Bravo," said Mack, who was apparently admiring her acting skills. He'd directed a play not long ago, and if he did another one, I wouldn't be surprised if he considered casting Betty in a part.

"It's nothing." Betty got to her feet and took a little bow as if she were making a curtain call. "Knowing how to pass out is a good way to avoid trouble sometimes when you're living on the street."

Mack and Betty were beginning to get along a little too well, as far as I was concerned, and they were straying off the subject.

"Back to the alley," I said. "Why didn't the police find the newspaper?" Of course maybe they had and Stan simply forgot to tell me or, let's face it, thought it was none of my business.

Instead of answering, Betty bent down and did a pretty good imitation of someone flipping over a body.

Oh, swell, Honest Abe had moved the body.

Then she swooped up the sheet of paper with the drawings on it. "So when he doesn't find anything else," she said, "he takes the newspaper. He thought maybe it was that day's paper, and he always did like to keep up on current events."

"But it wasn't that day's paper," I said. "It was from February."

"That's right." Betty nodded happily, apparently pleased

that I was following her little charade. "It was old news, so he chucked it."

Betty went over and threw the sheet of paper in her trash can. I went over and retrieved it, because this, after all, was something that definitely needed to be turned over to the police.

"So what was the date on the paper?" Mack asked from the couch.

I put the paper in my purse as I looked over at Betty, hopeful that she could supply us with an exact date without acting it out. Maybe there was something in that particular issue of the paper that had brought Jeremiah back to Denver. Why else would he be carrying a month-old newspaper?

"Don't you think I asked Honest Abe that? That's why he wrote down *February*, but he couldn't remember the date."

Well, at least February was a short month if I had to go through every paper page by page. And I knew I would—even though I would have to turn the information over to Stan as well. But he couldn't keep me from checking out all the papers, especially since I had a friend who could supply me with every one of the back issues. I was sure I could figure out a few favors Nat owed me, and if that didn't work, I could tell him that the papers might be a clue to the murder. That would bring him around when all else failed. I'd have to call him as soon as I got home.

"And you didn't tell Stan about Honest Abe's drawings?" I held out the sheet of paper in hopes she'd just been toying with me the first time.

"You kiddin'? I wasn't going to tell him about them and have him go right back in there to try to catch poor old Abe."

"You have to tell him, Betty."

"You tell him. I don't like him."

I wasn't looking forward to calling Stan about how Betty had held out on him. He didn't think too highly of me and my motley crew as it was, and I thought it might be best to wait until tomorrow to make the call. I was sure he'd want to talk to Betty again, and I didn't want to hang around waiting for him to show up here. Maybe tomorrow at work would be best, when he could talk to her at the plant where I could have people watching the doors so that she couldn't get away.

"Let's call it a day," Mack said.

"I'll drink to that," Betty said, winking at him.

Mack chuckled, and I frowned at both of them, but I was still thinking about Honest Abe as I started to leave. "So I wonder who went in the alley and called the police after your friend left."

"Oh, Honest Abe did that."

I turned around and came back in the room. "And just how did he manage that, seeing that he doesn't speak?"

This gave her another opportunity to act out one of her silly charades. She put her thumb to her ear and her little finger down beside her mouth as if she were talking on the phone. Then she pretended to dial a number.

Okay, maybe I'd asked for this, but I was getting downright irritated. "You told us Honest Abe couldn't speak," I protested.

"I didn't say he couldn't speak," Betty said, slamming down her imaginary phone. "I said he didn't speak."

"But I thought he was—" I tried to think of the politically correct phrase. "I thought he was orally challenged." It sounded dumb, even to me.

Betty began to shake her head. "I never said that. I never once said"—she sputtered for a minute—"whatever the heck it was you just got through saying."

"So what is he?" Mack asked, taking the direct approach.

Betty put her hands up, palms toward us, and began to move them around in a circle as if she were trying to get out of a glass house.

And if I'd had an imaginary stone, I gladly would have shattered a few of her imaginary windows. "Enough with the pantomimes," I said.

"Right," she said, waving her hand in excitement. "I knew you'd get it. He's a mime, not a deaf mute."

"A mime." Mack whacked his forehead. "Of course."

"A mime?" I asked as I wrung my hands in a pretty good imitation of someone wringing Betty's neck.

"I thought I already mentioned that," Betty said.

I was shaking my head in the universal symbol for no. She hadn't mentioned that important fact.

"Sorry," she said. "That's what he did back in the old days before he got to drinkin'."

"So he's actually the one who called the police?" I asked.

"Yeah, but he had to use his voice for that. It's pretty hard to do pantomime on a telephone." Betty looked at me as if maybe the reason I was having difficulty grasping this concept was that my wires didn't quite connect to my receiver.

CHAPTER 12

"Maybe we should have called Stan tonight?" I said, more to myself than to Mack as we pulled away from the curb in front of Betty's apartment building.

"It'll keep," Mack said, which is the kind of answer I wished he'd give more often, seeing that I do consider him a father figure. "Betty's friend is long gone from that building by now."

"I know, but Betty's information sounds important."

"What makes you think Betty told us everything?"

I looked over at Mack in surprise. "Why would she lie to us?"

Mack never missed a beat as he drove north on Lincoln toward Capitol Hill. "To protect her friend, and besides, how do we know Abe was telling her the whole truth?"

"*Honest* Abe?" I asked.

"Maybe he picked Jeremiah's pockets, and that's why there wasn't any ID on the body."

I couldn't argue with that. A nickname was no real evidence of Abe's veracity. "I guess I'll leave that decision up to Stan."

Mack had to stop for a light at Sixth Avenue. "And

speaking of being candid, what's the real story about your car?"

I looked over at him in surprise. Was I that transparent? I hadn't even itched when I'd told him my car was in the garage; I simply hadn't told him how it wound up there.

I sighed. "Okay, if you must know, the car went into a ditch Monday night when I took Rosalie down to Trinidad to see Jeremiah's aunt." Then of course I had to explain about the charge application, my part in discovering the aunt's name, the information we got from Maxine, and the torturous trip home through the snowstorm with the tractor-trailer on our tail.

"I keep wondering if the aunt sicced the truck driver on us when we left the truck stop where she worked," I concluded. "Anyway we wound up in the ditch on Monument Hill when I tried to outrun the guy."

By then Mack had pulled up in front of my building in Capitol Hill. "You know, don't you, that the whole trip to Trinidad was pretty stupid?" Mack said when I finished, now turning into the critical parent.

"Well, yeah, *now* I do," I admitted. "We even pulled off the highway in Colorado Springs to try to lose the guy, but it didn't work. Or at least someone else started following us. I remember seeing a truck pulled off at the side of the road a mile or so from the restaurant. I think it had a bird on the door, and I wondered if maybe it stood for Bird Trucking or something, but there was no company like that listed in the phone book."

"You ought to run these things by me before you go off half-cocked." Now Mack had turned into the protective mother hen, unlike my real mother down in Phoenix, who is more like a preening peacock.

Whoa. Back up. My mind flitted off to the logo on the

side of the truck. What if the symbol on the truck had been a specific kind of bird, not just a generic one?

Mack was still expressing his disapproval. "I figured you were up to no good when you didn't call me yesterday and tell me you were going to be out of the plant all day."

"I'm sorry." I opened the door and jumped down from the pickup.

"Want a ride to work tomorrow?"

"Okay, sure." I slammed the door and literally flew up the stairs to my apartment.

I would have liked to call Nat about supplying me with all twenty-eight issues of the *Trib* for February, but it was too late to do it without raising his hackles about why I wanted them. Still, I had a mission—as soon as I fed Spot, that is. He jumped down from the sofa, which he'd pre-empted recently as his *new* favorite place to sleep, when I added a few Friskies to his already half-full bowl. That satisfied him that I was still his slave and gave me a chance to convert the sofa into a bed when he wasn't looking.

Then I grabbed the Yellow Pages and hauled them over to the bed. I fell asleep with the phone book open on my lap, but not before I'd found something worth checking out as soon as I got my car back the next day: Robin Trucking, with offices in an industrial area just off Interstate 70.

I was exhausted when I arrived at work the next morning, and my overloaded brain was going off in a dozen directions. First I had to call Stan to confess that Betty had withheld some important information from him. Since he wasn't too happy with me anyway, I figured this would do nothing to enhance my popularity. Like bag lady, like boss lady. Of course there was always the possibility that he would be impressed that Mack and I had been able to wrest the information from Betty when he couldn't. Okay, so I was probably right the first time.

I made sure that Betty was at work before I called him. I was hoping that I'd get his voice mail, thus avoiding a real conversation with him. That's why I called at seven thirty, when I thought he wouldn't be in yet.

"Detective Foster here," Stan said after the first ring.

Darn. I had my "recorded message" speech prepared, but now I began to stutter. "Uh—this is Mandy. I—I was calling because, well, I have some evidence for you. Actually I guess you'd call it information, and uh—"

"What are you talking about?" Stan was obviously getting irritated with my hemming and hawing.

"Well, it's really Betty's information. She talked to Honest Abe last night—"

"She did what?"

I held the receiver away from my ear until I was sure he was finished. "She talked to Honest Abe, and he saw Jeremiah's murderer's—"

"Why the hell didn't she tell me that last night?" Even when he was mad, Stan seldom raised his voice; now he was practically screaming.

It made me defensive about Betty. "You ought to know by now that she doesn't trust cops. She was afraid you'd run back in the building and hunt down her friend."

"Damn." He was probably especially upset at that last remark because it was exactly what he would have done. After a pause to recover his composure, he continued. "So who'd he say killed Atkins?"

"If you'd have let me finish, what I started to say was that Honest Abe saw the murderer's shoes."

"His shoes?" Stan was almost sputtering.

"Yes," I said, "and they weren't *his* shoes. They were more likely *her* shoes because they were high heels." Before he had a chance to say anything more, I added, "And I want you to know that I've never seen Rosalie in high heels in my life."

He took a deep breath, as if trying to stifle a whole lot of other swear words that were bubbling up in him. "Okay, go on."

I explained how Betty had told Mack and me about the drawing of the shoes and the fact that Honest Abe had found a February issue of the *Trib* under Jeremiah's body.

"When he saw that it wasn't that day's paper, Honest Abe threw it away," I said. "He didn't remember the date, and"—I took a deep breath—"he also searched Jeremiah's pockets, but he didn't find anything else, no ID or anything."

"I'll be right down," Stan said, "and I'll want to talk to Betty."

I felt as if I should say "Yes, sir," and salute at the commanding tone of his voice, but I fought off the impulse. Instead I said, "Okay," and hung up.

It was a good thing I'd made sure Betty was here before I called. Now I went back to the dry-cleaning machines and asked Mack to keep an eye on her while I waited for Stan at the front counter.

I busied myself by helping my morning counter crew, Julia and Ann Marie, take care of customers. Best to keep busy while I awaited Stan's wrath. At least the wrath wouldn't be directed at me, but in a way it might be easier if it was. Betty would be hopping mad when she realized she had to talk to him again. "Jumpy as a rabbit in heat." Wasn't that the expression she'd used when she described the owner of the art gallery? Well, that would be nothing compared to this. Betty would probably think I'd betrayed her and was the worst kind of human being—a snitch.

Nope, I was really not looking forward to this. In fact I

was grateful when Arlene Whitney, who looked too young to be a bank vice president, came in with a load of clothes. She was one of our best-dressed "career women" customers and always kept her wool suits meticulous. In fact I suspected that she wore an outfit only once before she brought it back to be cleaned. That's the kind of customer I like. And with her mathematical mind, I visualized that she kept the freshly cleaned clothes in garment bags at home, all organized by day so that she'd never wear the same outfit twice in a single week.

"Hi, Arlene," I said. "How are things going at the bank?"

"We're having an audit this week. That's why I'm here early." She put a load of clothes on our counter. "I need this dress for a dinner tomorrow night." She held up a pale green chiffon that I was sure would bring out the green in her eyes and set off her reddish brown hair. "Can I get one-day service on it and pick it up tomorrow after work?"

"Arlene, for you, anything." Actually she knew darned well we always gave a one-day service—same-day on request—but she usually just came in once a week. And I never said anything about her having us store her things for a week because she was such a good customer. Besides, some people did it for a whole lot longer than a week.

I went to our conveyor and picked out the five outfits for her from her previous week's visit to the cleaners, then went to our separate shirt conveyor for her coordinated blouses and hung the accumulated outfits on our slick bar at the counter. I pulled up her order on our computer and gave her the price. She was writing a check when Stan appeared. He must have used his siren in order to get here so fast.

"I'll be with you in a minute," I told him.

Stan looked irritated, but I wasn't about to turn a cus-

tomer over to another employee in the middle of a trans-
action.

He glowered at me as I put the check under the change
drawer in the register, gave Arlene a receipt, and offered to
carry her clothes out to the car for her, as is our custom.
She said she could handle the clothes, and I said good-bye
to her. Did Stan have to watch every move I made as if I
were planning to steal money from my own till?

"So where's this drawing that Betty's friend made?" he
asked the moment Arlene was out the door.

"It's in my office." I put Arlene's incoming cleaning order in a laundry bag, tossed it in a cart under the counter
until Lucille at mark-in was ready for it, and then motioned him to come around behind the counter. "If you
want to come back with me, I'll give it to you."

He followed me through the plant, and just my luck, I
saw Betty turn from where she was pulling a load of shirts
out of the washer. I knew she saw us. She gave a little
reflex movement as if she was ready to bolt. I shook my
head at her and kept on walking. She relaxed when she
saw I was taking Stan to my office; still I was relieved when
I saw Mack move toward his station at the back door,
ready to head her off if she actually did try to make a run
for it.

Poor Betty. She probably thought my head shake indicated that she wasn't going to have to talk to Stan again.

When we reached the office, I grabbed a folder with
Honest Abe's drawings inside. I'd considered putting the
piece of paper in a large Baggie, but that seemed a little
like overkill. The sketch wasn't evidence that might con-
tain the murderer's fingerprints or anything.

Stan pulled out the paper and zeroed in on the stain.
"What's that?"

"It's not wine, if that's what you're thinking." Of course

Stan probably hadn't been thinking anything of the kind, not having had the experience of protecting a recovering bag lady from herself. "It's grape juice, and I spilled it on the paper."

He glanced up at me, and I thought there was just a hint of amusement in his eyes. After all, I'd started out our relationship by giving him advice on how to get ink and grease stains out of his shirts. Mandy's Helpful Cleaning Tips, I called them. I think he took pleasure in seeing that I was a klutz sometimes myself, but his enjoyment faded fast.

"Okay, can I use your office to talk to Betty now?"

"Sure," I said, "I'll go get her, but I think she might be more cooperative if I stayed here with her."

Stan started shaking his head even before I finished. "No, I want to talk to her alone."

"All right, but remember that time she refused to talk to you at the hospital and you had to come and get me."

I probably shouldn't have brought it up. It was over a year ago—a whole different set of circumstances, and he apparently didn't want to be reminded of it. "We'll try it my way first."

I could hardly wait to say "I told you so," but for the time being, I merely nodded and left the office.

Betty had removed all the shirts from the washer and was separating them by hanging them over the side of a laundry cart for the shirt pressers.

"How about a break, Betty? I'll get Juan to finish that for you."

She eyed me suspiciously and kept on working.

I decided it was time to get tough. "Betty, I need you to come to my office. Stan wants to talk to you."

"I don't want to talk to him."

"He's a policeman, and you have to talk to him."

"You orderin' me to talk to him?"

I sighed. "Okay, if that's the way you want it, I'm ordering you."

She glared at me, and for a moment I thought she was going to refuse. But finally she slammed a shirt over the top of the cart and started for the office. "Okay, but you got to stay with me to see that there ain't no police brutality."

"You tell *him* that. I already tried."

We were at the door by then, and she gave him a dirty look. She didn't request that I stay, however, and Stan asked that I close the door as I left. If she wasn't going to complain about being left alone with him, I wasn't going to hang around where I wasn't wanted.

I don't know what went on inside, much as I was tempted to eavesdrop from outside the closed door. Instead I couldn't find Juan. He must be on break. I went over and finished separating the laundered shirts for her and started another load of wash. I wanted to talk to Betty as soon as Stan was finished, and maybe after he beat her down, she'd be willing to answer my questions. All I wanted, after all, was to find out her life story and her next of kin. I'd been planning to ask her last night, but I'd been too flustered by the grape-juice incident and finding out that she'd withheld information from the police.

I'd barely finished loading the washer when the office door opened. I was ready to accept Stan's apologies, once he got through begging me to help him out. See, I would say, I told you she wouldn't talk unless I was there. I'm glad I didn't express my thoughts aloud. Before I had a chance to gloat, Betty emerged from the office, too, and started back to the laundry.

Dang her ornery hide. Despite her protest, she'd apparently answered his questions, but I knew she hadn't pantomimed her way through the conversation about Honest

Abe the way she had with Mack and me. There hadn't been enough time, and I have to admit that I was disappointed that Stan hadn't needed me.

I hurried over to them. "Betty, would you mind waiting for me in the office a minute," I said before she got away. "I need to talk to you."

Betty beat a quick retreat to my desk, but it didn't get me out of a brief private conversation with Stan. "Is there anything else you want to tell me while I'm here?" he asked as soon as she left.

Well, of course there was the trip to Trinidad, but *want* seemed to be the operative word here, and no, I didn't *want* to tell him about that, so I didn't. Rosalie was handling that revelation, and in fact I assumed she'd already provided him with the information about Jeremiah's relatives. Since he didn't mention the trip to me, maybe she really had kept my name out of it. I was sure he would have brought it up if she had.

But what if she hadn't talked to him? For just a minute I felt uneasy as I recalled that she hadn't returned my call the day before. Why not? What if something had happened to her after I'd taken her home? I made a mental note to call her again as soon as I talked to Betty.

Stan was waiting, and I finally realized that he'd asked me if there was anything else I wanted to tell him. "No, nothing," I said, and tried to smile, even though I was beginning to itch. "I'll see you later."

"Yeah," he said, and then he surprised me. "And—uh—thanks for getting Betty to talk."

"Sure. Anytime." And now my smile was genuine. He'd actually acknowledged the help Mack and I had given him.

I noticed he was carrying the grape-stained sheet of paper as he left. I turned back to my office.

"I got a bone to pick with you," Betty said the minute I was inside.

"Of course you do," I said, "and I have one to pick with you too."

Betty looked stunned. As if no one could possibly have a complaint against her.

"Look, Betty, you had no business going off by yourself last night to look for Honest Abe." Geez, I sounded just like Mack, but I went on. "It was dangerous, and Arthur was going to go out looking for you himself if I hadn't said I'd do it."

Betty was belligerent. "I coulda took care of myself."

"Arthur didn't know that."

For once Betty was silent.

"I didn't even have my car," I said, "but luckily I was able to get Mack to help me look for you."

"Yeah, and you almost blew the whole thing."

"Okay, maybe we did, but Mack and I were worried, too, and that made me realize something. I don't even know the name of a relative to notify in case something happens to you."

Betty ducked her head and stared down at her hands for a while. "That's because I don't have nobody."

I didn't know whether to believe her or not, but if it was true, it made me want to cry. I looked away.

She must have sensed my vulnerability. "Guess that makes you my next of kin, boss lady. I got nobody else."

I glanced back at her, but I couldn't see the normal twinkle in her eye. "You're serious, aren't you?"

"If you must know, I was married once, but we never had no kids."

"What happened to your husband?"

"He died."

"But how did you wind up on the street?"

Betty looked thoroughly irritated now, but she didn't clam up the way I expected. "If you must know, he and I had a tailor shop, like I said once, but he left me with all these debts, and I got to drinkin'. Finally the bank foreclosed, and his bookie was after me to pay his gamblin' debts, so I just took off. End of story."

"I'm sorry." What a pathetic response for me to make when I'd insisted on her telling me her life history. "Okay," I said finally, "I guess I can be your next of kin."

Once she'd pulled those begrudging words out of me, she got a twinkle in her eye. "Don't worry about it, boss lady. Maybe Artie can be my next of kin. He's been talkin' about wantin' to get married."

Dear God. Arthur and Betty married. It would be like Kewpie Doll exchanging vows with Raggedy Ann. I tried to figure out if she was kidding or not, but I couldn't tell, and frankly I didn't want to pursue the subject any farther. The only time I'd tried to play matchmaker, I'd inadvertently set up the gentle doll doctor with a retired bag lady. Better that I be her unofficial next of kin than for her to marry Arthur.

"Can I go now?" Betty asked.

"Sure," I said. She never brought up the bone she'd wanted to pick with me, and that was a relief. I think we were both just glad to have this conversation come to an end.

CHAPTER 13

I didn't know whether to worry about the fact that I hadn't heard from Rosalie or about the possibility of a marriage between Betty and Arthur. Now that I'd semiofficially adopted her, Betty would probably want me to be the maid of honor.

I decided not to focus on wedding bells but to call Rosalie instead. She still didn't answer her phone, so I left another message. I called Nat, too, and left him a message at his extension at the *Trib*. Sometimes it felt as if the whole world never bothered to answer its phone. I could have tried Nat's cell phone or pager, but I didn't want to tip him off that my inquiry about Joey Perez had been more than a casual interest about a job applicant at the cleaners. And I didn't want to act as if it was an emergency when I put forth my request for every issue of the paper for the last month.

I worked on the books, which weren't books anymore but spreadsheets on the computer. When I finished, it was time to go up front to relieve Julia and Ann Marie again for their respective lunch breaks. No one had called for me while I was in my office, and I resisted the impulse to leave another message for Nat. I did call Rosalie again. Still no answer. I tried the garage, where someone told me my car probably wouldn't be ready until midafternoon. I was anxious to get the car so that I could check on Rosalie and take a look at Robin Trucking.

I was waiting on one customer and had two more waiting in line when Rosalie did better than call. She showed up at the cleaners and started waving at me from just inside the door.

"I have a lot to tell you," she said when she reached the counter. She then moved back a respectful distance to wait until I was free.

"Have a chair," I told her. "I'll be with you as soon as I get caught up."

But I didn't get caught up. The customers kept coming, and I finally noticed Rosalie fidget in her seat and get up. "I'm going over to that Mexican restaurant we went to before," she whispered. "Meet me there as soon as you can."

I didn't think Ann Marie and Julia were ever going to return. When they did, I took off. I was afraid Mack would want to join me for lunch, so as I went out the back door, I pointedly asked if he'd like me to bring something back for him. He said he would be taking his lunch break later. That made me uneasy. I didn't want him to show up in a few minutes and add his conservative overview to whatever Rosalie had to tell me. I was assuming it had to do with Stan's reaction to her news about Trinidad.

She was seated at a back booth of Tico Taco's, sipping a Coke, when I reached the restaurant. It's just across the pavement in a strip shopping center behind our standalone cleaners.

"Sorry I made you wait," I said as I slipped into the seat across from her.

"That's okay, but I just couldn't stay there another minute," she said. "I was just bursting to tell you everything."

The first thing I wanted to know was how she'd been able to avoid telling Stan about my part in finding Jeremiah's aunt and learning about her son, Joey, who'd died in prison.

"Okay, I'm ready," I said.

Manuel, Tico Taco's genial owner, must have thought I meant I was ready to give my order. He appeared out of nowhere with a glass of water and a cup of coffee. I knew the menu by heart, and I told him I'd take the cheese enchiladas. Anything to get to Rosalie's news.

As soon as he headed for the kitchen, she leaned toward me. "Okay, are you ready for this? I went to see Jeremiah's sister."

"You what?"

"I went to see Juanita, Jeremiah's sister," she repeated.

Maybe it was because of Betty's reluctance to talk to the police, but I was beginning to have a bad feeling about Rosalie too. "And that was all right with Detective Foster?"

"Oh, I haven't talked to him yet."

Yep, another Betty.

"I wanted to check the people out first before I told him about them," she explained.

"Not a good idea, Rosalie. He won't like it that you're going around talking to people before he has a chance to interview them."

"Oh, but I had to discuss a funeral with her. You know how I told you the medical examiner is ready to release the body? I had to talk to his sister about it."

"And what did she want to do?"

Rosalie shrugged. "Nothing. She doesn't have much money."

I realized I was running my own hands through my hair in agitation. Now I thought I knew how Stan felt about me once in a while. Okay, a lot of times.

"But I found out one thing," Rosalie continued. "She seemed very nice, and I don't think she could have killed Jeremiah."

"But Stan—I mean Detective Foster—he isn't going to like this."

"I just had to find out about her, Mandy. It's my life that's on the line."

"Okay," I said. "But you need to go talk to Foster this afternoon and tell him what we learned. Please, Rosalie."

Behind me I heard someone clear his throat. "I don't want to interrupt. . . ." Oh, right.

"You remember Mack, don't you?" I asked Rosalie.

She nodded.

"I just wanted to tell you how sorry I am about everything that has happened," he said.

She thanked him, and for a moment I thought she was going to invite him to join us. Before she had a chance, Manuel brought my order of enchiladas along with Rosalie's combo plate, which she'd apparently ordered earlier.

Mack asked him for fajitas, then turned back to us. "Now if you'll excuse me, I have some manuals to read, so I'm going to grab myself another booth."

"Another booth" turned out to be right behind us, and I had a feeling Mack had chosen it so he could eavesdrop on our conversation. He and I had done that one time ourselves.

I leaned toward Rosalie and said softly, "Promise me you'll go see Detective Foster."

"All right, I promise, and I'll try to keep your name out of it." Rosalie's voice reverberated around the booth, and I winced at the thought that Mack was probably hearing every word.

"Okay, good," I whispered.

"But first," Rosalie continued, still loud enough to be heard by anyone within twenty feet, "I was wondering if I could talk you into going over to see if Joey's bimbo still lives at the address Maxine gave us."

I stabbed into the enchilada and, despite my best intentions, yelled, "No, absolutely not. You need to talk to Detective Foster first."

"*Then* will you go with me? Please."

"I don't think it's a good idea. He's not very happy with me right now."

"Why? What could he possibly be mad at you about?"

Well, for not telling him about the trip to Trinidad, for one thing, and he hadn't even heard about that. "It's about the employee of mine who thought a friend of hers might have witnessed the shooting."

"Oh, please God, tell me they found the witness."

I could see why she would get excited, and I had to head her off. "No, but my employee was withholding some information about his whereabouts."

"Why?"

"She seemed to distrust the police—just like you do."

Rosalie ignored my point. "So where is this witness?"

"That's the problem. He isn't at the same place anymore, and I have to tell you, Detective Foster isn't happy about it."

I could see Rosalie's disappointment in her eyes, but at least she understood what I'd been getting at. "Okay, I'll go see the policeman, but you have to promise me one thing."

I wasn't about to make a commitment until I knew what the favor was. I took a bite of enchilada and waited.

"Would you go to the funeral with me? Please. I really need the support."

"What funeral? I thought you said there wasn't going to be a funeral."

"No, I said Juanita couldn't afford to help pay for one. She has a bunch of kids, her husband left her, and she's on welfare. What could she do to help?"

"So who's paying for the funeral?" Of course I knew the answer.

"Well, I couldn't very well let his body go unclaimed," Rosalie said. "I had to give him a proper burial, so I've just finished making the arrangements. The service is tomorrow at ten. You'll go with me, won't you? Please."

That word again, but this time her plea was so plaintive, I couldn't refuse. Besides, if the murderer always returned to the scene of the crime, why couldn't she—I was remembering the high-heeled shoes—also turn up at her victim's funeral?

It was worth looking into. Only trouble was that Rosalie told me in the next breath that she wasn't sure the service would have time to make the funeral notices in the paper. How could the murderer show up at the service if she didn't know there was going to be one?

I had a solution for that. Nat. But first I had to sneak past Mack in the next booth. I was afraid he might want a private word with me to "critique" the conversation he'd just overheard, but he merely nodded at Rosalie and me and returned to his operational manual about our dry-cleaning machines. As if he didn't know everything there was to know about them already.

As soon as I returned to the plant, I called Nat again at the *Trib* and listed the time and place of the funeral on his voice mail. I was sure he'd be doing a follow-up story for the next day's paper, and he could tack the information about the service at the end of the article. That would give the time and the place of the service greater visibility than a listing in the obituaries. I gave Nat another reminder to call me when he got back in the office.

I continued to play catch-up all afternoon—that is, until the predictable appearance of Mack in my office when he'd finished work for the day. He showed up while I was taking a call from the garage that my car was ready. The mechanic assured me that there was no serious damage to the car, although he'd had to replace the tailpipe.

"I'll give you a lift," Mack volunteered as if that had been the only thing on his mind when he came in to see me.

I told Theresa at the front counter that I wouldn't be back for the rest of the day and that if Nat called, to tell him to leave a message at my apartment.

It had been my intention, after I retrieved my car, to drive up to Robin Trucking Company to check it out for crazed truck drivers and cab doors with bird logos on them. It wasn't to be.

Mack was on a tear. "I know you feel sorry for Rosalie, but you need to stop messing in this," he said as soon as I was inside his truck. "She's manipulating you, and you're getting in way over your head."

"You were spying, huh?"

He was innocence itself. "I couldn't help overhearing what she was telling you."

In my own defense I said, "Well, she's my friend, and she doesn't have anyone else."

"That's no excuse for not telling Foster about your ill-conceived trip to Trinidad when he was in this morning."

"Okay, I know, but I still think she should be the one to tell him."

Mack still wasn't through with his "parental" advice by the time we got to the garage. It hadn't occurred to me that he would want to come in with me. But why not? He prides himself on his mechanical and automotive skills.

I tried to head him off by saying my car wouldn't be ready for another hour. That brought the slightest tickle to my nose, but oh, well. Besides, Mack ignored me.

And be careful what you lie about—it may come true. The car actually wasn't ready for an hour and a half because the mechanic had forgotten about the new set of tires I wanted.

Mack hung around while the tires were being put on the car and finally proclaimed that everything had been done properly and I wasn't getting cheated on the bill.

"And let this be a lesson to you," he said as we finally parted. "You need to quit messin' in other people's problems."

I felt like saying "The same goes for you, buddy," but I decided to look on the bright side. Even though it was too late to go to the trucking company that night, I could do it on my way to work the next morning, and at least I had a new set of tires. Let it snow, let it snow, let it snow.

Nat still hadn't called by the time I got home in my Hyundai with the best treads in town. It was already dark, and I was getting irritated at Nat's lack of attention. I fed Spot and myself tuna fish—from our respective Purina and Chicken of the Sea cans. Then I beeped Nat on his pager. He showed up at my apartment about fifteen minutes later. I knew it even before I saw him because he played his own particular form of Morse code on the door.

Nat's a skinny guy, just a few inches taller than I am but with what he thinks of as an uncanny resemblance to John

Lennon, and he has been my best friend since junior high school. God knows why.

He's the classic Type A personality but with no aspirations to become managing editor of the newspaper. He's found his niche in life, which so few of us ever do. When we were in junior high, we used to make up comic strips, which he wrote and I illustrated. He always devised the most heinous crimes for me to draw, but now he writes about real ones as the primo crime reporter on the *Trib*. And with only peripheral help from me.

"Okay, what the hell's going on?" he said when I opened the door.

I took a step backward, not so much to let him enter as to show my surprise at his surly disposition. "No hello or anything?" I asked. "Just 'What the hell's going on?' "

"That guy—Joey Perez—that you wanted me to look up in the morgue . . ." Nat always used the term *morgue* for the library of a newspaper because he lived in a time warp that dated back to pre–World War II when newspapers practiced yellow journalism and reporters said things like "thirty," which meant the end of the story and not the year. "You know," he continued, "the guy who was supposedly applying for a job at the cleaners? Well, that must have been a little hard for him to do, don't you think?" He moved his head back and forth as he spoke. "The guy died in prison three years ago."

"Whoops," I said.

"So come clean, Mandy. What's going on?"

"Okay," I said, knowing when to give up, "he was a cousin of Jeremiah's, and—uh—it's possible the two of them were involved in some sort of scam just before Jeremiah disappeared."

"Yo," Nat said, which would have sufficed as a greeting

when he first came in, but now was used as an exclamation. He squinted his bespectacled eyes—in Lennon-type granny glasses—at the printouts of old newspaper clippings he had in his hand. "Well, what do you know?"

"What?" I said. "Do you have something about that in the clips?" I didn't see how he could because I was sure someone would have picked up on it at the time and told Rosalie.

Nat went over to my dining room table, which is across the counter from my tiny kitchen. He shrugged out of his leather Harley jacket and sat down in one of the chairs, running his finger down the column until he found what he wanted.

"Here it is," he said. "This Joey guy was sent to prison for pulling off an art heist that went bad. It says the burglary had a similar MO to a big art theft a few years earlier except that Perez got caught, and the other case was never solved."

"Let me look at that." I bent over the table and saw where his finger had stopped near the end of the article:

Perez was arrested Saturday night coming out of the home with several valuable paintings after a neighborhood security guard spotted the suspect with the art treasures.

Perez had successfully deactivated the home's security system and would have made his escape within seconds if the security guard hadn't apprehended him. A car was seen speeding away from the scene just after Perez's arrest, but no other arrests have been made.

I couldn't help wondering if Jeremiah had come back home to help in the burglary and then returned to Mexico with no one the wiser. Maybe he'd made many clandestine trips back to Denver throughout the years.

I read on:

> The police questioned Perez about a possible accomplice, but he denied that a second person was involved. They also questioned him about an earlier burglary in which several Picassos and a Chagall were stolen from the home of Edward Longworth, wealthy Colorado cable tycoon. The burglary two years ago was never solved.

I checked the date of the article and subtracted two years. The earlier burglary could have taken place just before Jeremiah disappeared.

I also noticed the byline. It had been written by someone other than Nat. "How come you didn't write this article?"

"Yeah, I wondered about that too," Nat said, "but that was the time I went on that vacation to Acapulco with the gorgeous blond TV anchorwoman."

I looked over at him, remembering how he'd come back home and cried on my shoulder about it. "Oh, right, she dumped you for a bullfighter when you got down there."

He'd long since gotten over the broken heart, and he grinned. "TV and newspaper reporters just don't mix. Besides, she got canned by the station manager a couple of months later and went to Minneapolis, so it wouldn't have worked out anyway."

"Right," I said, and got back to the burglaries. "So why does it say they had a similar MO?"

He flipped to another article, also written while he was on his disastrous trip South of the Border. If he'd only known that Jeremiah might have been hiding there at the time, it would have made the trip worthwhile.

Nat moved his finger down the second article and para-phrased, "Well, both houses were on the market at the time and were being discreetly shown to other millionaires, al-though there were no tacky signs out on the front lawns, believe me. Perez had an airtight alibi for the time of the first break-in, though. He was in jail for getting into a bar fight."

I'd just had an epiphany, if a brilliant thought can be considered a divine revelation. The lightbulb above my head, like the ones I used to draw for our comic books, must have lit up my face.

"What?" Nat asked. "What are you thinking?"

I wasn't sure if an epiphany was meant for public con-sumption, and that's what would happen if I shared it with Nat.

But Jeremiah had been a real estate salesman at the time he disappeared. What if he'd had some insider information about that first house being on the market and had been the mastermind behind the still-unsolved art heist? That would be a reason to clear out of Denver—once he'd col-lected his money for the paintings. All this made Laura Deverell or some other art dealer a possible suspect in Jeremiah's murder.

CHAPTER 14

Despite my best intentions to keep the idea about the real estate connection to myself, Nat pulled it out of me.

Well, actually I shared it with him because of the favor I planned to ask him. With Nat you usually have to give something to get something. He's a firm believer in the quid pro quo.

So I told him how it had just occurred to me that Jeremiah, in his job as a part-time realtor, could have had information about the house being on the market and that that could have enabled him to pull off that first burglary. I didn't know how the second burglary fit into the equation, but maybe Jeremiah still had contacts in the realty business, even long-distance, that had allowed him to send Joey on his botched break-in. And maybe he'd even been the driver of the getaway car.

"Hmmm," Nat said. "I'll have to check out the clips about that first theft."

"That could have been why Jeremiah disappeared right about then," I added.

"Hmmm," Nat said again. "I'd better get going." He

jumped up from the chair, and I knew I wouldn't be able to keep him here much longer.

He was like a bloodhound when a piece of clothing from a missing person was waved in front of it. I had an idea Nat would be down at the *Trib* all night sniffing through the files of that earlier burglary.

I stopped him at the door. "Did you use that information about the funeral for an article in tomorrow's paper?"

Nat turned to me with a blank look on his face. "I thought it was just a tip for me to follow up on tomorrow."

"No, dammit, I wanted you to use it in the paper so that maybe some of the suspects would show up at the service. Doesn't the murderer usually show up at the funeral just to make sure his victim's really dead?"

Nat looked amused. "You mean, like 'the murderer always returns to the scene of the crime'?"

His attitude irritated me. "Yeah, something like that."

"I think those theories are highly overrated." He was grinning as he said it, and I realized he was leading me on.

"You put the notice in the paper, didn't you? You're just trying to pull my strings." When I talked to Nat, I tended to fall into the habit of using clichés. That's because Nat is the cliché king of Denver when he's engaged in normal conversation. I've always suspected that he uses the same hackneyed expressions in his writing, and that some copy editor has to spend hours deleting them from his stories.

"Okay, you got me, Mandy. I just wanted to see you jump through a few hoops." See what I mean about the clichés? "I was a little peeved about you telling me Joey Perez was someone you might be thinking of hiring."

"I didn't say that. I said I was trying to do a better job of checking out job applicants, and that's true."

Nat gave me a disgusted look and turned the doorknob. I had to catch him before he got away.

"While you're checking into things," I said, "I was wondering if you could do me one more favor and get me a copy of all the newspapers from February."

"All the newspapers from February? You have to be kidding."

I wondered if he would fall for the old business-as-usual excuse again. "Oh, you know," I said, "Victor's Cleaners—the one that always advertises 'to the victor belongs the soils'—was running an advertising campaign all month that I've heard good things about. I wanted to check it out."

I'd gone too far this time, and I could tell Nat wasn't buying it. "Come on, Mandy, give me a break. You read the papers all the time. You wouldn't have overlooked something like that."

I had to admit defeat. "Okay, but this is off the record unless you get it from a police source. You have to promise."

"Fine. I promise."

"Put your hands out in front of you so that I can make sure you don't have your fingers crossed."

"Okay, okay." He dangled his hands in front of him as he came back to the table. "But you'll have to feed me while you're at it."

"Tuna fish is all I have."

"Fine," he said, and plopped down in a chair to wait.

If I hadn't wanted those newspapers so badly, I might have been tempted to give him the tuna with the Purina label on it. He was wearing that smug look similar to the one that Spot gets sometimes.

The cat, hearing the word *tuna,* came out of his hiding place in my walk-in closet and began to ingratiate himself to Nat. The cat rubbed against his leg, and Nat put an indifferent hand down to pet him. Now, why would Spot let Nat pet him when he wouldn't let me do it? I decided maybe it was a testosterone thing, even though one of them was fixed.

"Okay," Nat said. "So what about the papers from February?"

"Apparently the only thing Jeremiah was carrying when he was killed was a copy of the *Trib* from last month, but I don't know the date."

"How do you know this?" I could tell by the tone of his voice that Nat was a little insulted that he hadn't found out the information himself. "Did his wife tell you about it?"

"I can't say." I didn't see any reason to tell him about Betty and her friend, the Marcel Marceau of street people, and I must have managed to look sneaky enough that Nat decided his guess was right.

"So what's your take on the newspaper?" he asked.

I finished making his tuna sandwich and brought it over to the table. "I'm wondering if there was something in that paper that might explain why Jeremiah came back to Denver."

"Hmmm," Nat said, partly because his mouth was full and partly because I knew darned well he'd go over all the papers with a magnifying glass before he brought them to me.

"You have to promise me you'll tell me if you find anything, and I'll do the same with you."

"Deal," he said, taking another bite. "You wouldn't happen to have a beer, would you?"

"First, you have to agree to bring the papers over to me tomorrow night." Once I'd extracted that promise from him, I got up from the table to get the beer. When I came back, he had taken a piece of tuna off the bread and was feeding it to Spot. Maybe that's why Spot liked him best. Table scraps.

* * *

I put on the skirt and blouse that I'd recently proclaimed the uniform for our front-counter personnel. Before I headed for my car, I put on my long tan coat, careful to cover my embroidered name and the name of the cleaners on my blouse. I carried my basic black dress in one of our plastic garment bags, but I deliberately laid it out on the backseat with the Dyer's Cleaners' logo facing down. No way was I going to hang it over the hook behind the front seat and advertise my place of business when I was going snooping.

It was already seven thirty in the morning, and I knew I didn't have much time to check out Robin Trucking before I went to work. After all, I'd promised Rosalie I'd be ready by ten o'clock to accompany her to Jeremiah's funeral—hence the all-purpose black dress. With all the time I was taking off, I would have to go to the plant on Sunday to catch up on paperwork.

I drove out east on Colfax, turned north on Colorado Boulevard, and merged into the traffic on Interstate 70 going east again. Luckily I was heading in the opposite direction to most of the rush-hour traffic, and I made it to the Peoria interchange before eight o'clock.

I found Robin Trucking without any trouble, but I stopped across the road from an open gate that led to the compound where a dozen huge semis were parked. I didn't want to be too obvious as I rolled down the window to take a look at the trucks through the eight-foot-high chain-link fence. I was too far away to see the logos on the sides of the cabs, but just as I was about to get out of my car, one of the rigs rolled out of the yard. For a minute I thought it was going to broadside me as it made a wide turn in front of me and headed toward the freeway.

As it swung out, I got a good look at the side of the

truck, and there it was: the bird emblem on the side of the door that I'd glimpsed through the snow just outside of Colorado Springs. It was similar to the one I'd doodled on my sketch pad the other day. Okay, so I was right about that, but it didn't necessarily mean the trucker who'd pursued us up Monument Hill had been driving a Robin's rig.

I sat in my car for a few minutes watching several more trucks pull out of the yard. I squinted to see if any of the drivers looked like Maxine's friend. None of them did. The bald-headed driver with the fierce eyebrows was probably long gone from Denver by now.

The yard was abuzz with activity at this hour in the morning. How dangerous could it be to go into the office just beyond the gate and make an innocent inquiry to see if the company had an employee matching the description of Maxine's friend?

I got out of my car and crossed the road that provided access to Robin Trucking and some warehouses in the area. I pulled my coat collar up around my neck to keep out the cold wind that whipped across the yard.

"Hey, little girl, can I help you find someone?" a deep voice yelled from out of nowhere.

I jumped guiltily and turned around, ready to escape if it was Maxine's friend. Instead I saw a skinny, weathered middle-aged man who appeared to be checking out the tires on his truck.

I could tell him I didn't like being called little girl or I could ask him about Maxine's friend. I thought better about both options and said, "I'm looking for the office."

"In there." He pointed in the direction I'd been going. "Audrey can help you."

Audrey. That was a relief. The name sounded like someone who wouldn't call me little girl and might be willing to help me. Unfortunately Audrey turned out to be a heavyset woman with unruly brown hair and a bad disposition.

"What?" she asked, not even bothering to look up from the paperwork she was doing.

I waited for her to finish, but when she did, she gave me a dirty look. "Can't you see I'm busy? What d'ya want?"

Not a good start. "I promise not to take up much of your time, but I was wondering if you have a driver who was on a run up from southern Colorado Monday night during the snowstorm."

"We have a lot of drivers, honey, and they're spread out all over the country from here to hell and gone."

I took her use of the word *honey* as a sign that she was warming to me. Not so.

"He was bald and looked like Mr. Clean—only meaner."

"Look, I don't have time to play games with you."

"He was really big. Sort of like Paul Bunyan, maybe."

She didn't seem to be making a connection.

Okay, so maybe my last description threw her off. I was pretty sure Paul Bunyan had a full head of hair.

"He was kind of a combination of a sumo wrestler and a skinhead."

Her eyes narrowed. "Why do ya want to know?"

I decided the suspicious look meant she'd probably been playing dumb all the time. I didn't think it would help my cause if I said he'd nearly run me off the road that night. "He stopped to help me during the storm Monday night, and I wanted to thank him."

"Oh, well." She looked relieved. "That sounds like Hulk Harrigan."

The Incredible Hulk. Now, why hadn't I thought of that?

I felt a sudden draft from behind me as the front door opened.

"Someone lookin' for me?"

A chill ran up my spine, but it wasn't from the open door.

"This lady was asking about you," Audrey said. "Claims you helped her out the other night, and she wants to thank you."

I turned around to look into the narrowed eyes below the shaved head of Maxine's friend.

"Oh, I'm sorry, but this isn't the man." I looked at the woman behind the counter for help, but she'd gone back to her paperwork.

I looked back at Hulk. We both knew I was lying. The chill along my spine turned into an enormous itch, and I began to sweat. I wanted to rip off my coat, but I didn't dare. Not with the walking "menu board" of a blouse I was wearing underneath. I started for the door, but Hulk blocked the way.

"Yeah, I remember you," he said. "Maybe we should have a cup of coffee and talk." He was surprisingly soft-spoken for a guy who looked like a bald Paul Bunyan. He put up a huge hand and motioned me to a break room that was right across the main entrance from Audrey's station.

I gave a tentative nod of my head to signify agreement. How dangerous could it be to have coffee with him, what with Audrey right across the hall? I glanced over at the woman for reassurance, but she seemed to be totally engrossed in her bills of lading or whatever they were.

Still, I could always scream for her if things got scary, so I let myself be herded into the break room, which was not unlike the one we had at the cleaners. Hulk motioned me to a table, and once I took a seat, I watched every move he made as he poured some coffee into two Styrofoam cups and came back to the table. He offered me a bowl with packets of cream and sugar in it before he sat down.

I declined and glanced out the door to Audrey's cubicle. She had disappeared from sight, but I prayed she was still within earshot.

"I saw you down in Trinidad," he said. "Maxie pointed you out to me. So what do you want?"

I felt a momentary satisfaction. I'd been right. He was the driver of the *Duel*-like rig, even if that's not exactly what he'd said. How did I get him to admit it?

I started to speak, but no sound came out. Too bad I wasn't like Honest Abe and could pantomine my way through this. I decided to lubricate my throat, but when I took a sip of the coffee, it was so hot and strong, it threatened to burn out my voice box. I began to cough.

"You okay?" Hulk asked. "Want a glass of water?"

I nodded and waited for the water. That gave me a chance to pull myself together. I took a sip, then lied as if my life depended on it. "Look," I said, "I know Maxine asked you to follow us back to Denver, and I wondered why."

Hulk began shaking his head so hard, I was surprised the room didn't tremble. "No, that's not true."

Time to try a bluff. "Please, how do you think I found you if Maxine didn't tell me?"

His head quit shaking as he pondered this question.

I didn't dare let up now. "You almost ran us off the road on Monument Hill, and I'm going to have to report you to the police if you don't tell me why she wanted us followed."

"I didn't run you off the road. You were going too fast and skidded off the road all by yourself." The moment he finished, he looked appalled at what he'd said.

I felt like yelling "Gottcha," but my voice had given out again. All I could do was look at him sadly as I fought off the urge to scratch all the nerve endings in my body.

Hulk's whole demeanor changed. It was an awesome sight to see a man of his size act contrite. "Please," he said finally, "I'm sorry you ran off the road. I was afraid to try and stop for fear I'd jackknife or plow off right on top of you."

I had to admit there was a certain logic to that. I wouldn't have wanted his eighteen-wheeler to land on top of us either.

"And when I went by," he continued, "I could see that there was no real harm done to you or your car, but I did call the state patrol to let them know about the accident."

"Well, thanks for that, but why did you—" My voice was shaking, and I took another sip of water so that maybe he wouldn't notice. "But why did you follow us all the way from Trinidad?"

He shrugged, as if it were the most natural thing in the world to tail someone for two hundred miles. "Maxie asked me to do it. She said she'd give me a couple of big ones if I found out where you were going."

"Big ones?"

He looked at me as if I didn't understand English. "A couple of hundred bucks."

"But why?" And where did Maxine, who couldn't even afford a phone, get that kind of money?

"Didn't she tell you that, too, when she told you where to find me?"

I stumbled around a little before I figured out an answer to that. "I just wanted to see if she gave you the same explanation she gave me—uh—that she wanted to find out if we were really who we said we were."

"Sorry, but I didn't ask her," he said, "and I couldn't very well collect the money when you went off in a barrow pit at the side of the road."

I tried to decide whether Hulk was lying. I seemed to be

having trouble reading people these days; after all, I'd bought Maxine's story about Jeremiah and her son, but now I was convinced she knew a lot more than she'd told us.

I tried one more question on Hulk. "But didn't you wonder what was going on?"

He shrugged his massive shoulders and swigged down his coffee in a single gulp. "Not really, and like I said, I felt bad when you took a header off the highway, but I didn't have anything to do with that." He got up, a lumbering motion that went with my original Paul Bunyan image of him. "You believe that, don't you?"

I was still convinced I wouldn't have skidded if his truck hadn't been bearing down on us so fast, but I wasn't going to argue about it. "Yeah, sure," I mumbled, and followed him out of the room to the front door.

Audrey still wasn't at her booth. Fine lot of good she'd have been if I'd needed her.

"I got to tell you, ma'am," Hulk said when we got outside. "You need to get a better car if you plan to do much drivin' out on the open road. That little tin can of yours doesn't have enough ummph to get up a hill, much less a mountain."

Of course he didn't know about my new set of tires. I thanked him for his words of advice and beat a fast retreat to my car before he had time to think over our conversation.

I patted the dashboard of the Hyundai when I was safely away from the trucking yard. I now believed I could go anywhere, do anything. I felt invincible. I had a new set of tires and the knowledge that Maxine had hired him to follow us home.

Even if Rosalie had kept my name out of it when she

talked to Stan, I would have to tell him the whole story about our trip and Maxine's part in our accident. How mad could Stan be? After all, I'd found him a high-heeled suspect in Jeremiah's murder, who now was at the top of my A-list.

CHAPTER 15

As I hurried in the front door of the cleaners, I heard Ann Marie saying, "I'm sorry she's not here right now."

I waved at her, but she couldn't see me because of several customers waiting in line. It had taken me longer than I'd expected at Robin Trucking, and I was in a rush to change clothes so that I would be ready to go to Jeremiah's funeral with Rosalie.

In fact I fully expected to see Rosalie when I worked my way past the waiting customers, but instead Ann Marie was talking to a blond man in his early twenties.

"I'm here," I said. "Where's Julia?"

"She called in sick." Ann Marie, who's only nineteen and a bit of a scatterbrain, eyed the handsome customer as if she was disappointed that I'd shown up just when she'd met the man of her dreams. "Here's Ms. Dyer now."

"I'll be with you in a minute." I took my black dress, still in its Dyer's Cleaners bag, and hung it over a rack at Lucille's mark-in table just inside the door to the back of the plant. Lucille, who'd worked for my uncle for years, gave me an irritated look. It was nothing compared to what she was going to do when I told her she'd have to help out at the counter later so that I could go to a funeral. She was not a people person.

"It's about time," she said in a voice that implied that my uncle would never have been late to work. "I was afraid Ann Marie was going to need me out front."

I went back into the call office. "What can I do for you?" I asked, trying to place the man who was obviously the object of Ann Marie's newfound affection.

She was still talking to him instead of moving on to another customer. Meanwhile one person had already given up and left.

"I'll handle this. Why don't you wait on Mrs. Woods?"

Ann Marie sighed, and turned to the next customer in line.

I couldn't place the guy, even though he looked familiar. And I was the one who insisted that my counter personnel remember all the customers' faces and try to match them with their names.

"Do you have some special problem?"

"I wanted to talk to Mandy Dyer, the owner," the man said. "That's you, right?"

I nodded and realized I was still wearing my coat over the uniform that had my name embroidered on it.

"I wondered if you could remove this stain from my new ski jacket," he said.

A skier, huh? It didn't help me put a name with the face, but it explained his bronzed good looks and his hair bleached to gold by the sun. No wonder Ann Marie lusted for him.

"What is it?" I asked about the stain.

"Red wine."

"That shouldn't be a problem." If I could remove grape juice, I could handle wine, and I wondered why the customer had felt it necessary to talk to the owner about something that simple.

"Maybe you'd like to have the jacket weatherproofed while you're at it," I suggested.

He nodded, and I asked his name.

"Sean Thompson," he said.

"Have you been here before?"

He shook his head, which made me feel better about not recognizing him. I put his address and phone number in our computer and told him the jacket would be ready the next day at four.

Just then Rosalie entered the cleaners. I glanced at my watch. She was right on time, and unfortunately she didn't know that I wasn't ready, since I was still wearing my coat.

I handed Sean his computer-generated ticket as she came over to the counter. "Just wanted to let you know I'm here," she said. "I'll be so glad when Jeremiah's funeral is over."

Sean glanced at her curiously, then grabbed his ticket and left.

"I'll be ready in just a couple of minutes," I said to her.

"I'll wait in the car." She started for the door, exiting just after Sean.

I turned to Ann Marie. "I have to leave, so I'll tell Lucille to help you."

Once Ann Marie had quit fawning over Sean, she'd managed to take care of the three other customers who'd been waiting, and now she had her hands on her hips. "That really makes me mad," she said as I started to leave. "Guys are such jerks."

I looked back at her in astonishment, stunned that she seemed to be talking about the guy she'd been flirting with only a few minutes earlier.

"He's a liar just like all of them."

"What do you mean?"

"I met him at this singles' bar the other night," she said, and I could only hope that it was one of those clubs for people under twenty-one. If she'd used fake ID, I didn't want to know about it. "Anyway he told me his name was Kevin, not Sean."

Kevin. That's when it hit me. The blond beach boy from the art gallery. I could still recall Laura Deverell saying, "Kevin, will you show these women something that might be more in their price range."

"And he seemed like such a hunk too." Ann Marie sighed.

First Hulk Harrigan and now the Hunk. Just when the burly trucker had convinced me that Maxine was the number-one suspect in Jeremiah's murder, the guy from the art gallery shows up and gives a fictitious name. Why? To verify that I was the one who'd been making inquiries at the gallery about Jeremiah's painting? He looked too young, but could his boss have been the fence who handled the stolen paintings from the art thefts years before? Worse yet, he'd heard Rosalie mention the funeral, so he knew that I had more than an art lover's interest in Jeremiah's work.

It was a lot to think about, but I had a funeral to attend first. I ordered an irritated Lucille to help at the counter, and I checked the pockets of Sean's ski jacket while I talked to her. Unfortunately there was no copy of a receipt for delivery of a stolen painting inside, so I put the jacket back in a laundry bag with a copy of the ticket and tossed it in a cart so that Lucille could mark it in later.

She calmed down a little when I said I had to go to a funeral. I asked her to phone Theresa, who normally comes in at one, to see if she could come in early so that Lucille could go back to her work behind the scene. Then I hurried to my office with my black all-purpose dress dangling from its hanger. Even though I kept on the pair of black flats I'd been wearing at the trucking firm, I would have made a quick-change artist proud at the speed with which I slipped out of my uniform and into the dress.

The old adage about being late for one's own funeral is nothing compared to being late for someone else's. I rushed back through the plant and out the front door to Rosalie's waiting car. She had the motor running.

"I'm sorry," I said as I jumped inside. "I hope we won't be late." Fine friend I was. I was supposed to be giving her moral support, and instead I might be responsible for making her miss the service.

"That's okay," she said. "I just appreciate the fact that you're taking time off from your job to come with me."

She was more magnanimous than I might have been, and maybe that was her plan. It was a technique I used myself. Never confess your own transgressions until you have the other person at your mercy.

"I need to tell you something, Mandy," she said as she sped out of the parking lot. "I discovered that the girlfriend of Maxine's son, Joey—the one Maxine called the bimbo—still lives at the same address."

"Detective Foster told you that?" It was definitely a question, but I was afraid I already knew the answer.

"No." She ducked her head, and for a minute I was afraid she wouldn't see where she was going and would plow into another car. "I went to the apartment complex. Unfortunately the bimbo wasn't home, but I found out from one of her neighbors that she still lives there. Remember how Maxine said Joey always called her Suzie Q? Well, her real name's Susan Quigley."

Despite the fact that I found this information interesting, I was fixated on what Rosalie hadn't said. "So you're telling me you still haven't talked to Stan?"

She bit her lower lip. "I tried once, but I hung up when I got his answering machine. I just couldn't deal with it before the funeral."

I made an effort not to show my irritation. Not right now. "Okay, but we have to go see him as soon as this is over."

"You'll go with me? Oh, thank you, Mandy."

Why not? It was about time I took responsibility for my actions. Besides, I needed to tell Stan a few things that Rosalie didn't even know about.

"I staked out the apartment building for a while, but the bimbo never came home," Rosalie continued. "Maybe we could drop by one more time on our way to see Detective Foster."

"No."

"Well, at least I'll be interested in what you think of Juanita."

"We're not going to go see her either." God, how many times did I have to tell Rosalie that?

She pulled into the parking lot of the mortuary. "Oh, we don't have to go anyplace to see her. She's going to be here at the service."

Swell. Now I would be consorting with another suspect, but at least I could find out if Juanita wore high heels, the way Maxine and Laura did. As far as I could tell, that was the only real clue to Jeremiah's killer.

"Juanita managed to talk Maxine into coming up from Trinidad for the funeral," Rosalie continued, climbing out of the car.

She seemed taller somehow as I walked around from my side of the car to accompany her into the chapel. I looked her up and down until I reached her feet. I stared at her shoes in horror. The woman I'd told Stan *never, ever* wore high heels was wearing them now.

I should have backed out right then, and I would have if I'd realized that Stan would be at the service too. Apparently he shared my view that the murderer sometimes shows up at the funeral of her victim. God, I hoped he didn't think it was Rosalie. Not after I'd made such a point about the shoes.

The chapel of the mortuary was empty when we got inside. Rosalie must have allowed some extra time for the trip when she'd arranged to pick me up. No wonder she'd been less nervous than I was about my being late, but now her face was pale, even with the now-peeling remains of her sunburn.

"I hope I can get through this," she whispered just as the funeral director approached to escort us to our places in the front pew.

When we were seated, the man bent down to her. "When the service is over, would you like to leave the chapel first so that you can greet people in the vestibule, or would you prefer to wait here until the other people file out?"

"Wait here," she said as she looked straight ahead at the small altar.

Fortunately she'd decided to have a closed casket. I was glad because I didn't want to have to look at Jeremiah throughout the service. The memory of seeing him at the morgue still brought back waves of nausea to me.

I heard the funeral director's voice behind me a few minutes later, and I looked around. That's when I saw Stan. Our eyes met, but I couldn't read his expression. After that I didn't want to turn around.

"I wish they wouldn't put the family up front," Rosalie

said, echoing my sentiments. "This way everyone can see you grieve, and if you don't, they think you're some sort of monster."

I nodded and wished I had sat someplace else myself, but why come if I wasn't going to offer Rosalie my support?

"You'll have to look back and tell me if anyone's here," she said.

"I don't think that's a good idea. You can check on the other people when they get up to leave."

Despite herself, Rosalie looked around at the main door, and she noticed Stan. "Oh, dear," she said. "That policeman is sitting in the back row."

"I know." I scrunched down in my seat as if I could hide from him that way.

"I hope Juanita and Maxine make it. I don't want us and the policeman to be the only ones here."

She had nothing to worry about. Despite her best intentions, she kept looking around and giving me a body count. I finally took a quick look over my shoulder too. A number of people had filed in, but it was impossible to tell if they were acquaintances of Jeremiah's from long ago or merely curiosity seekers who'd read about the service in Nat's article in the morning paper.

"I don't recognize anyone," Rosalie said. "Who can all these people be?"

I shook my head as the organist began to play.

Rosalie faced forward again, but suddenly someone tapped her on the shoulder. She jumped.

When I glanced back to the next pew, I saw a plump but attractive dark-haired woman who was probably in her late thirties. It had to be Rosalie's recently acquired sister-in-law.

"Aunt Maxie never showed up," the woman said, "and I had to take the bus. I thought I was going to be late."

"Juanita, this is my friend Mandy. Remember, I told you about her?"

Juanita nodded at me and continued. "It makes me mad. Maxine is always doing this to me, but I really thought she'd come this time as a favor to me."

The organist quit playing, and the funeral director moved to the lectern. He delivered a generic eulogy. It was sparse, like everything else about the service. There were no flowers except for a spray that Rosalie must have felt compelled to buy for the casket. There were no personal eulogies by any of the mourners and not even a little sheet that was handed out at the door about the deceased. But I guess Rosalie hadn't known what to put in it—the name Jeremiah or Luis—much less his date and place of birth.

Rosalie sat there stoically, her face a picture of control, but at one point when the funeral director said something about Jeremiah's art, I saw her tremble. She squeezed her hands together as if that would keep her from crying. I felt my own eyes tear up, not so much for Jeremiah as for Rosalie.

I didn't think the funeral director would ever finish, but he finally invited us to pray. Afterward the organ music—a generic song that sounded familiar even if I couldn't place it—filled the small chapel again. The other mourners began to file past us and out a side door. I don't think Rosalie had realized they would come by us on their way out of the chapel. I know I hadn't.

A few people stopped to express their condolences, but Rosalie didn't seem to know them. One bearded man in a red flannel shirt, jeans, and Birkenstocks said he'd been an artist friend of Jeremiah's. A well-dressed woman in her fifties said she'd worked with Jeremiah at the realty office. Hmmm. I wondered about them, especially the realtor, who could have been in contact with Jeremiah after he'd disappeared.

I was a little disappointed that Maxine wasn't there. She'd been my prime suspect until Kevin/Sean came into the cleaners this morning. But maybe Nat was right. Maybe the killer didn't show up at the funeral of his victim or even return to the scene of the crime. Nat hadn't come to the service to check out my theory, and Laura Deverell and Kevin, my second most likely suspects, hadn't shown up either.

For an instant I thought I'd been wrong about the gallery owner, but only because I noticed a flash of blond hair as a tall woman came around the end of the pew. On more careful inspection, I realized she was younger than the gallery owner and less sophisticated-looking, not to mention more well-endowed.

The woman, gliding along on high-heeled boots, cut a wide swath around us as she moved by the casket. Rosalie let out a loud gasp and started out of the pew before I could stop her. I followed, hoping to prevent a scene. Rosalie looked as if she wanted to gouge the other woman's eyes out.

I put a hand on her arm. "What's the matter?"

Rosalie shook her head in disbelief, releasing the locks of brown hair that she always tucked behind her ears.

"Who is it?"

She yanked out of my grasp. "It's her. I'd know that bitch anywhere." She started to follow the blonde out the side door of the chapel, but it looked as if conversation was the last thing on her mind.

Stan stopped her when she crossed the threshold.

"Don't let her get away." Rosalie tried to push past him. "It's Bambi, that model I was telling you about—the one who was Jeremiah's lover."

CHAPTER 16

"**G**ood job," Stan said, "but I'll handle it. Did you see anyone else you knew?"

Rosalie shook her head violently. Her hair was in her eyes now, and she brushed it back, probably unaware that she was even doing it. "Didn't you hear me? I said it was Bambi. Don't let her get away."

"Yes, I heard you, and we'll take care of it." Stan put a hand on her arm to keep her from going after the blonde.

"Come on, Rosalie. He'll deal with it." I led her back inside the chapel, where Jeremiah's sister was still standing in the second pew.

"He'd *better* talk to her," Rosalie mumbled, more to herself than to me.

I'd wanted to tell Stan that Rosalie and I needed to talk to him, but this wasn't a good time.

"Do you want to go to the grave site?" I asked her. Rosalie had already told me there wasn't going to be a graveside service.

"I'd like to," Juanita said.

Rosalie seemed surprised that Juanita was still there, but

she finally gave up her quest to accost Bambi and agreed to go with Juanita and me to the grave.

As soon as we returned to the hall, however, she glanced around for Stan and Bambi. "I'm sure she's the one who killed Jeremiah," Rosalie said. "After all, she was the spurned lover and had the most reason to kill him." I wasn't about to point out that Jeremiah had dumped them both.

The funeral director was still at the side door, and he told me how to get to the cemetery plot, where we could see the casket lowered into the ground. When we got outside, I was relieved to see that Stan had caught up with the blond model. Rosalie saw them, too, and I thought for a moment she was going to make a break for them.

"I'm sorry Maxine never showed up," Juanita said, momentarily diverting Rosalie's attention. "She said she'd come up right after work last night. She could at least have called."

I pointed at Rosalie's car. Luckily it was in the opposite direction from Stan and Bambi, and I took a firm hold of her elbow as I steered her away from them.

"Would you mind driving, Mandy?" Rosalie asked when we reached the car. "I'm too upset to think straight right now."

I agreed, but I waited on the passenger side of the car until Rosalie pulled the front seat forward so that Juanita could get in and then climbed in herself. I didn't want her to get any sudden ideas to bolt in the direction of Bambi.

This also gave me an opportunity to observe Juanita. She was wearing a navy blue dress, a gray tweed car coat, and—yes—a pair of black pumps, similar to the ones Rosalie had on. The shoes had thick heels unlike the slimmer variety that I'd seen Laura wear and Maxine carry in her plastic bag. And now there was Bambi in her high-heeled boots. I wished Honest Abe had been a better artist. The shoes he'd drawn in the sketch had been somewhere between the thick and thin heels of my suspects.

By the time I got around to the driver's side of the car and fastened myself in behind the wheel, Juanita had leaned forward from the backseat. "Who was *that* woman, anyway?" she asked.

Rosalie turned to her, fire still in her eyes. "You already know what a bastard your brother was, so I guess it doesn't hurt to tell you. She was Jeremiah's lover."

Juanita reached over and put her hand on Rosalie's shoulder. "I'm sorry. He shouldn't have treated you that way."

For some reason her words seemed to trigger a delayed reaction from Rosalie. She began to cry.

"That's all right," Juanita said, patting her shoulder. "It's good to get it all out."

I decided she was a better caregiver than I was, so I eased the car out of the parking lot and drove the short distance to the cemetery.

"That bearded Casanova didn't deserve someone like you," Juanita added. "He always thought he was such a ladies' man."

Rosalie had stopped crying by the time I entered the gate to the cemetery. "Thanks, Juanita," she said as she wiped and then closed her eyes. She reached up and held Juanita's hand.

Once I was inside the cemetery grounds, I tried to follow the funeral director's instructions, but I must have taken a wrong turn somewhere. The place was a maze of roads branching off in all directions to the various grave sites. Finally I saw a pickup truck and some men working across an older section of the cemetery. The tombstones sat up on end, unlike the newer ones that were flat to facilitate easier mowing of the grass in the summer. At this time of year the grass was brown and the limbs on the trees were bare, awaiting a spring rebirth. The sky was gray. Wind whipped the car as I tried to get to where the men were working so that I could ask for directions.

I made several attempts to reach them before I found the right way. This appeared to be a new part of the cemetery, and there was a canopy beside a freshly dug grave. Folding chairs had been set up under the canopy. Apparently a graveside service was scheduled for later in the day. When I drove closer, I saw that the workmen had moved on to another grave site.

The men, wearing jeans and work jackets, were taking a casket from the back of the truck. It didn't take long for me to realize that it must be Jeremiah's, and I didn't think any of us was prepared for such an unceremonious ending.

Before I could turn the car around, Juanita said, "Oh, there it is. Isn't that Jeremiah's casket?"

Rosalie opened her eyes and watched in revulsion. The casket was being removed from the truck by grave diggers in grungy clothes, not by well-dressed ushers, who would have taken the casket from a hearse if there had been a graveside service.

"Do you want to stop?" I asked as we neared the truck.

"No, please," Rosalie said. "Let's go on."

Juanita didn't object, so I turned the car around and wended my way back. That included a few wrong turns, but eventually we exited the cemetery. I drove past the mortuary chapel, but everyone had departed by then. I'd been hoping Stan would still be there so that we could make arrangements to talk to him later.

Rosalie had promised to take Juanita home, and since I was already at the wheel, I decided to keep on driving. I knew Rosalie was upset, but I wasn't about to have her drop me at the cleaners and ignore once again my advice that she call Stan.

I asked Juanita for directions to her house, and she mentioned an address on the west side of town, just off Colfax. "I've lived there for fifteen years, but Luis never even came to see me." She was talking of course about Jeremiah, using the name she'd known him by.

I was afraid she might want us to come in when I got her home, so before she extended an invitation, I pointed out to Rosalie that we needed to visit Detective Foster as soon as we dropped Juanita off.

"I know," she said, apparently resigned to the inevitable.

We were silent for a while as I drove across town on Eighth Avenue, then over the bridge above the railroad tracks and the Platte River to West Denver on the Sixth Avenue Freeway.

I kept thinking about Jeremiah, and I looked back at Juanita. "Do you mean you never saw your brother in all those years and he never contacted you when he got back to town just now?"

She shook her head. "No, never."

"What about your cousin Joey?" I continued. "Did you see much of him?"

"Oh, yeah. In fact he's the one who introduced me to my husband, Carlos. He and Carlos liked to watch football and drink beer together down at a bar near us."

As long as I would be talking to Stan soon, I might as well see if I could get any more information from her. "What about Joey's girlfriend? Did you ever meet her?"

"No, I guess she was too fancy for us."

I swung north on Federal toward Colfax. "So did you see her at Joey's trial?"

"No, because I didn't go to it. I was pregnant at the time and due any day."

"Did you ever visit Joey in prison?"

"You kiddin'? By then I had four kids under six and no husband. Carlos walked out on me about the same time that Joey was arrested. Just went out for a beer and never came home."

I glanced back at her quickly. "Did he give you any indication he was thinking of leaving?"

"Not really, but he was all shook up when Joey was arrested, and I always wondered if that had something to do with why he walked out on us."

Maybe it did, I thought, if the article Nat and I had been reading the night before had anything to do with it. What if Juanita's husband, not Jeremiah, had been the mysterious driver of the getaway car in Joey's botched burglary? It was worth thinking about, along with the possibility that Carlos had joined Jeremiah in Mexico.

I wondered if I should ask her about that, and I finally forged ahead. "Did you ever wonder about the coincidence of both your brother and your husband disappearing?"

Juanita looked stunned. "I knew Luis changed his name, but"—she gave an apologetic look over at Rosalie—"to be honest, I thought he was dead. I just figured Carlos couldn't handle all the kids and the responsibilities."

I didn't want to call Stan from Juanita's house, so as soon as we dropped her off, I pulled in at a convenience store and made the call from a phone booth outside the entrance.

Stan must have gone back to work immediately after the service because he caught the phone on the first ring.

"Rosalie and I need to talk to you," I said.

"Good thing you called. I was planning on calling you. Who was the woman you left with?"

I guess that's what homicide officers are trained to do:

know what's going on around them even when they seem to be involved in something else. He'd seemed to be totally engrossed in talking to Bambi when we left the chapel.

"Oh, that was Jeremiah's sister."

"I thought Rosalie didn't know anything about Jeremiah's background or relatives."

"That's what we want to talk to you about. If you aren't tied up right now, maybe we could meet for coffee and Rosalie and I could tell you what we know."

"Where did you want to meet?"

I was envisioning someplace public where we could talk to him together and where he wouldn't be so apt to show his displeasure with us and me in particular. "How about that coffee shop on the corner or Speer and Colfax?" I suggested. "That's not too far from the police station, is it?"

"No," he said, "it isn't too far, and no, it won't work."

I guess he'd known what I was after all the time.

"I want you down here at police headquarters in half an hour or else I'll send someone out to bring you here." I could almost picture his clenched jaws as he spoke. "Do you understand?"

"Sure," I said. "We're on our way."

I knew the drill. He would separate us, put us in separate rooms without any windows, and question us one at a time to see if our stories jibed. Always looking for discrepancies.

I returned to the car, and since Rosalie had made no attempt to get into the driver's seat, I got behind the wheel again.

"He wants to see us at the police station, so I'll drive us there," I said. "I already know where to park." Oh, yes, I'd been there before. Too many times, as a matter of fact, for a law-abiding citizen such as myself.

Rosalie was staring out the window. "I wish I was in a

position to help Juanita," she said. "Did you see that house she lives in? It's so shabby and not nearly large enough for her and four children, now that they're growing up."

Actually it hadn't been too different from Maxine's place in Trinidad with the peeling paint and weeds in the front yard. Only difference was that Juanita's house had a bicycle with only one wheel and a few dilapidated toys out front.

"Well, maybe you could buy the kids some toys," I said.

"I just keep thinking if that lout of a brother of hers had left any money in the bank when he took off, I would give it to her."

I didn't point out that Rosalie probably would have spent the money by now, and theoretically he had left her some money.

She remembered this without my mentioning it. "Of course he did leave me five lousy dollars and eighty-nine cents in that checking account," she said, then gave a bitter laugh. "It never drew any interest after that, but maybe I should get it back from the state anyway."

I knew she'd told me all this before, but now something bugged me about it.

"And why did you say the state has it?"

"Because it was an inactive account for five years."

That explanation didn't seem to help me much.

We'd reached the police headquarters, and I pulled into the parking lot across the street.

"Can you hold on for a minute?" Rosalie said as I got out of the car. "I want to change shoes. These heels are killing me. I never wear them except to weddings, funerals, and special events at work."

What about to a killing? Dear God, don't even think that way, I cautioned myself. I hadn't said anything to her about the shoes, even though I'd been tempted, but I was glad she'd decided to change. Of course she didn't know

about Honest Abe's sketch of the high heels, but Stan did.
I'd been afraid he would zoom in on them when we got
inside instead of the other things we were going to tell him.
With any luck, he hadn't noticed her high heels at the
funeral, but with *my* luck, he probably had.

Rosalie reached under the driver's seat and pulled out a
pair of flats. I waited while she changed out of the heels,
and then she set out at a pace that I could hardly match.
But she was an outdoor person, after all.

"I'm really dreading this," she said. "I think I'll go up to
my cabin as soon as we're through. I need to be alone for a
few days to decompress."

We were rounding the corner of the building to the
wide plaza in front of police headquarters. I stopped. "Before we get inside, I just want to say that you don't need to
try to protect me. Tell Detective Foster the whole story.
Don't leave anything out, not even our accident on the way
back from Trinidad."

"I thought you didn't want him to know that you went
to Trinidad with me."

"No, tell him everything. You never know what's going
to be important." And of course at that moment the thing
that seemed most important to me was that Maxine had
asked a truck driver to tail us home.

"Okay, if you're sure." Rosalie followed me through the
double doors, where Stan was waiting for us.

"You got here with three minutes to spare," he said.
"Congratulations."

He was still wearing the dark suit he'd worn to the
funeral, and he looked great. Until now I'd never really
seen him in anything but slacks and a variety of sports
jackets, apparently the uniform of choice for homicide
detectives.

Despite the suit, he still had the homicide mentality. He

whisked us through a secured gate to the third-floor Crimes Against Persons offices, where the homicide department was in one big room. It had a bunch of desks where the detectives did their paperwork, a private office in the back for the head of the department, and a hallway that led to a bunch of other little rooms. I knew from personal experience that the rooms had video cameras where the police could videotape interviews with their suspects.

Before we had a chance to catch our respective breaths, Stan took Rosalie away to one of the rooms. I sat across from his desk staring out the window at the increasing darkness of the clouds. The last time I'd been here there had been a thunderstorm. This time the clouds threatened snow.

I tried to think of something to get my mind off the upcoming interview. What? The thing that had bothered me when Rosalie brought up the money that Jeremiah had left in their account. Five dollars and eighty-nine cents. Five dollars and eighty-nine cents month after month in a joint checking account. That was it.

Where were the service charges? Why the heck hadn't the account been reduced to a zero balance within a few months of his departure?

CHAPTER
17

I kept wondering about the missing service charges on Rosalie's meager checking account as I waited for her and Stan to emerge from the interview room.

Her account should have been at zero in a matter of a few months if it had been assessed service charges the way my interest-bearing account was when my money dipped below five hundred dollars. After all, she'd indicated that it had once earned interest. Did some banks have different kinds of checking accounts that didn't add on monthly fees for being poor? That's the kind of checking account I needed.

I vowed to ask Rosalie what bank she and Jeremiah had used just as soon as we left here. That's about the time I saw her and Stan come out of the room where he'd been talking to her.

Rosalie looked tired. I would, too, if I'd been through everything she'd been through in the last few days. As a matter of fact I had been through a lot of what she'd been through, and I probably didn't look my best either. I didn't even remember if I'd combed my hair after my quick-change into the black dress this morning in my office.

And while I was at it, I noticed that Stan didn't exactly look like a model for *Gentleman's Quarterly*. He had loosened his tie the way he always did when he was particularly agitated.

"You can go now," he said to Rosalie, running his finger around the collar of his shirt. It was the only sign that he was getting ready to give me the third degree. Otherwise he had a stony look on his face, kind of like one of the heads on Mount Rushmore. "You have your car, don't you?"

She nodded.

He'd apparently noticed that we'd been driving her car at the funeral, so I figured he'd also been aware of her shoes. God, he never missed a thing. It was going to be up to me to convince him that someone else had killed Jeremiah—namely Maxine.

"Okay, we'll be in touch, and I'll see that Ms. Dyer gets back to work once I finish talking to her."

But, hey, I wanted to talk to Rosalie some more. Ask her about that good-deal checking account that allowed her to keep five dollars in the bank indefinitely.

I started to ask if Rosalie could wait around for me so that Stan wouldn't have to worry about getting a patrolman to take me to the cleaners. One look at her, and I decided to let her go. Now that the interview was over, there was such relief on her face that I didn't want her to have to hang around any longer.

Stan was flipping through his notes. "You want to come back to one of our interview rooms now, Mandy?"

I could only hope that I would be filled with relief, too, after I finished talking to him.

Rosalie was on her way to the main door before I was even out of my chair. "You have my phone number up at the cabin, don't you?" she asked.

Stan nodded, but he didn't look up. He headed back

toward one of the little rooms without any windows. Interview rooms. Ha. Inquisition rooms were what they were, and somehow that had a more sinister sound.

He ran his hands through his curly blond hair as soon as the door was closed. "What the hell were you thinking of when you went to Trinidad with Rosalie, and at the very least why didn't you tell me about it as soon as you got home?"

"I thought Rosalie was going to tell you." Geez, I sounded like the kind of person I disliked most—someone who was always blaming other people for her problems. "I'm sorry. I should have told you right away."

"I should have known you were up to something that day at the storage locker," he continued. "You looked so guilty when I showed up."

"I didn't really think I'd find anything when I looked at the old charge applications," I said, "and when the million-to-one shot paid off, Rosalie was adamant that she was going to go running off to Trinidad right then. I didn't think she was in any condition to drive." I was doing it again. I was saying everything was Rosalie's fault instead of taking responsibility for not calling the police myself. It *was* my fault, and I should shut up and take the blame for it.

"Tell me about Maxine"—Stan flipped through his notes—"Maxine Perez. What does she look like?"

I thought that was an odd place to start. "She has dyed red hair, is probably in her fifties, kind of wrinkled, weighs about one hundred ten pounds, and is, maybe, five-one without her high heels, which were in a plastic bag as she left for work, probably because she had a date later on that night." I threw in the part about the shoes so that Stan would know her shoes could have been the ones in Honest Abe's sketch.

Somehow Stan seemed a little off his stride. He stared at what he'd written instead of battering me with his usual rapid-fire questions.

"Okay, tell me everything you remember about the conversation with Ms Perez." He ran his finger around his collar again, then unbuttoned the top button on his shirt. "Start at the beginning."

Actually I started with finding the charge application, the trip to Trinidad, and our stop at the Colorado Visitors Center once we got there to ask for directions.

Then I described how we actually found Maxine, what she told us, and how we lost her on the way to the truck stop but found her again after a fifteen-minute wait in a booth. "When she showed up," I continued, "she said she had to take some orders. She talked to one of the drivers before she finally came over and gave us Juanita's address. Oh, yes, and she asked me for my name and for Rosalie's phone number in case she ever wanted to call her. She said she didn't have a phone."

Stan seemed antsy the whole time I was talking, and I wondered why. The person being interrogated should be the nervous one, which isn't to say I wasn't.

"And there's something I just found out this morning," I said, leaning over the table toward him as I began to describe the trip back from southern Colorado and the eighteen-wheeler that was behind us most of the way. "It followed us like the crazed machine in Steven Spielberg's *Duel*."

Luckily Stan must have seen the TV movie because he seemed to understand what I was talking about. Sometimes only Mack and I could connect on that level of expertise about movies and television.

I explained about the bird I'd seen painted on the side of a truck after we'd thought we lost the driver in Colorado

Springs, and how, through my deductive skills, I'd finally found the same logo on the side of the cabs of Robin Trucking. Unlike some other times I'd talked to Stan, I didn't expect any praise for my cleverness; I was too busy trying to redeem myself in his eyes.

"Anyway I went out to the trucking firm this morning and found the driver I'd seen talking to Maxine in the truck stop. His name is Hulk Harrigan"—whoops, if I'd been on the ball, I probably would have gotten his real first name—"and he said Maxine asked him to follow us home and see what we were up to."

I paused to catch my breath.

"What was this Harrigan's first name?"

I knew I should have gotten it, but I had to admit defeat. There were just too many aliases and nicknames floating around this case. Even nicknames for nicknames in the case of Honest Abe/Harpo.

"So my feeling is," I continued, "that if Maxine had him follow us, she must know a whole lot more than she told us, and therefore she must have something to hide. Ergo, she seems like the number-one suspect in Jeremiah's murder."

Good grief, where did that *ergo* come from? It wasn't even copspeak, but I'd said it and I couldn't take it back.

Stan didn't respond, just kept writing in his notebook.

"So don't you think that makes her a prime suspect?" I prodded.

He ignored my question. "Have you told me everything?"

"Everything about our trip, yes. I already covered what Maxine said about Juanita and Joey and Joey's girlfriend, Suzie Q, whom Maxine called the bimbo. But I haven't told you about my trip to the art gallery."

I then spent at least ten minutes explaining about Laura

Deverell and Jeremiah's fifty-thousand-dollar painting, and the fact that there was a big art heist just before Jeremiah left, and how Joey was arrested for the same type of crime. "So I'm wondering if Laura Deverell is a fence who disposes of stolen paintings." Again I paused for breath. "She wears stiletto heels, by the way."

Stan zeroed in on the part I didn't particularly want to explain. "How do you know about the art thefts?"

"Uh—I read some newspaper articles about them."

"Oh, yeah, your good friend, Nat, right?"

I winced as I nodded ever so slightly.

"Why the devil can't you just let us do our business and stay out of things?" He ran his hands through his hair again.

"I'm through now." I meant with what I had to tell him, but I guess Stan assumed I meant I was through looking into the case.

"That'll be the day."

"Oh, no, I meant that's all I have to tell you."

Stan started to put his notebook away. It must have been almost filled by then between the statements Rosalie and I had given him.

"Oh, there is one other thing." The moment I started to speak, Stan opened his notebook again. "Maybe Laura Deverell isn't the fence. Maybe it's her assistant, Kevin, but I think he's probably too young." Before Stan had a chance to ask, I added, "And no, I don't know his last name. But anyway, it was very curious. This morning he came into the cleaners, wanted to talk to me about a ski jacket he needed cleaned, and then he gave me a phony name—Sean Thompson."

Then I had to explain to Stan how I found out who Kevin really was from my employee, Ann Marie, who'd met him at a singles' bar. "So what would be your take on that?" I asked.

Stan didn't miss a beat. "That he gave Ann Marie a phony name at the singles' bar. Men do that, you know."

"No, that's not it. When Ann Marie mentioned the name he'd given her, I realized where I'd seen him before. I remember distinctly that Laura Deverell called him Kevin."

Stan finally finished writing, and before he closed his notebook a second time, he asked, "So is that it—you can't think of a single other thing, no matter how remote, that might pertain to this case?"

I stared off into space, which was easy to do since there was nothing but blank walls to stare at. "Oh, yes, there is something else."

Stan was beginning to look even more irritated than he had during other parts of my "interrogation."

"Remember how I told you about the newspaper article about Joey's arrest for the burglary he was sent to prison for? It said there may have been a getaway car, but that the driver was never arrested. Juanita said on the way home from the cemetery that her husband deserted her just about that time, and I'm wondering if he might have been the guy in the getaway car. Maybe he even went and hid out with Jeremiah."

I waited for him to finish writing.

"That's it," I said. "Everything I can possibly think of."

He closed the notebook at last. The guy probably had writer's cramp.

"Now can I go?"

He fidgeted in his seat. "Not yet." He made a vague gesture toward the main room. "I have something I need to check before you leave. Would you mind waiting here for just a minute?"

Well, yeah, I did mind, but he'd taken my confession so well—for him—that I decided to cooperate. "Okay."

But why didn't he let me come out into the other room with him or else let me wait in the lobby? I wondered what he had to check that was so all-fired important it couldn't wait. And why did he want me where he could keep an eye on me to make sure I didn't leave?

After about fifteen minutes Stan returned to the room or what I'd begun to think of as "solitary confinement." Before he could get inside, I was on my feet. "Can I leave now?"

He shut the door behind him. I took that as a no.

"There's something else I need to talk to you about." He sat down at the table across from me.

Uh-oh. Surely he wasn't going to talk to me about that personal thing that had been hovering over our heads since Monday in the storage locker when Rosalie showed up. This wasn't the place where I would have thought a professional like Stan would want to discuss our relationship. But what else could it be? I'd already told him more than he probably wanted to know about my involvement in the case, so I girded myself for the worst. The *personal* problem.

"Would you like a cup of coffee, by the way?" he asked.

I shook my head. I wasn't going to give him the chance to delay any longer, and besides, the memory of the diesel fuel that had masqueraded as coffee at Robin's Trucking this morning still left a bad taste in my mouth. So get on with it, fellow.

"How about a Coke?" he asked.

"No, nothing."

Frankly our relationship had never gone very far because of Stan's delaying tactics. Stan wouldn't let it, because of his fiancée who'd died—I didn't even know how

long ago it was. Of course the real impetus to the disinte-
gration of our floundering romance had been that I'd
promised to stay out of another case, and inadvertently
wound up being taken for a ride by the killers.

I have to admit I still found Stan attractive, but I could
get over him if he'd just spit it out. I sure wasn't expecting
the conversation to lead to a renewed romance. What I
figured he planned to say was that we didn't have a future
because he still mourned for his fiancée. Well, we weren't
exactly having a *present,* either, so why did he feel compelled to explain at all?

"So what did you want to talk to me about?" I asked.
"I've told you everything I can think of."

Darned if he didn't get out his little notebook again—
the one in which I presumed he'd been taking down my
statement a few minutes earlier. Don't tell me he had a
speech written down that he was going to read to me?

He cleared his throat. "I need a little more information
about Maxine Perez."

I was dumbfounded. "What?"

"Information on Maxine Perez," he explained as if I were
not only dumbfounded but dimwitted. "You said you saw
her at the truck stop. What was she wearing?"

Frankly who the hell cared? Apparently Stan did. He
had his pen ready, its point pushed out.

"Well, if you really must know, she had on a two-piece
uniform. Short red skirt, a white blouse with red piping on
the collar, and a red-and-white-striped headpiece. She was
wearing white orthopedic shoes, but she had high heels in
a plastic bag." I paused to reinforce the fact that I'd already
told him that. "Oh, yes, and her first name was monogrammed on the pocket of her blouse in red.

"The uniform didn't do a thing for her, by the way," I

added, just in case Stan wanted a fashion critique from a dry cleaner. "It wasn't the same color red as her hair."

"That's too bad," he said, putting his pen away.

I looked at him in surprise. "What? You think the uniform would have been better in blue?"

He didn't even try to clear up my confusion. "You said she'd been planning to go to the funeral with her niece, Juanita, but she never showed up. Do you know when she'd planned to come up here from Trinidad?"

I was getting really suspicious of Stan's motives. "Juanita said Maxine told her she would be up last night after work. Why? What's this all about?"

Stan bent over toward me. "I need to ask you a favor. You probably aren't going to like it."

"What do you want—to wire me and have me talk to Maxine?" Actually that sounded kind of interesting.

He sat back in his chair. "No, where'd you get a crazy idea like that?"

"From you. You've been asking so many questions about Maxine that I figure you must think she's the prime suspect in Jeremiah's murder too."

At that moment he looked as if he wanted to get out of here as much as I did. "No, Mandy, she isn't. I've been asking questions about her because we found a woman's body in another alley not too far from here." Suddenly I wanted to put my hands over my ears so that I wouldn't hear the rest. "She had red hair, no purse, and she was wearing a waitress uniform with the name Maxine stitched in red on the pocket."

CHAPTER 18

"**T**hat can't be true," I said. "There has to be a mistake. It can't be Maxine."

The body the police had found couldn't be the feisty woman I'd thought would probably become the oldest living waitress in Trinidad. She was too tough and street-savvy to die, although I'd recently begun to think she might spend her old age in prison for the death of her nephew.

"It's true, Mandy," Stan said. "At least the part about the body, and it really threw me when you and Rosalie started talking about a waitress named Maxine. That's why I asked you to wait while I checked the report for details about the body."

"But you still don't know for sure that it's *our* Maxine."

"Not until we get someone to ID the body at the morgue."

I started shaking my head even before he finished. "No, don't even think about it."

"It would really help us out."

"What happened to her? Was it some kind of sex killing?"

"She was shot in the chest."

"You mean just like Jeremiah?"

"We'll have ballistics check out the bullet to see if it came from the same gun."

My hands began to shake. If I didn't watch out, I might even start to cry.

Stan moved to my side of the table, sat down in a chair, and put his arm around my shoulder. "I'm sorry I had to tell you this way."

I pushed away from him. It wasn't as if Maxine and I had been bosom buddies, but it was still a shock.

"I wouldn't have mentioned it at all unless everything checked out," he said.

"It's all right." I gripped the edge of the table and took a deep breath. "I understand, and I'll be okay in a minute."

Stan returned to his side of the table. "Look, I'll ask the niece to see about the ID."

I shook my head. "No, I'll check it out first. Maybe it isn't her."

But how many waitresses could there be named Maxine whose names were emblazoned on their uniforms? And how many bodies could there be where the only clue to their identity was their clothes?

As we left police headquarters, I was glad I hadn't accepted Stan's offer for a cup of coffee or a Coke. If I had, I might have thrown up. As it was, my stomach was still burning from the remains of the trucker-coffee and was making gurgling sounds because I hadn't had any lunch.

I followed Stan to his car. It didn't take long to get to the morgue across the street from the Denver Health Medical Center. As I said before, it'll always be Denver General to me, but then the Denver Broncos' home jerseys will always be orange, not navy blue. And their logo will be a white bucking horse inside the letter *D,* not a wild-eyed one with an orange mane.

We went through the same procedure we had when I'd identified Jeremiah. I first talked to an investigator in the conference room at the medical examiner's office and signed some papers. This time I had to look at the victim's picture while we were in the conference room, probably to shield me from the trauma of viewing the body if I didn't think it was Maxine.

Why did this bother me even more than it had with Jeremiah? Maybe because I hadn't really expected it to be Jeremiah, and this time I knew from the photo that it was Maxine.

The investigator escorted Stan and me down a hallway to the viewing room and turned on a light switch that lit up the area behind the room's glass window. The body was already in place, and again a sheet covered all but the victim's head.

Although I'd only met her once, it had been just a few days ago. I didn't have to account for a change in her appearance, the way I'd had to do in the seven years since I'd last seen Jeremiah.

Besides, Maxine had been such a memorable character with her sassy red hair. Even so, it might as well have been seven years since I'd seen her last; there was nothing sassy about her anymore. Her face seemed sunken and old, as if it had been the eye shadow and bright lipstick she'd used when she was alive that had given her face the fighting spirit.

"It's Maxine," I confirmed again, although I'd already identified the picture. "I hope they'll put some makeup on her before the funeral." I didn't ask if I could leave. I just turned abruptly and headed for the door.

Stan and the investigator followed me. "Are you going to be okay?" Stan asked when he caught up with me.

"Yeah, I just want to get out of here."

First I had to sign some more papers, verifying my identification, and I provided Juanita's name, which I assumed was Maxine's next of kin. Fortunately I remembered her address because I'd just driven her home a few hours before.

When I was free, I went outside and down the few steps to the sidewalk. Stan didn't come out for several more minutes, and by then I'd walked by his car and down to the end of the block.

"You all right now?" he asked when he reached me.

Yes, but I would never be able to handle seeing dead people day after day. I wondered how he and the people from the medical examiner's office stood it. I wished I still smoked. A cigarette was the only thing I could think of right now that would calm me down and relieve the stress.

In lieu of that I just kept walking. Stan didn't point out that we'd already passed his car. He fell in step with me as we crossed the street and walked up the other side. Finally I stopped. "Okay, I'm ready. Will you take me back to work?"

"Sure, and thanks. I owe you for this."

Nat and I talked about owing each other favors all the time, and we called them in on special occasions. But how could Stan ever repay me? How could you ask a man to fall in love with you just because he owed you a favor?

We didn't say much on the way back to the cleaners. What was there to say? Who's laundering your shirts these days? Who's the prime suspect in Jeremiah's murder now that Maxine is dead? I'd been so sure she was involved somehow, and it appeared that I'd been right. Only problem was that Maxine was dead and couldn't tell anyone what her involvement had been.

Stan pulled his car up in front of the call office. "Thanks again."

I nodded. I sure wasn't about to say "Anytime."

"We'll get together when this is over and have dinner."

"Sure," I said, but right then I didn't feel as if I would ever eat again.

Getting back to work helped, and I quickly changed back into my uniform. We were having a particularly busy day. It sometimes happens when the weather forecast calls for snow. People run out to the grocery stores to stock up on food, and they decide to run their other errands at the same time.

When there was a lull at the counter, I went back to my office to catch up on the calls I needed to return. But I stopped at Mack's spotting table and told him what had happened.

I was careful not to say it in front of Betty because she might get worried about Honest Abe, and I didn't want her to go off looking for him again to make sure he was all right.

"Do you want to get together after work and talk about it?" Mack asked.

"I can't leave until seven," I said, "I have too much to do."

"That works for me," he said. "We'll go over to Tico Taco's and grab a bite."

Bless him. I knew he'd probably go home and then come back to meet me, but I needed to talk to someone and Mack was the best thing there was next to having my own private psychiatrist. Only trouble was that he voiced his opinion frequently instead of letting me arrive at my own conclusions.

That afternoon I worked up a storm, just like the one brewing outside, and at four when people started getting off work, I went out front again to help at the counter.

Arlene Whitney, the bank vice president, came in for her green chiffon cocktail dress at four thirty.

"Hope you aren't going to have to rush to get changed for your big party tonight," I said.

"No, I left myself plenty of time."

That was good because I had something I wanted to discuss with her. First, though, I asked if she wanted to pick up the rest of her clothes.

"If you don't mind, I'll leave them here and pick them up next week."

That's what a lot of people do, which is why customers wind up forgetting some of their clothes at the cleaners. I knew Arlene wouldn't do that, though, not with her orderly mind. I had a picture of her as being super organized and always correctly accessorized.

I went back inside the plant to grab her dress off the conveyor. Luckily I'd noted that she wanted it earlier than the rest of her clothes, so our inspector had bagged it separately when she made up the order.

"I was wondering about something," I said as I came back to the counter, relieved to get my mind off Maxine and my visit to the morgue. "Does your bank have any interest-bearing checking accounts that don't have service charges, even when the account drops down to, say, five dollars?"

She drew back in astonishment. "Maybe if it's a senior-citizen account, but otherwise show me the bank that does that, and I'll transfer my own account."

"I have a friend who said she had an account like that. It just stayed at five dollars and eighty-nine cents month after month until it was finally turned over to the state because she'd never deposited or withdrawn any money from it."

Arlene nodded. "Yes, banks have to do that if an account hasn't had any transactions for five years. I think the state felt that banks were just holding the money and not doing enough to find customers who may have forgotten that they even had an account. So the state takes the money, and every year it puts out a list of all the missing account holders in the paper."

"But why would a checking account like the one I mentioned have lasted for five years without being eaten up by service charges?"

She shrugged as she grabbed her dress from the slick rail where I'd placed it. "May I pay for this when I pick up the rest of my cleaning next week?"

"Sure, I'll make a special exception for you." I smiled at her, but I was still puzzling over Rosalie's mythical five-dollar account.

Arlene must have been too. She was halfway to the front door when she stopped and came back to the counter.

"I've been thinking about what you said." She hung the dress back on the rail. "You know, it's possible there was another account at the bank, and it had enough money in it to cover the monthly charges. Do you know if she had a second account?"

I shook my head.

"Was the one she had a joint account?"

"Yes, as a matter of fact it was. Her husband cleared out all but the five dollars, apparently so he wouldn't have to get a signature from her to close out the account. Then he took off."

She grabbed her dress again. "That might explain it. Maybe he had another account in that bank that she knew nothing about, and if both accounts had his Social Security number on them, the bank could have waived the service charges on their checking account."

"Really. You think there might be money in the bank that she knew nothing about?"

"Could be. You'd be surprised at the things we see between spouses when it comes to money, and if a spouse's name isn't on one of the accounts, we can't even let that person know about it."

Okay, so I wouldn't avoid a nasty service charge by getting an account at Rosalie's bank. But maybe Arlene's information would help Rosalie.

"It's worth looking into," Arlene continued. "Of course if the five-dollar checking account was turned over to the state, then I suppose the other account would have been, too, unless the husband continued to make deposits and withdrawals in it." Arlene frowned. "But if her scoundrel of a husband does have money somewhere, she probably could go through the courts and get her share, whether it's still in a bank or the state has it."

I watched Arlene leave, and then I went back to work with the first good feeling I'd had for days. Maybe Rosalie had money coming from Jeremiah. She deserved a break.

CHAPTER 19

"Is it possible to have an order of toast?" I asked Manuel, the owner of Tico Taco's, after he'd taken Mack's order for fajitas.

I still wasn't sure I could handle stronger fare, but both he and Mack looked at me as if I were nuts. Asking for toast in a Mexican restaurant was probably a little like asking for steak in a doughnut shop.

"That won't do," Mack said. "What you have to do is order a chicken salad sandwich." Mack slipped into his best Jack Nicholson voice. ". . . then all you have to say is 'hold the chicken, bring me the toast, give me a check for the chicken salad sandwich—and you haven't broken any rules.' "

Manuel looked at us as if we were both nuts, but I knew what Mack was talking about. "Just ignore him, Manuel," I said. "It's a quote from a movie called *Five Easy Pieces,* and he's just trying to give you a hard time."

Mack motioned his head toward our host at Tico Taco's. "Well, what did you think you were doing, asking for an order of toast in a Mexican restaurant?"

"I guess you're right." I looked at Manuel. "I'm sorry.

Just bring me the usual—cheese enchiladas and maybe some soup."

Of course I was thinking of some comfort soup like chicken noodle. I knew, whatever the soup of the day was at Tico Taco's, it would probably blow off the top of my head and clear out my nasal passages all in one fell swoop, but maybe that's what I needed. Something to clear the cobwebs out of my brain.

"You gringos—*muy loco*," Manuel said in his best South of the Border accent as he circled the side of his head with his index finger, but he was smiling as he left to get our orders.

Mack always did have a way of cheering people up, even when he didn't know he was doing it. Somehow the game we played about movie quotes was a welcome return to normalcy.

I thought sometimes that Mack had missed his calling. He should have been an impersonator with his ability to imitate voices, but thank goodness he'd chosen to be a part-time actor and full-time dry cleaner. This way I had someone to tell my troubles to. Never mind that I wasn't always pleased with the answers or the fact that they sounded as if they were being delivered by John Wayne or Marlon Brando.

"So you want to talk about this latest shooting victim now or wait until after dinner?" Mack asked.

"Now," I said, "I have a lot of rethinking to do." The peaceful familiarity of sitting across the table from Mack seemed a long way from that afternoon at the morgue. "You see, I was so sure Maxine was the one who'd killed Jeremiah." Then I told him about visiting the trucking firm this morning and how Hulk Harrigan had told me Maxine had offered to pay him to find out what we were up to.

"Why would she have done that if she didn't know something about Jeremiah's death?"

Mack dipped a chip into a bowl of salsa that Manuel had brought to the table when he came to get our order. "She must have known who the murderer was, and it got her killed."

"That would be the logical conclusion, wouldn't it?" I took one of the taco chips, sans salsa, and nibbled at it. The chips might be as good as soda crackers for calming my nervous stomach.

So who did that make the most logical suspect now? I decided it was Laura Deverell, although I didn't have any real evidence against her. Only the articles Nat had dug up about the art theft before Jeremiah disappeared, plus her assistant's puzzling visit to the cleaners this morning.

I told Mack about the alias Kevin had used when he came to the cleaners and about the earlier occasion when I'd gone to the gallery in the unwanted company of Betty and seen one of Jeremiah's outrageously expensive paintings.

"Maybe this Kevin didn't think you would recognize him from the gallery, and he was just checking you out to see if you had the money to actually buy the painting."

"Oh, right," I said. "The owner had us pegged the moment we walked in the gallery. She said she was going to show us something more within our price range, even though I don't think there was one thing there I could have afforded."

"Don't sell us dry cleaners short," Mack said. "I know one guy who's so rich, he spends eight to ten months a year on his yacht sailing the Seven Seas."

I gave him a dirty look. "I'd settle for a weekend in the mountains in my Hyundai." I looked outside where I thought I saw a few ominous flakes of snow. "Well, maybe not at this time of year."

"Be that as it may, the gallery owner might have been trying to decide if she missed out on a hot prospect."

I didn't agree with Mack, mainly because it was getting us off the subject I wanted to discuss. "Anyway, about the time she was going to steer us to the cheaper stuff, her assistant came out and said there was someone—" I stopped midsentence and tried to remember his exact words. "He said there was an angry woman at the back door who was demanding to see her. I wonder if it could have been Maxine, demanding blackmail money for something she knew about."

"That's pure speculation," Mack pointed out.

"I know," I said. "Geez, I wished I'd gone around in back and waited for the person to come out. It might have solved everything, but at the time I figured it was just some disgruntled customer that she'd insulted the way she had Betty and me. I know we were pretty disgruntled by the time we left."

"It could have been anyone," Mack said.

"You're right. It's just that I was so sure this morning that Maxine was the killer."

Manuel brought my soup right then, and darned if he didn't have an order of toast with it. I wondered if he'd run to the nearest Safeway to buy a loaf of bread. I thanked him for it, and I was more grateful than he knew after I tried a spoonful of soup. My whole mouth and throat exploded. The more water I drank, the worse it became.

"You must have gotten a chili pepper," Mack said as my body burned from the inside out. "The only thing that helps is to eat some bread."

Thank God for the toast. I ate a whole slice before the

fire subsided. By then Manuel had returned with Mack's fajitas.

"*Muy picante,* eh?" he said, and winked at me. "I knew it would be good for what ailed you."

Mack and I ate in silence for a while, which was good. The inside of my mouth was too seared to talk.

"Does anyone claim to have seen Jeremiah when he came back to town?" he asked finally. "He must have contacted someone when he got here. He had to have come back for some reason."

I waited until I swallowed. "Rosalie didn't see him, and the gallery owner said she hadn't seen him either. She said the painting we saw was something a private owner had put back on the market when the story broke about his murder. Profit-taking by death, I guess."

"What about his aunt or the sister you were telling me went to the funeral with you?"

"Nope. Both of them claimed they hadn't set eyes on him in years, either before or after his disappearance seven years ago." I nibbled on my toast as something niggled at my brain. "Hey, I have it," I said as I put the toast back on the bread plate. "The sister, Juanita, said something about . . ." I paused to think of how she'd phrased it. "She called him a bearded Casanova. How would she have known he grew a beard? He didn't have a beard when he disappeared."

Always the devil's advocate, Mack said, "She could have seen it at the funeral."

"No, it was a closed casket. Dammit, she must have seen him after he came back."

"I don't want you running off to see her when you leave here," Mack said. "That Rosalie has gotten you a whole lot more involved in this than you should be."

I put my hand up to stop him. "Look, I'm through. I

promise. Besides, Rosalie has gone up to her cabin in the mountains, and I don't even know how to reach her."

The dinner with Mack, aside from a few of his usual words of caution, had lifted me out of my black mood and gotten my mind working again. Now I had something I could pass along to Stan that had nothing to do with any clandestine activities on my part.

I started up the stairs to my apartment, intent on calling him at his police number, when I saw an apparition on the third-floor landing by my door. Actually all I could see was a human head behind a stack of—what? When I was halfway up the steps, I realized that it was a stack of newspapers with a person in the shadows behind it. If I hadn't known better, I would have thought it was the homeless man who wandered down our alley every week looking for recyclables.

"Hi, Nat," I said as I reached the landing.

"Where have you been?" he asked, getting to his feet with the enviable agility of a permanently skinny person. "I was going to ask you out to dinner, but I bet you've already eaten without inviting me along."

I put my key in the door. "Who would have known you were available? Your idea of dinner is usually a midnight snack at some greasy spoon."

"How can you be insulting to the person who has just brought you, at the cost of much time and effort, I might add, every single issue of the *Tribune* from February?" With that he handed me one of the papers, which he'd apparently been folding into thirds, suitable for hurling at front porches.

The guy couldn't sit idly and do nothing for the life of him, but this must be a throwback to junior high, when he'd been a paper carrier for the same newspaper that now employed him as a reporter. I knew about his early days because I'd been his helper on Sundays until I came to the conclusion that the pay sucked. Having the pint-sized entrepreneur buy me a McDonald's at the end of our route wasn't exactly the way for him to share his wealth.

Once I opened my door, I stood aside while Nat lugged the rest of the newspapers into the room. "I took out all the ads and stuff so they wouldn't be so heavy," he explained as he dropped them on the floor by my kitchen table.

Spot jumped off the sofa and eyed both Nat and the newspaper suspiciously. The cat always looks warily at anything new or different, and of course he had to sniff the papers as soon as Nat deposited them on the floor.

"Put them on the table," I ordered before Spot decided to mark them in his own inimitable way or mistook them for the lining of his litter box. That satisfied the cat, too, who turned his attention to food, which was his only long-term interest.

While I went to get the cat food, Nat sat down at the table. "I gotta tell you, Mandy, I can't find anything in these papers that could have brought Jeremiah back to Denver."

Hadn't I predicted that Nat would go through every issue with a magnifying glass before he turned them over to me? And with his bad eyesight, that wasn't just a figure of speech.

"You can give them a look-see," Nat continued, "but if you find anything, you gotta share it with your good buddy."

I bent down to spoon cat food into Spot's dish. "And who, pray tell, might that be?"

"The guy who searched out all the stories on that art theft in Denver seven years ago"—he waved a sheaf of papers at me—"and went to the trouble of bringing them over to share with his oldest and dearest friend."

"Oh, that good buddy." I put the cat food back in the refrigerator and joined Nat at the table.

He had the articles spread out in front of him. "There really isn't much here that we didn't already know. The art theft took place while the house was on the market and the owners were out of town—"

I interrupted. "There was a woman at the funeral today who said she'd worked with Jeremiah at his real estate office. Maybe she kept in contact with him after he left and alerted cousin Joey to prospective houses to burglarize."

Nat looked interested momentarily, then continued. "There was never an itemized accounting of what was taken other than to say several Picassos and a Chagall were among the missing paintings."

"But when exactly did the theft occur?" I asked, more interested in the date of the theft than in what had been taken.

"Well, our hunch was right about that." Nat pointed to the date on the paper. "It occurred just a couple of days before Jeremiah disappeared."

I tried to read the rest of the story, but Nat's hand was in the way. "Was there ever a follow-up story about any of the artwork being recovered?"

"Zilch," Nat said in that irritating way he has of throwing in one of his slang expressions during an otherwise normal conversation. "The suburban police promised a quick recovery of the stolen items, but there was never anything about finding them."

"So we can only assume," I said, throwing in my smattering of art expertise, "that they were acquired by a private collector and hidden away for his own personal enjoyment."

"Bingo, and I'd think there would have to be a middle-man somewhere to fence the stolen merchandise."

Or "middlewoman," I thought, which brought me back to Laura Deverell.

Nat fidgeted in his seat, perhaps because Spot was sitting nearby and staring at him, hoping for some people food from the sucker who'd fed him the night before. It must have reminded Nat that he was hungry. "Want to go out and grab a bite?" he asked.

"No," I said. "I just ate, and I want to start looking through the newspapers before I go to bed."

Nat looked at me as if he were trying to size me up for a proposition he wanted to make. It couldn't be sex, because we knew each other too well for that.

"What?" I asked. "What devious thing is on your mind?"

He glanced at his watch. "Well, I'm on a pretty tight schedule, if you must know, and I was wondering if you'd be willing to feed me in exchange for my taking you on an interview I have set up for ten o'clock."

"Ten o'clock tonight? I don't think so." I was not only amazed at his offer—Nat fancied himself the Lone Ranger of the newsroom—but I didn't feel like feeding him from my woefully understocked larder. I couldn't imagine that he was dying for another one of my gourmet sandwiches after last night's fare. He had to have an angle.

"So what gives?" I continued. "Who are you interviewing, and why do you want me along?" After all, before he got on the police beat, I'd begged him to let me go along when he interviewed Mick Jagger years ago, and Nat had said in no uncertain terms that, unlike Mick, he worked solo.

"I just thought you might find it interesting," Nat said. "I found out that Jeremiah's cousin, Joey, had a girlfriend named Susan Quigley."

The mysterious Suzie Q, whom Maxine had dubbed the bimbo. This was getting tempting.

"She was at Joey's trial every day," Nat said, "and I tracked her down."

Never mind that she still lived in the same place where she'd stayed with Joey. I already knew that because of Rosalie's stakeout of the place yesterday.

"I thought you might find it interesting to see what she has to say," Nat continued.

The only possible motive he could have for asking me along was that he thought I knew more about this case than he did and might contribute some valuable questions during the interview. For once I thought he might be right.

"Want to tag along?" he asked.

I probably shouldn't do this, I told myself, not after the scolding I'd given Rosalie and the problems we'd caused Stan. But now that we'd spilled our guts to him, and he'd forced me to identify Maxine's body, it seemed like he ought to be able to overlook a few indiscretions. As for the promise I'd made to Mack, this had nothing to do with Juanita or Rosalie.

I sighed. "Okay, will chicken noodle soup do?"

"Okay," Nat said, "if you don't have any more tuna fish."

I put on the soup and changed into slacks and a blazer. It wouldn't do to wear my uniform with my name monogrammed on the blouse.

We arrived at Susan Quigley's apartment at quarter to ten. The apartment complex where she lived was in Lakewood, one of Denver's western suburbs, and it had all the yuppie amenities, including a swimming pool, now covered with a tarp, and a fountain with a frozen spray of ice.

I'd insisted on taking my car instead of Nat's Harley, so

at least we weren't out in the cold. I'd sworn last summer, after a disastrous trip to the mountains on Nat's bike, that I would never ride shotgun for him again. Tonight the heater in the Hyundai wasn't adequate for the wind that whipped out of the north, but it was better than sitting on the back of a Hog. Except for the few flakes of snow I'd seen outside Tico Taco's, the snow was still playing tag with Denver, apparently staying up in the foothills west of town.

"What does Susan Quigley do?" I asked.

"I think she's a bartender somewhere, and she said she gets off her shift at nine-thirty."

About that time we saw a woman get out of a car, the collar of her coat pulled up against the cold. She approached the building and headed for the door to the apartment we'd already scouted out as being Suzie's.

"Here," Nat said, and thrust something at me.

I looked down at the dark object in my hand. "What is it?"

"It's a point-and-shoot camera," Nat said. "I'll tell her you're my photographer."

Oh, swell. Although I sometimes took color slides of landscapes to use later as inspiration for my paintings, I didn't know anything about this camera.

"You'll have to show me how to use it."

"It's a camera for idiots," Nat said.

We were out of the car by then, and he gave me a quick lesson in how to operate it. "Just act like you're taking a few candids. The paper probably won't use them, but occasionally they surprise me."

I followed Nat to the door of Apartment 22C, looking not at all like a press photographer. At the very least I should have had a press pass tucked into the band of a fedora.

Nat knocked on the door. A minute later it opened, but

something was seriously wrong here. The woman at the door wasn't Suzie Q, the bimbo that Maxine had described as Joey's girlfriend.

"Susan Quigley?" Nat asked.

She nodded.

I shook my head. No, this couldn't be Suzie Q, Joey's girlfriend. This was Bambi, the nude model whom Rosalie had found in bed with her husband just before he disappeared seven years ago. I knew because I'd seen her earlier today at Jeremiah's funeral when Rosalie took off after her, ready to scratch her eyes out.

And then it finally hit me. Well, I'll be damned. Jeremiah's Bambi and Joey's bimbo were one and the same.

CHAPTER 20

Suzie Q the Bimbo aka Bambi the Nude Model asked us into her living room once Nat introduced himself. However, he had to grab my arm and give me a shove to make me ambulatory. I seemed to have lost all ability to move because of the shock of my discovery, and I had to work hard to mask my surprise as I followed Nat through the door.

The apartment was Danish modern, and it was nicer than mine. There was even a stairway that led up to bedrooms on the second floor. Suzie Q must get a lot of tips as a bartender, and I couldn't help wondering if Jeremiah's nude model of old worked in a topless joint nowadays.

Suzie Q tipped her head to one side when Nat introduced me as his helper. "Haven't I seen you somewhere before?" she asked, looking directly at me. Her little-girl voice and her buxomy, blond sexiness reminded me of Melanie Griffith and Judy Holliday rolled into one.

I felt like confessing, Yeah, as recently as this morning at Jeremiah's funeral. Instead I gulped and started to say something unintelligible.

"You probably have," Nat said, never at a loss for words. "Mandy's my assistant, and she gets around."

"Oh." Suzie was still staring at me. "Won't you sit down?" She gave an exaggerated gesture toward a beige sofa, which sat on a beige carpet. Realtor's beige, someone had called it, which seemed to be the color of choice if you planned to sell or rent residential property these days. "Would you like a drink?" she asked.

"No, we're still on duty," Nat said, continuing the myth that we were both bona fide members of the press.

"If you don't mind, I'll just fix myself a short one, then."

She went over to a liquor cabinet behind the sofa and poured herself a shot of bourbon as Nat gave me an inquiring look. I was sure he was wondering where she'd seen me and if he might have to reevaluate his opinion about my nonexistent social life. Just in case I'd been out carousing at the place where she tended bar.

I frowned, and he looked over his shoulder at her. "I understand that your boyfriend, Joey Perez, was closely connected to Jeremiah Atkins, who was—" He didn't get to finish.

"That's where I saw you," Suzie Q said. Apparently she'd been studying the back of my head from her position at the liquor cabinet. Too bad, because that's the view she'd had of me at the funeral. "You were at Jeremiah's funeral, weren't you, sitting with Rosalie Atkins?"

"Well, uh—"

Nat, more quick-witted than I, jumped to my rescue again. "Oh, yes," he said, "I sent Mandy to talk to the widow."

"I thought you said she was a photographer," Suzie Q pointed out in that breathy little-girl voice, but it sounded as if she might have been smarter than Maxine gave her credit for when she dubbed her the bimbo.

I looked at Nat to see how he would answer that. "She's an apprentice reporter too. I'm training her." Personally I thought that Nat was piling it on a bit thick, but he continued. "Why don't you take some photos of Miss Quigley, Mandy, while I talk to her?"

Suzie had come back over and was sitting in a matching beige chair. She had crossed her legs, managing to expose a large expanse of thigh. Nat's eyes wandered to her legs, the lout, and I was afraid he was appraising her as a potential date. She was tall and blond, which were his only criteria for the perfect woman. It didn't matter whether the women were thin or well endowed like Suzie, as long as they were at least four inches taller than he was. No wonder his relationships didn't last.

I grabbed the point-and-shoot camera and took a picture. The flash exploded in the room, and it brought Nat back from wishful thinking to reality.

"We have reason to believe Jeremiah and Joey were in some sort of business together before Jeremiah disappeared," Nat said. "Do you have any idea what it was?"

I took another picture. The camera had a motor-drive that whirred after each picture, moving the roll to the next frame. This was kind of fun. Snap, whir. Snap, whir.

"No, I don't," Suzie said. "But I didn't know Joey that well back·then."

I guess not, I thought. You were too busy having an affair with Jeremiah. How could I break into Nat's interview to ask a subtle question about that? It was too bad I hadn't known Bambi and the bimbo were the same person before we arrived at her apartment. Then I could have filled Nat in on the proper questions to ask.

"But you knew they'd been friends, didn't you?" Nat asked.

"Well, yeah."

"Actually they were cousins, weren't they?"

"So what?" Suzie shrugged dismissively, and I recorded it for posterity. She glared at me. Snap, whir.

"Joey was sent to prison for the theft of an art collection," Nat continued. "It was similar to an unsolved art heist two years earlier. Do you think Joey might have been involved in that too?"

"I didn't know anything about his business," Suzie said. "All I know was that he was a good provider, and he bought me this condo." She gave a smug little smile of satisfaction.

Snap, whir. Now her expression was recorded for the ages.

"That'll be enough pictures for now, Mandy," Nat said, and I could tell he was getting irritated at how much I was getting into my role of photographer.

"What did he do for a living?" Nat asked.

"I don't know. He said he had some investments down in Trinidad." She readjusted her skirt in a flirtatious gesture sure to raise Nat's testosterone level.

I took one final shot, moving the camera so that both Nat and Suzie were in the picture. For Nat's memory book.

Even through the viewfinder on the camera, I could see Nat give me the evil eye. For a minute I thought he was going to demand that I give back the camera.

My brain whirred to a decision. After all, Suzie already knew I'd been sitting by Rosalie at the funeral, so I put down the camera and looked directly at her.

"Mrs. Atkins said at the funeral today that you'd been Jeremiah's lover."

The statement threw both Nat and Suzie off their stride. Suzie uncrossed her legs, and slouched in her chair.

"I don't have to answer that, do I?" She looked beseechingly at Nat.

"Look, this is off the record," I said. "Okay?"

She looked at Nat again.

"Okay," he agreed, glaring at me. I could tell he was going to have a few well-chosen words for me after we left.

Apparently Nat's answer satisfied Suzie, and I'd have to make sure that Nat upheld the journalist's code of honor after we left, even though he hadn't been the one who suggested it.

"So maybe I *was* his lover," Suzie said, "but he dumped me just the way he dumped his wife. He kept promising that we were going to run off together, and then the bastard left without me."

"Then you knew he hadn't actually died when he disappeared?" I asked.

"I figured he hadn't, but I didn't know until later." She jumped up, went over to the liquor cabinet, and poured herself another drink straight up.

"So why'd you go to the funeral?"

She tossed her long blond hair over her shoulder as she came back to the chair. "It wasn't out of no respect for the dead, I'll tell you that. I was so blown away when I heard he was back in town and had gotten himself killed that I wanted to see for myself. But they had the lid down on the casket, so I couldn't even find out if it was him. I can see now I never should have gone to the funeral."

"Did you tell the detective that you were Jeremiah's lover?"

She threw her head back as if I were out of my mind. "You kidding? I told him I'd been working for Jeremiah as his model. That's all."

"And you didn't mention that you were also his cousin's girlfriend?"

"Why should I? He didn't ask."

"It seems like you must have had a lot of reasons to hate Jeremiah. It might make you a suspect in his murder."

Suzie gulped down her drink. "I didn't kill him. I didn't even know he was back in town until I read about the shooting in the paper."

Poor Nat was sitting directly across from Suzie, but for once he was speechless. Finally he said, "Let me get this straight." It must have cost him dearly to utter those words; he always wanted to be in control of the interview. "You were Jeremiah's lover, but when he disappeared, you took up with his cousin Joey?"

Suzie had recovered sufficiently to bat her eyes at him. "Why not? Jeremiah left, and Joey said he'd always been in love with me, only he hadn't wanted to cut in on Jeremiah's turf."

Honor among thieves, I thought. "And you went by the name Bambi back then?" I asked, just to double-check Rosalie's facts.

"Oh, yeah." Suzie smiled at some private memory and recrossed her legs for Nat's benefit. "Bambi Deere. That was my professional name when I was a model, but Joey wanted me to give up my career." She shook her head sadly. "He wanted me to go to work at a real estate firm because he said it was more respectable."

Whoa. "So did you work for a realtor?" I asked. "The same one where Jeremiah had worked?"

"Well, yeah," Suzie admitted.

I immediately scratched off the real estate agent who'd come up to Rosalie at the funeral this morning as a suspect. Joey'd had his own personal spy in the firm, if that was indeed how he'd gotten his leads on houses to burglarize.

"But as soon as Joey went to jail, I had to quit and go into bartending. There's no money in being a flunky in an office."

"You mean because Joey wasn't around to support you anymore?"

"Yeah, but he promised as soon as he got out of prison, he could get his hands on some money. Right after that he gets himself killed, and poor li'l Suzie Q is on her own again."

Nat had once told me "to follow the money," so I did. "What money was he talking about?"

Suzie hesitated for just a tad too long. "I wish I knew. Do you think I'd be bartending if I did?"

"Did you have any reason to believe that Jeremiah was behind Joey's attempted art theft?" Nat asked.

"No, why should I? He wasn't even around by then."

I didn't want to get sidetracked from the money, and if I didn't keep asking questions, it sounded as if we were headed for a derailment. "You're sure you don't know about any stash of money?"

"No." She shook her head a little too hard, but I didn't seem to be breaking her down.

"But what about after Jeremiah left? Did you have any reason to believe that he and Joey were in contact?" I asked.

Suzie Q leaned back and closed her eyes. I didn't know if she was in deep thought or trying to figure out how to get out of this whole conversation. "Well, if you must know," she said finally, "I used to wonder about his trips down to Trinidad to see his mother. He always came back with what he said was merchandise from Mexico."

Aha. So when Maxine professed to know nothing about what Jeremiah and Joey were up to in Mexico, she was lying.

"Was it drugs?" I asked, remembering Maxine's speculation about that.

Suzie Q shrugged. "I never saw any. I went down there

once with Joey, but his mother said the delivery hadn't arrived. She hated me on sight, and I have to say the feeling was mutual, so I didn't go back no more. After that Joey always kept whatever it was locked up in the trunk of the car and then he disposed of it as soon as he could."

"If you had to guess," Nat asked, "what would you say it was?"

"I don't have any idea. All I know is that Joey promised me that if I'd be faithful to him while he was in the joint, he'd see that I was taken care of when he got out."

"Anything else you want to get off your chest?" I asked, figuring that was a good way to end the interview and still leave it open for discussion.

I lost my momentum a little when I saw Nat grimace. I guess he thought I was being sarcastic about her not inconsiderable bra size.

Suzie shook her head, and Nat didn't seem to have any more questions either, which surprised me. Perhaps he was still reeling from the answers to the questions he hadn't known to ask.

"Okay," I said, rising from the sofa. "And thanks for your help."

Nat got to his feet too. "If we need anything else, I'll give you a call."

Suzie Q rose and escorted us to the door, although how she could do it with the liquor she'd slugged down was beyond me. I was already outside, when she put her hand on Nat's arm and pulled him back into the room.

"Maybe we could have a drink sometime," she said, "when you don't have your *assistant* with you. I might remember something else."

Grrr, I thought, and decided I'd better rescue Nat before she seduced him right then and there. Besides, I'd thought of another question.

She still had her hand on his arm when I got back to the door. "Oh, by the way," I said, "I was wondering if you remember if Jeremiah had a beard the last time you saw him?"

Nat and Suzie both looked irritated that I'd interrupted their little mutual-admiration society.

She stroked the sleeve of Nat's leather jacket, then moved her hand to her face as if the very thought of a beard gave her whisker burn. "No, Jeremiah never had a beard. I would have remembered that." Then she looked back at Nat and patted his cheek. "I like my men clean-shaven, like you."

Nat had a kind of goofy look on his face by the time I managed to pull him away from the seductress, and I decided to go on the offensive before he attacked me for taking over the interview. "Please, Nat, I hope you're not going to be dumb enough to fall for her line."

"What are you talking about? That was no line. She adored me." He flashed me a wicked grin as he practically skipped his way to the car.

Men! It took so little to please them.

"Unfortunately," he said, "I never date the people I interview. That would be against my journalist's ethics." He opened the door and plopped into the passenger's seat of my car. "And while we're on the subject . . ."

I had a feeling he was about to yell at me for taking over the interview, and I was right.

". . . what was the idea of telling her the interview was off the record, and why the hell didn't you tell me before we got here that she'd been Jeremiah's lover?"

"Because," I said as I strapped myself into my seat belt and put the car into reverse, "I didn't know she'd been Jeremiah's lover until we got here, and the only way I knew then was because I saw her at the funeral. You should have come and then you would have recognized her."

"I was working on a story about another murder last night, and like I said, I don't think killers show up at the funerals of their victims."

"I wouldn't be too sure. That's how I found out about Suzie. If Rosalie could have gotten to her, she would have pulled her hair out by its dark roots."

"Shame on you," Nat said, "making cracks about a beautiful woman like Susan." I refused to respond to that, and he continued. "So what's your excuse for forcing me to promise that everything would be off the record?"

I tried for the philosophical approach. "Aren't you more interested in getting at the truth than in writing a story that is just a bunch of innuendoes?"

Nat snorted. "Well, no, I'm interested in quoting what people say and letting the readers decide for themselves if it's truth or fiction."

"Look, I'm sorry, but I don't think she would have talked unless we promised not to write about it."

"We?" It wasn't like Nat to pout, but that's what he proceeded to do. His lower lip pooched out, and he crossed his arms and closed his eyes as if he were trying to shut me out.

I decided to put the interview in perspective for him from the point of view of the other things I knew. "Did that story you were doing this morning involve a woman who was shot and dumped in an alley downtown?"

Nat's eyes popped open. "How did you know that?"

I made a left turn at West Colfax, heading back to downtown Denver. "Okay, this is a tip from an unidentified source, understand? The woman's name is Maxine Perez, and she was Jeremiah's aunt as well as Joey's mother. The one we went down to Trinidad to see."

"Damn, how do you know these things?" Nat was sitting upright now, all thoughts of sulking forgotten.

I filled him in on the details, all from the viewpoint of "a usually reliable source."

"What I think is interesting is that Maxine apparently knew what was in the deliveries from Mexico, even though she denied any knowledge of it," I said, skirting the downtown area on Speer to get home.

"And what about the money?" Nat said, getting excited and presumably forgiving me for the off-the-record commitment. "Didn't I tell you once 'to follow the money'?"

I nodded, hoping to boost his deflated male ego.

"That's right," Nat continued, "and since I'm presuming Jeremiah knew where the money was hidden, I wonder if Suzie might have wanted it bad enough to kill him for it."

"Except I don't think she saw Jeremiah after he returned," I said, bursting Nat's bubble.

He gave me a dirty look. "Why do you say that?"

"She didn't know he'd grown a beard in the last seven years," I said. "Rosalie said he didn't have one when he disappeared."

Nat wasn't willing to give up on his number-one suspect. "She could have been lying."

"That's possible, but another person to consider is Juanita."

"And who the hell is Juanita?"

"It's Jeremiah's sister. Rosalie had looked her up, and she went to the funeral service with us."

"God, maybe I really should have gone," Nat said, forced to reevaluate his whole theory about funerals.

"She said something about his beard, and the service was closed-casket. So how did she know about the beard if she hadn't seen him after he got back to Denver?"

By then we were pulling up in front of my apartment

building, and Nat leaped out of the car, eager to get to the newsroom and start checking out the facts.

His motorcycle was parked just in front of my walkway, so I waited for him to move so that I could take the space.

But first he came over to the driver's side of the car, forcing me to roll down the window.

"What do you want now?" I asked as the wind whipped into the car. "I'm waiting for you to leave so I can take your parking space and get upstairs."

Nat reached his hand in the car. "Give me my camera—oh, yeah, and you passed your test as an apprentice reporter."

Coming from him, I considered that a high compliment. "What about as a photographer?" I asked as I handed him the camera.

"We'll have to see what develops on that."

As far as I was concerned, that was worse than my "getting it off your chest" remark, and I made a face at him as he left. However, I couldn't help feeling pleased with myself as I climbed the steps to my apartment. After all, it wasn't every day that someone like Nat complimented me on my reportorial skills.

The good feeling was shattered by the shrill ring of the telephone just as I opened the door, and that was nothing compared to what happened when I picked it up.

"Mandy," someone screamed. "You've got to come up here quick."

Up where? Who was it? I couldn't tell by the hysterical sound of the woman's voice.

"Who is this?"

It took a while for me to get her calmed down enough to understand that it was Rosalie. "I can't believe it," she said. "It's the last straw. I can't take any more."

CHAPTER 21

"Please, you have to come," Rosalie pleaded.

"What's wrong?" I asked. "Where are you?"

"I'm at the cabin."

Oh, great. I was sure it was snowing in the mountains. I had to talk her down literally as well as figuratively. Get her back to Denver where we could meet in a Denny's over some more comfort food and talk out whatever was bothering her.

"Can't you at least tell me what's the matter over the phone?"

"No, you have to see it to believe it." I had a feeling she was afraid if she told me, I wouldn't come.

"Is it money? Did you find some money?" I was visualizing a hidden stash of cash that only Jeremiah and Joey had known about. That was based on Suzie's comments a few minutes before.

"No, not anything like that," Rosalie said.

I thought about the information that Arlene, my drycleaning customer from the bank, had told me. If Rosalie's checking account never had a service charge, maybe it was because it was hooked on to another more sizable account.

Maybe that possibility would cheer her up. I started to say something, but Rosalie wasn't listening.

"You have to come," she said. "I can't believe it was here all the time, and I didn't even know about it. The police are going to think I killed him for sure. Oh, Mandy, I need you. I'm at the end of my rope, and I don't think I can go on." She began to cry.

Well, of course no matter what Mack said about people manipulating me, that was just the thing to pull me in as if I were a calf in a roping contest. She sounded—God forbid—suicidal, and I couldn't have that on my head.

"Okay, where are you? You'll have to give me directions."

It took a while to get them from her, but by the time I wrote them down, she sounded better.

"Flash your headlights when you get down to the main road in front of my place," she said. "You can't miss it. There's a bunch of mailboxes right across the road."

"Why should I blink my lights?" I still didn't think she was making sense.

"I'll come down and get you on foot. The road isn't plowed up to the house."

Just what I needed—an unplowed road.

"But what's it like on the main road?" I asked. "Can I make it up there all right? I don't want to skid in another ditch."

"You'll be fine. The snowplow went by right before I got here."

This was not what I wanted to hear, but before I could list my multiple concerns, she said, "So I'll see you in about an hour, and thank you, Mandy. You don't know how much this means to—"

The phone went dead. I spent a few minutes trying to

jostle the disconnect button on the phone and wondering why it always worked in the movies and never in real life.

"Hello, hello." The line was definitely dead, and finally I heard the familiar dial tone. I didn't even have her telephone number. She'd given it to Stan at the police station, but not to me. Well, I sure wasn't going to call and ask him for it.

And I decided not to get myself bent out of shape by the fear of driving in the snow. Just because I'd run off the road coming back from Trinidad didn't mean I was going to be permanently intimidated by winter weather. After all, that was because I'd tried to accelerate going uphill to keep from being run over by an eighteen-wheel monster. And besides, now I had a new set of tires. I was woman. I was invincible.

Let it snow. Let it snow. Let it snow. Hadn't those words reassured me the other day when I'd purchased my new tires? Yeah, I argued with myself, but that was because I was thinking of driving in the city, not setting off in my Hyundai up an unfamiliar mountain road.

I changed into jeans and a sweatshirt and put on a pair of boots, my heaviest jacket, and a knit hat that was not unlike the one Betty used to wear. Okay, I was ready for my assault on Everest, or the Colorado equivalent. Actually I wasn't even heading for the mountains, only a cabin in Coal Creek Canyon on the way up to the real mountains. So how difficult could it be to get there?

I had to turn the light on in my walk-in closet to find a pair of gloves and my flashlight. Spot had vacated the couch as soon as I turned on the lights and was now curled up on a blanket in the corner. He put his paws over his eyes to shield them from the light, and he looked so cute, I wanted to go over and pet him, but he'd been known to attack at even a lesser show of affection. So instead I rewarded him for his inconvenience by putting another scoop of cat food in his dish in case he got hungry while I was gone.

Just as I started to leave, I thought of the newspapers. I went back inside to get them. All twenty-eight issues. I stuffed them in some plastic bags, the better to carry them downstairs and from the car to Rosalie's cabin. Once she calmed down, I could put her to work helping me check them out.

It still wasn't snowing in downtown Denver or even when I got to Interstate 70, heading west. Now that I was equipped with new tires, I probably wouldn't even need them.

I relaxed about the weather and began to wonder what Rosalie had found at the cabin. If not money, what? Oh, God, what if it was the gun that had killed Jeremiah? No, it couldn't be a gun. She said it had been there ever since Jeremiah disappeared.

I reminded myself to tell her about the checking account and the possibility of another account somewhere, and of course she didn't know that Maxine was dead. I'd have to evaluate Rosalie's condition when I reached the cabin and make my decision to tell her about Maxine at that time.

I didn't even hit snow when I took the cutoff from I-70 into Golden. Instead of continuing west into Clear Creek Canyon, I took a right at the mouth of the canyon and headed toward Boulder along the edge of the foothills. Highway 93 between Golden and Boulder is known for a grade that continually slips downhill, thanks to the unstable soil underneath.

Beyond that there's a windswept expanse known as Rocky Flats where some of the highest winds in the state— perhaps the nation—have been recorded. The wind shook the car and whipped snowflakes across the road as I reached Highway 72, the turnoff into Coal Creek Canyon. It's just south of the now-defunct Rocky Flats atomic plant that once produced nuclear warheads but is now the controversial repository for the nuclear waste it produced. There's an ongoing battle to find a better home for something no one wants, and I tried to see if I could come up with a solution, just as a way to keep my mind off the storm.

Snow had begun to stick to the road, but I was optimistic that I could actually make it to the row of mailboxes Rosalie had described. At the entrance to the canyon I stopped and turned on the flashlight to double-check the instructions. Rosalie had told me the exact distance from here to the graveled road I was to take to her place. I noted my odometer and the reading it should be when I got to the turnoff. She'd said it would be another mile to the bank of mailboxes. All I had to do when I reached it was to flash my headlights and wait for her. Piece of cake.

When I was a short distance into the canyon, the wind died down, and the snow started to come down harder. Fortunately I wasn't going up in elevation too fast. If I just kept driving at a steady speed, I was sure I could make it, even if my car was notable for its lack of umph. When I'd driven the specified distance, I began to peer through the rapidly increasing storm. The graveled road was barely visible to the right, but as I got closer, I could see where the snowplow had made a run up it.

The Hyundai strained ahead on an increasingly steeper grade. You can make it, I urged my car. I felt as if I were talking to *The Little Engine That Could*. I just hoped my car was as good as the locomotive. Only a quarter of a mile to go. Only an eighth. And finally I saw the mailboxes as well as her car parked across from them. I patted the Hyundai's dashboard to signify that it had done a good job.

Then I flashed the headlights, and while I waited for Rosalie to appear, I wiggled the car back and forth in the road until I'd turned it around, hugging the mailboxes and facing downhill. I thought it was smart of me to have such foresight. By then I could see Rosalie, or at least a light that I assumed was attached to Rosalie. It was coming down a steep hill.

I bailed out of the car and yelled toward the light. The storm seemed to swallow up my voice. Rosalie's flashlight twinkled in an erratic arc as it was deflected by a veil of snowflakes. I headed toward the light and finally heard Rosalie calling my name. I waved my flashlight in response, then remembered the pile of newspapers I'd brought with me and returned to the car.

By the time I'd managed to get them out of the car, Rosalie was waiting for me on the other side of the road. I struggled over toward her with the newspapers.

"Thank God, you're here," she yelled so that the wind wouldn't carry away her words.

I was hoping she'd give me a hand with the newspapers, but her hands were full already.

"What's that?" she asked, looking at the bags of newspapers.

"What's that?" I asked, eyeing what looked like a couple of giant tennis rackets in her hands.

"Snowshoes," she said. "You need to put them on. It'll be easier to walk up to the cabin if you wear them."

Oh, right. Like I didn't have enough to contend with, what with all the newspapers. "I can't put them on," I said. "I'm loaded down with all these newspapers."

"Why?" Rosalie asked.

"I'll tell you when we get to the cabin." With that I took

several steps up the trail before I broke through the crust of the snow and went in to the top of my boots.

Okay, snowshoes it would be, but how I was going to get them on was beyond me. I wasn't a snowshoe-type of person.

Fortunately Rosalie plopped them down in the snow and directed me to step into them. She bent over and strapped them to my feet, then took half the newspapers and started up the hill.

The ascent was just as bad as I'd feared. The snowshoes were like a couple of giant platters, each capable of holding an eighty-pound turkey. They could only be made to work with my legs spread apart as if I were straddling a horse.

"Follow me." Rosalie motioned me onward and upward.

Much as I wanted to know what could possibly be so important that she had called me out in the middle of the night, that could wait until we got to the cabin too.

We waddled along up the hill like two ducks who couldn't get airborne, and the duck holding down the rear was at a decided disadvantage. Rosalie, after all, did this kind of thing all the time. I was a neophyte in the snowshoe department, and I huffed and puffed like the little engine that couldn't, despite all its good intentions.

We curved around on what I presumed was a private road, although the only reason you could tell was that there were no trees in our path. Why didn't the person who'd whacked out this road have the good sense to go straight up the hill? Finally we made our roundabout way to the cabin, which looked like Shangri-la by the time we got there. It wasn't actually that far from where I'd parked my car except that someone, in his infinite wisdom, had decided to provide access via the scenic route. Not that I would have been able to enjoy the view, even if it weren't obliterated by snow.

I'd broken out in sweat under my layers of clothes, and when Rosalie opened the door, she didn't even give me a chance to take off my outerwear, put down the papers, or catch my breath.

"Look," she wailed. "I couldn't believe it. That's what I found when I got here."

I blinked in the bright light of the cabin. At least the electricity hadn't gone off and the place was warm, partly from a fire in the fireplace. I looked around as her hand swept across the room.

Paneling had been pulled away from one wall and a suitcase was open on the floor with—what? I clomped over to it, still in my snowshoes, and saw a shirt box from Dyer's Cleaners on the floor. Beside it was an open suitcase.

"The bastard came here when he got back to town," she said. "Before he disappeared seven years ago, he apparently stashed this suitcase in the wall"—she pointed at the gaping hole—"along with the clothes he didn't want to take with him."

At least that explained how a guy could be wearing a neatly pressed and folded shirt from seven years before and yet be killed only a few weeks ago.

"He must have wanted a more 'hip' type of clothing for his getaway than what I'd packed for him," Rosalie said.

I looked back at her in amazement. "But surely that wasn't why he came back here—to reclaim some old clothes he left behind." And surely that wasn't why I had come all the way up here in a raging snowstorm.

Apparently it was—at least as far as my trip was concerned. I stared at the empty shirt box from our cleaners as Rosalie went over to a knotty-pine chair, sat down, and whipped off her snowshoes.

"But he violated my space," she said. "It wasn't bad

enough that he rose up from the dead after seven years. He came back here to our cabin—my family's cabin—and hid out for a while."

I stood in the middle of the room, trying to decide the best way to remove my snowshoes. Finally I dropped my bag of newspapers on the floor and clomped on over to another chair, where I was able to bend down and un-buckle the snowshoes. I felt like a Mafia hit man's victim who'd somehow managed to get out of her cement foot-wear.

"But there must have been some reason for him to hide out here," I said. "I still think we need to figure out why he came back to Denver in the first place."

Now that I was able to move again without looking like Charlie Chaplin on a bad day, I stood up and walked around the room. "That's the only thing you wanted me to see—an empty suitcase and a box for one of our shirts?"

Rosalie nodded, and I like to think that she looked a little ashamed. She should. "But if they see this, the police are going to think I saw him once he got back to town," she said.

"But you weren't here," I said. "You were on a cross-country ski trip higher up in the mountains." I thought about it for a minute. "No, there has to be more to it than the fact that he hid his suitcase here for seven years and then came back for a change of clothes."

I looked over where the paneling had been removed from the wall. "Was there anything else inside?"

She shuddered. "I didn't want to look. I know he's dead, but I was afraid he'd booby-trapped the place."

I went over to the hole in the wall and took a peek. I could see what looked like a board leaning against the inside wall.

"There's something here." I motioned to her, then

pulled my head out of the recess. "Bring a flashlight and come over here."

It would have been easy enough to stretch out and grab whatever was leaning against the interior wall, but I have to admit that I wanted the flashlight to make sure there weren't any cobwebs or creepy crawlers between me and the board. Not to mention booby traps.

She handed me the flashlight, and I ducked my head back inside. There didn't appear to be any obvious spidery obstacles, so I reached in with my hand and pulled out the board. Only it wasn't a board.

"It's just an empty picture frame," Rosalie said, sounding disappointed.

I wasn't disappointed, though. Once I got it out, I could see that there was something else inside the wall. I ducked back inside the hole and retrieved it. Another frame. Both of them were ornate, gilded frames, and when I inspected them, I could see that someone had used a sharp object to cut out the canvases that had once been inside them.

The paintings must have been the real things Jeremiah had come back to the cabin to reclaim.

CHAPTER 22

"**W**hat do they mean?" Rosalie asked, staring at the picture frames. "Jeremiah never had any frames like those."

"I think they might be from some paintings that he stole before he disappeared," I said, and then had to explain to Rosalie about the art heist just before Jeremiah left. "Maybe the owner of the paintings that were stolen will recognize these frames."

But there was something wrong here. The empty frames raised more questions than they answered. The newspaper article that Nat had shown me from seven years ago indicated that more than two paintings had been stolen, although an exact number was never specified. If Jeremiah had been the thief, where were the other paintings?

I grabbed the flashlight and went back to the recess behind the ripped-out paneling. I swept the beam to either side, and I could see all the way to the corners of the building. There was nothing more.

When I crawled out of the hole, Rosalie was staring at the empty frames as if the paintings that had once been inside were gaping holes in her past. "I can't believe that

Jeremiah could have been an art thief." Then she let out a strangled laugh. "But why not? Nothing about him was what I thought it was."

I turned the frames over. There obviously wasn't enough of the canvases left to identify the paintings.

Rosalie went over and collapsed on an Early American sofa that was so worn, it looked as if it had actually been used back in the Revolution. "But if he stole some valuable paintings, why wouldn't he have disposed of them before he disappeared?"

I could only speculate. "Maybe they were too hot to handle at the time, and he couldn't risk getting caught taking them to Mexico. So he must have stashed them here until he could arrange for a buyer."

The only problem was where were the other paintings if indeed these empty frames were part of that seven-year-old art heist? If Jeremiah hadn't been able to dispose of these, how had he gotten rid of the others? Well, maybe there had been no others; maybe the owner had claimed there'd been more just to collect the insurance on them.

And that of course meant I'd been falsely accusing Laura Deverell and her sidekick, Kevin, of being fences. And it sure didn't explain about those packages Joey kept going to Trinidad to pick up at his mother's after Jeremiah disappeared. It also didn't explain the phantom money that Joey had promised Suzie after he got out of jail. Unless of course Jeremiah was planning to come back once Joey was released, sell the paintings, and split the profits with his cousin.

"We need to call Detective Foster and tell him about this," I said, looking around the room for the phone.

"I'm sorry," Rosalie said. "The phone went out while I was talking to you. I'm so thankful I got through to you before the line went dead."

I was always the optimist. "Maybe the phone company has it fixed by now."

Rosalie was shaking her head. "Not until the storm is over." Nevertheless she pointed to the phone on a small table by the entrance.

I went over and picked it up. I prayed for a dial tone, but there was nothing. I guess I'd been expecting a miracle, and a wave of claustrophobia or some other more obscure fear swept over me. We were cut off from all contact with the outside world. I wasn't used to that. I'm a city girl, and I wanted to go home.

I glanced outside at the storm that had picked up in intensity, and I was afraid we'd be truly snowed in by morning. It reminded me of Agatha Christie's play, *The Mousetrap,* where a bunch of people are snowbound with a murderer. I pressed my face to the window even though I couldn't see but a few inches in front of me and tried to keep from hyperventilating. Calm down, Mandy, I told myself, as I put my face against the ice-cold pane. It wasn't as if there was a whole houseful of would-be murder victims with a killer running amok among us. I breathed deeply and turned back to Rosalie, who looked somewhat less hysterical now that she had me here as her protector.

Fine help I'd be. I was the one with the strong desire to grab my coat and flee into the night. Anything to keep the walls from closing in on me.

I finally remembered the newspapers. If he'd come back for the paintings, then why was he carrying a month-old newspaper with him? I still thought the paper must have something to do with the timing of his visit.

"Okay," I said. "I have a project for us to do while we wait out the storm."

Rosalie didn't pay any attention to me. "So what do you

think happened to the paintings that were inside the frames?"

"Obviously Jeremiah came here to get them. He must have cut them out of their frames, rolled them up, and taken them with him when he left. Picking up the clothes was just incidental."

"Maybe we don't need to tell the police about this. They're going to think I met him here, helped him collect the paintings, and then killed him when we got back to town." She began to get agitated again.

She might be right, but I wasn't about to tell her that. "They're not going to think anything of the kind, and we *are* going to tell them."

What she needed was to get her mind off this. And what I needed was some help looking through the newspapers. After she'd dragged me out in a raging storm, it was the least she could do.

"Look, I found out that the one thing Jeremiah was carrying when he was killed was a copy of the *Tribune* from February," I said, "and a friend of mine got me all the back issues."

Rosalie glanced over at the papers she'd asked about earlier. "How do you know that?"

I said the police had found out about it. Never mind that they found out from me, who found out from Betty. "Anyway there could be something in them that doesn't have anything to do with you and the paintings. Something that brought him back to Denver at this specific time. I was just getting ready to go through them when you called. Now you can help me."

"Anything is worth a try." She came over to where I was dividing the papers into two piles and grabbed the first half of the month. I took the second, and for about an hour we plowed through the papers page by page.

"I haven't found a thing," she said finally.

"Neither have I, but we need to keep going."

She shook her head. "I can't even see anymore. I have to close my eyes for a few minutes." With that she went back over to the sofa, where she pulled an afghan up over her legs.

It was getting cold in the cabin, which may be why my claustrophobia had receded, but when it came to hyperventilating or freezing to death, I opted for the first. I went over and threw another log on the embers in the fireplace.

"That feels good," Rosalie said a few minutes later. "I finally think I can get some sleep—now that you're here, and I don't feel like I'm alone with Jeremiah's ghost. You can have the bed up in the loft."

I glanced over to where a ladder led up to a half-floor that jutted out from under the eaves. Just what I needed. A space so narrow that it looked like a berth in one of those old "train" movies that Mack liked so well.

I felt myself begin to get short of breath again, and rather than try to sleep in such close quarters, I went back to the newspapers. I finished the ones that Rosalie had been looking at, then went back to the last week and a half of my pile.

It was a strange, eerie experience when I finally saw what could have brought Jeremiah back to Colorado. I hadn't really expected to find anything obvious, but the moment I saw it, my mental antennae went up. Yes, this could be it. The headline popped out at me because it had to do with money: AS GOOD AS HITTING THE LOTTERY! it said, CHECK THE TRIB ON SUNDAY.

I continued down to the story:

The *Tribune* will try to help the state give back more than $16 million to Coloradans this Sunday, when it publishes a 12-page Great Colorado Payback section with the names of 18,000 persons on the state treasurer's lost-and-found list.

The next paragraph continued,

The Great Colorado Payback is a result of the state's unclaimed property law, adopted by the legislature in 1987, which seeks to locate owners of inactive accounts from banks and other financial institutions, as well as insurance firms and companies that issue stock and dividends. The accounts must have been inactive for five years.

This was more than a lightbulb above my head. This was like a whole laser show. Rosalie had said that her five-dollar account had been turned over to the state. And Arlene, the banker, had speculated that maybe the reason no service charges had ever been taken out was that it had been hooked up to another account.

I was almost sure I'd found the missing money, and what's more, the article said,

If someone sees his or her name or the name of a relative on the list, the person should check at the state treasurer's office and the money will be returned to the rightful owners at no charge.

When I glanced over at Rosalie, she was sound asleep. No need to wake her until I was positive. I rushed ahead to the Sunday paper and grabbed out the special section, which luckily Nat hadn't removed. He apparently hadn't read it either.

I ran my finger down the first column of 8-point type. Then up again. And there it was. So tiny I could hardly see it. *Jeremiah Atkins*. But it might as well have been in 72-point type, the way it jumped out at me.

"Hey, Rosalie." I was so excited I couldn't keep my voice down. "I found it."

She was on her feet immediately, her hands to her chest as if I'd shot her or else given her a heart attack.

"I'm sorry," I said. "I didn't mean to scare you, but I found what I think may have brought Jeremiah back to Denver."

I ran over and gave her the paper, my finger at the place where his name was.

She turned the newspaper over and looked at the front page, and then she said a strange thing. "Damn, so there was another account." Her face paled as if she thought she'd said something out of turn, and then she appeared to try to cover for it. "So what is this?" She punched at the front of the special section.

I got the distinct impression she knew exactly what it was and that she'd been searching for the money all the time.

The last thing I wanted to do was let her know the vibes I was getting. Instead I answered her question. "Remember how you said the five dollars from your checking account was turned over to the state?" I watched her as I spoke. "Well, apparently it was connected to another account that Jeremiah had, and that's why you never got any service charges."

She didn't react the way I would have thought someone would if they'd just found a hidden cache that they might inherit. "I'm sorry, Mandy," she said. "I think I'm too tired to grasp this tonight. If you're not going to use the bed upstairs, then I think I'll go up there. Maybe I'll be able to understand what you're saying in the morning." With that she went over and turned off the light switch and climbed the ladder to the half-attic. "You should try to grab some sleep too." She disappeared over the top.

I went to the sofa, sat down, and stared into the fireplace. What had just gone on here? It definitely sounded as if Rosalie had known about the money all the time, although maybe not how to get her hands on it, and she hadn't wanted to admit that to me.

And then I had a spooky thought. What if Rosalie had gone up to the loft to figure out her next move? What if she'd decided I knew more than I needed to know? Not much was making sense, and I knew part of it was because I was so tired.

But I couldn't help thinking of Mack's warning to me that Rosalie was manipulating me. He'd meant that she was getting me more and more deeply involved in her problems, and it had made me irritated. But what if she had been manipulating me in a more sinister way to uncover all these other suspects so that she wouldn't look like the only one with a motive for his murder? What if she'd killed Jeremiah because he wouldn't tell her where the money was? What if she decided to kill me, too, now that I knew about the money? What if she were waiting in the loft right now for me to fall asleep?

I glanced up above me, but all I saw was the beam across the edge of the loft and the ladder going up to it. I went over to the window and looked out. The snow had quit. I didn't know if I was imagining things or if my suspicions had some validity; all I knew was that I wanted out of the cabin and I wanted out now.

The snowshoes were leaning against the wall by the side of the door, and I went over and picked them up. I somehow managed to strap them to my feet, once I got my boots on. Then I put on my heavy parka, stuffed the single issue of the newspaper into the back of my jeans, clamped my knit cap down over my ears, and grabbed my flashlight and purse.

I looked up to see if Rosalie was noticing any of this. So far, so good. If she missed me later, maybe she'd think I was just out for a breath of fresh air. I studied the ladder for a few seconds. Oh, what the hell. I walked over as quietly as a person wearing snowshoes can walk and removed the ladder.

It wasn't until I was a few yards from the house that I realized she'd never buy the "fresh air" story once I'd removed the ladder. Besides, the air might be fresh, but it was like ice when it hit my lungs. When I exhaled, it came out of my mouth like fire from a dragon.

I didn't know at exactly what point I'd decided to try to get back to Denver. All I knew was that there was something so weird about the way she'd acted that I didn't want to stay in the cabin to find out what it was. Probably I should have just left a note that said I couldn't sleep and was going to try to get home, snow or not. And I knew one thing for sure, when I got there, I was going to throw everything in Stan's lap and let him figure it out. It was way beyond me at this point.

Luckily I'd turned my car around when I got here. It was heading downhill, and surely I could plow through the drifts to the main road with my new tires. If worse came to worst, I could abandon the car and snowshoe the rest of the way to the main road and try to hitch a ride from there.

I could tell that a lot more snow had fallen since I'd gotten to the cabin, but my snowshoes skimmed across the surface as if I were walking on water. Why bother with the road that had annoyed me so much on the way up to the cabin? Instead of wending my way down to the car by the scenic route, I beamed my flashlight straight down the hill and cut through the trees.

When I was about halfway to the car, I saw a sharp drop-off in the snow, probably a gully that hadn't filled with snow. The only way to get across was to go down one side and then up the other, not an easy task on snowshoes. I half slid and half jumped into the trenchlike depression, but I landed a lot harder than I expected. The snow gave way underneath me, and my right snowshoe kept on going. The next thing I knew my foot, snowshoe still attached, was wedged into the rocks somewhere down below.

CHAPTER 23

"This is another fine fix we've gotten ourselves into," I muttered when I managed to pull my backside up out of the snow. But the words from the old Laurel and Hardy movie didn't cheer me the way they'd cheered Mack on a long-ago occasion when I'd said them to him.

Damn, I was probably going to die here, unable to get myself out of the hole I'd gotten myself into. I tried to pull my foot out of the rocks down below, but the snowshoe was wedged into a crevice I couldn't even see. The more I tried to pull myself free, the tighter the snowshoe seemed to be held in place by the rocks. I was afraid to move my other foot for fear it would break through the crust of snow and throw my whole body down even farther into the crevice.

I should have brought the ski poles I'd seen leaning against the wall of the cabin or at least followed the trail, which any smart person would have done. Better yet, I should have stayed in the cabin. What did I really think would happen—that Rosalie would kill me? Even if she'd known there was money somewhere, that didn't mean she'd killed Jeremiah and Maxine. It was just my over-wrought imagination playing tricks on me.

But what if she'd gotten me up here so that I'd think that I discovered the picture frames when she'd known they were behind the wall all the time? What if she'd been at the cabin when Jeremiah showed up a week ago?

She could have killed him. She sure had enough reason to hate him, and she didn't have an alibi for the time of his death. I couldn't figure out an explanation for Maxine's murder, but maybe the waitress had a good reason to have us followed from Trinidad. Maybe Jeremiah had told her something about Rosalie that had sent her to Denver for a confrontation with my friend.

I was thinking about this in a fragmented way as I kept trying to wrest my foot from its prison, but I was as help-less as a rabbit caught in a hunter's snare. At one point, when I finally decided to bear down with my other foot, the snow began to crumble beneath me just as I'd feared. I held my breath and stood still for a moment, hoping the snow wouldn't give way completely.

So far I didn't think I'd sprained my ankle, but I was afraid that would happen if I wasn't careful. It was proba-bly the least of my worries. I was going to freeze to death unless I could manage to find something to give me lever-age to pull myself out. I attempted to move forward in the hope of reaching a bush that was sticking out of the snow on the other side of the gully. If I could just grab it, I could hold on to it as I tugged at my foot. It didn't work. It was just barely out of my reach.

I stood up again, then tried to twist around so I could put my hands against the slope I'd just slid down. That was an even worse idea. I fell backward against the side of the slope, loosening a miniavalanche that came down on top of my head. I spat flakes out of my mouth, but crumbs of snow clung to my lips and eyebrows.

"What the devil happened to you?" Rosalie asked from somewhere up above me.

I cowered in the snow. I couldn't see her because I couldn't turn around, but the glow of her flashlight was shining down into the pit. She must be Superwoman, able to leap tall buildings at a single bound or at least jump down from an attic loft.

I shook the snow out of my face and managed to swivel my head around enough to see her shadow behind the light. She was standing right above me on the edge of the bank. What was she going to do—watch me die?

"What are you doing here?" she asked.

"I went for a walk." I realized it was a feeble explanation, but it was the best I could come up with when my insides were a frozen lump just like the rest of me. "My snowshoe is stuck in some rocks—" My anger finally overcame my fear. "So are you going to help me out of here or just let me flounder around?"

Rosalie didn't answer for a few seconds, and it scared me to death. "Okay," she said finally. "Grab this ski pole and maybe you can use it for support." She slid the pole toward me and I grabbed it and stuck it in the snow. Eventually I managed to right myself, but so what? I was now in approximately the same position I had been when I crashed through the snow in the first place.

"Now, see if you can lean on it and reach down and unstrap the snowshoe," Rosalie said.

Easy for her to say. She could probably touch her toes with the flat of her hands as well. I squatted down and dug in the snow until I reached my foot, but I didn't have enough dexterity with my gloves on to free it from the snowshoe. I ripped off the gloves and tried again. It was like trying to fix a piece of equipment at the cleaners while wearing a blindfold. I couldn't see what I was doing, but miracle of miracles, I finally managed to unhook the clasp and part company with the snowshoe.

"I have another pole here, and I want you to turn around and grab it. Then I'm going to try to pull you up the side. Use that other pole to help."

For a few seconds I thought of trying to get up the other slope and make a run for my car. Then I turned around and faced her, despite the fact that only minutes before I'd thought she might be a killer. Anything seemed preferable to freezing to death.

"Grab your purse," she said.

I looked around to where it had landed when I fell. "Got it," I said as I put its strap over my shoulder and grabbed the ski pole.

With her pulling and me using the other pole to push myself up the slope, I managed to get to the top. I stood beside Rosalie for a minute and shook the snow off of every part of me. My near-death experience seemed to have lessened my earlier panic about Rosalie. A grateful person such as myself now reasoned that she would never have rescued me if she was going to kill me. If she wanted me dead, she could simply have waited for rescuers to find my frozen body in a trap I'd created for myself.

"Come on," she said, picking up the flashlight that had been focused down into the gully.

I'd lost my own flashlight, not to mention the snowshoe, and I was left to hobble along on the one remaining snowshoe while my other foot broke through the crust of snow with every step I took. It was not a pretty picture, and I was both contrite and embarrassed by the time we reached the cabin.

"Thanks," I said, once we'd both shed our winter garb

and I'd taken off my remaining snowshoe. "I'll buy you another pair when we get back to town."

Rosalie waved off the offer and went over and stirred the fire. I followed her and warmed my frozen body in front of it. "This makes up for every favor I've ever done for you," I said. "You don't owe me for anything after this."

"What the hell made you go for a walk in the middle of the night?" Maybe she really had bought that pitiful explanation of my midnight stroll.

"Claustrophobia," I said, and it was partly true.

"But why did you move the ladder? I woke up and you were gone and so was the ladder."

I looked over and there was another ladder, although somewhat more dilapidated, in its place.

"Luckily I stuck that one"—she motioned to the rickety ladder now leaning against the edge of the loft—"upstairs when I had a carpenter make me a new one last summer."

Okay, she wasn't Superwoman, but I no longer thought she was a killer either.

"I woke up when I heard the door close," Rosalie said, "and then I discovered that the ladder was missing. It took me a while to realize that I still had the old one stashed up there."

"All right, I'll tell you," I said. "You reacted so funny when I told you about the money that I couldn't help thinking you might actually have killed Jeremiah."

She drew back from me. "You couldn't think that about me, could you, Mandy?"

"Well, yeah, I could, and all I wanted to do at that moment was get to Denver and dump everything on— uh—Detective Foster's desk and never think about it again."

"I could never kill anyone." Rosalie looked as if I'd slapped her in the face.

"So why did you act so funny when I showed you Jeremiah's name on that list?"

"If you must know, after my money was turned over to the state, someone wanted to know why it had never had any service charges." Rosalie began to pace nervously. "We finally decided that the charges could have been waived because it was hooked into another account. I inquired at the bank, but they wouldn't tell me anything, and then I realized that the other account could have been turned over to the state too." She stopped and came back to where I was standing by the fire. "So two years ago I went through the same kind of list you just showed me, but the only account they would tell me about was the five-dollar-and-eighty-nine-cent one that had been in my name too. It really startled me when you showed me the current list. Why would his name show up again?"

I was glad I had a possible explanation for that. "Because I think he and his cousin Joey might have had a joint account, and it ceased to have any transactions when Joey went to prison."

Rosalie nodded, but she didn't seem happy. "You know, Mandy, the first thing I thought about when you showed me his name on that list was that now people would think for sure I killed him, and the terrible thing is you did."

"Well, I don't anymore."

"Thank God for that." She went into the kitchen alcove and started looking through a cupboard. "I think I need a drink. I have some brandy somewhere. Would you like one too?"

"Sounds good," I said, but I didn't budge from the fire.

She found the bottle and poured the brandy into two snifters, then came over and handed one to me. Between the fire and the brandy, I finally began to get warm.

"The trouble is most other people are going to remain

convinced I'm guilty"—she smiled for the first time all night—"since I won't have the opportunity to save their lives."

"You'll never let me live this down, will you?" I picked up another log and put it on the fire, then turned and stood facing her. "So what we have to do is figure out who did kill Jeremiah, based on what we've learned."

Rosalie didn't even have to think about it. "I think Maxine did it. She didn't show up at his funeral, and that's suspicious."

I knew the time had come to tell her about Maxine's death, and it took about fifteen minutes before she recovered from the shock.

"Now that you're aware of that," I said, "we need to analyze everyone else we've met and try to figure out if any of them had a motive to kill Jeremiah."

"Then it's Bambi," Rosalie said. "Actually I've always thought it was her."

At this point I decided I might as well tell her about my trip with Nat to see Susan Quigley, and how Bambi Deere, Jeremiah's lover, and Suzie Q, Joey's girlfriend, were actually the same person.

"Oh, my God," Rosalie said. I was afraid she couldn't handle many more revelations, but the news seemed to start her adrenaline pumping. "That clinches it. It has to be Bambi, doesn't it? She had the most reason to hate Jeremiah."

"I don't know, but I did find out that she once worked for the same realty firm where Jeremiah worked. There was the art burglary just before Jeremiah left. Plus, the break-in Joey was arrested for two years later was also art related. So I'm wondering if the three of them might have been involved, using information from the realtor's office."

"Oh, she was, I'm sure of it."

I nodded. "If the newspaper is what brought Jeremiah back to Denver, there's also the question of who sent it to him," I continued. "Since Joey's name might have been listed on the account, it's possible Bambi knew where Jeremiah was and sent him the paper. She acted kind of funny when she talked about the money, and it would probably have been the only way for her to get Joey's part since they weren't married."

Rosalie was really getting into this now. "Of course, and she killed him because he wouldn't share the loot with her."

"But there's one thing that bothers me. She didn't seem to know that he'd grown a beard while he was in Mexico, and even though no one claims to have seen him when he returned, Juanita let something slip about his beard."

Rosalie drew back, almost as appalled as when I said I'd suspected her. "No, not Juanita. You'll never make me believe that she could kill her own brother."

"Just hear me out. She called him 'a bearded Casanova' in the car after the funeral. How would she know that if she hadn't seen him after he got back?"

"No, it can't be Juanita," Rosalie protested.

"But think about it. Her husband disappeared about the same time Joey was arrested, and one of the articles about his arrest mentioned the possibility of a second person involved in the crime. It could have been her husband, and if the whole burglary thing went back to Jeremiah, she could have hated him for that. For that matter, maybe Juanita's husband joined Jeremiah in Mexico."

Rosalie shook her head, but she didn't put up any more of an argument.

"Then there's the owner of the art gallery I was telling you about," I said. "The one who was selling Jeremiah's painting for fifty thousand dollars. Someone at another gallery told me she'd been a friend of Jeremiah's, and I've wondered if she could have been the fence for the stolen paintings. Still that's no real evidence, except that something suspicious happened yesterday just as you came by to get me for the funeral." I told Rosalie about the assistant who gave me the fictitious name at the cleaners. "That really made me wonder. . . ." I'd come to the end of my list of suspects, and I looked over at Rosalie.

"There isn't a lot to go on with any of them," she said.

"Yes, but it's little things that usually trip up a killer." I waited for her to respond, and when she didn't, I continued. "Do you know anyone else to add to the list?"

"No, just Bambi. I tried to ask Detective Foster what he found out from her, but he wouldn't tell me."

"Did Jeremiah ever mention the gallery owner, Laura Deverell?"

Rosalie shook her head.

"There's the one thing we haven't considered—whatever Jeremiah was shipping to Joey from Mexico. It could have been drugs, but it doesn't make sense that he would send that through the mail—so it was probably something else. Maybe his paintings, which he continued to turn out from there. They would have brought a lot more money once there was all the publicity about his disappearance."

"I guess."

"I know I asked you once, but are you sure there isn't some way you could tell the difference between the paintings he did while the two of you were together and any he might have turned out after he disappeared?"

"No, not really. They all looked pretty much alike to me. Prehistoric monsters hiding in primeval forests." She thought for a moment. "And he always hid a little horse somewhere down in the corner of each painting."

I remembered reading that Al Hirschfeld, the famous

New York Times cartoonist, had done the same thing. He hid the name of his daughter, Nina, in all his cartoons as his trademark. So why wouldn't an artist whose speciality was hiding dinosaurs in ancient forests have done the same thing?

"You mean that it was kind of like his signature?" I asked.

"That's right," Rosalie said, "sort of like the little bunny they always have somewhere on the cover of *Playboy* magazines."

That was interesting, and it might explain the little horse that Betty saw that day in the art gallery, the one that led to our precipitous exit from the gallery.

It wasn't until late the next afternoon that I thought to ask Rosalie more about the horse, which led to the weirdest conversation I have ever had with Betty.

CHAPTER
24

We were snowbound for the rest of the night and much of the next day. The enforced captivity finally allowed me to get a good night's sleep, although most of it was done during daylight hours. I guess I'd gotten to the point where I couldn't think about Jeremiah's murder anymore, and I was content to give it up, knowing it was really Stan's problem.

Although I declined to accompany her, Rosalie managed to snowshoe over to a neighbor's house in the morning. The neighbor had a cell phone, and Rosalie was able to call Mack at the cleaners to tell him about my predicament and that I wouldn't be in that day.

"He didn't sound happy," she said when she returned.

"That doesn't surprise me," I said from the Early American couch where I'd been napping. After all, I was sure Mack was already thinking "I told you so" about how Rosalie had manipulated me. And I guess maybe that was true, but if a friend can't manipulate you once in a while when she needs your help, who can?

I went right back to sleep and continued to doze throughout the day until the snowplow finally made it up the hill in the late afternoon. Then I had to spend another hour trying to dig my car out from under last night's snowfall and the snow that the plow threw on it. Rosalie was busy on the other side of the road clearing the snow away from her car.

While I was shoveling out the Hyundai, I began to wonder about the little signature horse that Rosalie said Jeremiah had always hidden somewhere in his paintings. Had it been a prehistoric eohippus—the "dawn horse"—as I'd suggested to Betty that day at the gallery, or had it been some latter-day horse like a pinto pony?

"What kind of horse was it?" I yelled across the road at Rosalie.

"What?" she yelled back.

I walked over to her, ready to use any excuse to take a break. "The horse that you said Jeremiah used as his signature?" I asked. "I was thinking maybe he changed it to an armadillo or something when he moved to Mexico—you know, his own personal little joke."

I knew it was an off-the-wall thought, but if he had done something like that, the police might be able to search for any paintings that were from his postdisappearance era seven years before. I was convinced an artist wouldn't just give up his art, especially when there weren't a lot of other things he could do in exile.

"No, it was just a horse." She took off her gloves and leaned against her car, which, unlike mine, was nearly uncovered by now. "It was a white horse," she said, "and he told me once that it symbolized the West and the Denver Broncos. He was a big Broncos fan and always went over to a friend's to watch the game, but he never wanted me to go along."

She looked sad for a moment, and I couldn't help remembering how Juanita had said her husband and Joey would meet down at some sports bar to watch the game. I wondered if Jeremiah met them there; then I had an even more interesting thought.

"You mean it was like the Broncos' logo?"

"Well, no, not exactly. I think he didn't want to get in trouble about copyright infringement. It was just a white horse, rearing up like the Lone Ranger's horse, Silver."

"Really," I said. I started back to my own car, glad that I was no longer wearing the extra set of snowshoes that Rosalie had found for me to wear down the road from the cabin.

Halfway to my car I had another thought. Suddenly my energy level was at warp speed. I needed to get back to Denver and see Betty. I attacked the remaining snow as if I were a woman possessed. When Rosalie finished with her car, she came over to help me.

Within twenty minutes we had the snow cleared away. I handed her the snowshoes so that she could return them to the cabin before she headed back to town herself. She said she didn't want to stay at the cabin right now, and I was glad of that.

"I'll call you later tonight." I held my breath as I climbed into the car and tried the ignition. I was relieved when the car started, and I patted the dashboard. "Good car."

Now I had to spend some time rocking it back and forth in its tracks since I hadn't been able to get all the snow cleared away from around the tires. Finally it lurched forward, and I was off. It was all downhill from here, and I was optimistic I could get home with no more trouble. Wasn't that Newton's theory of gravity, after all—what goes up must come down?

I made it out to the main highway and then on into Denver in record time, but still it was nearly seven thirty and already dark when I got there. I whipped by my apartment to feed Spot, who jumped down from the sofa when I switched on the light. He made it known that he wasn't happy with me. Every bit of food in his bowl, even the dry stuff he normally disdained, was gone.

He didn't seem disappointed that I wasn't staying once I had restocked the feed bowl. I didn't bother to change clothes, just headed over to Betty's apartment as fast as I could. She would have left work more than three hours ago, and I was hoping that she'd be home, not out on a date with the doll doctor.

When I reached the entryway of her blocklike apartment building, someone was just leaving. I caught the door before it closed and went inside. That way I didn't have to wait for her to buzz me in.

I thought I heard murmurings from inside the apartment when I reached her door. I knocked, and there was dead silence. I knocked again and heard a shuffling, like mice scurrying back to their holes. Still no one answered the door.

I knocked a third time. Still nothing.

"I know you're in there, Betty," I said, "so let me in."

"Who is it?" I recognized her voice, and she sounded as if she was just on the other side of the door.

"It's Mandy. Let me in."

"Just a minute." Now she sounded farther away. There was a muffled sound of words I couldn't understand and then what sounded like "—pull out your shirt."

I must have misunderstood. All this had started with a shirt, yes, but her words didn't make any sense.

"Are you going to let me in or not?" I yelled.

More shuffling, and I could have sworn I heard Betty say, "Now look like you're tucking it in."

"Betty, I don't have all night," I yelled.

The door opened, but darned if she didn't have it on a chain.

"Betty, it's just me—not the vice squad."

Little did I know that I might have been closer to the truth than I would have liked to think.

"Uh—just a minute," Betty said, peeking at me with one eye through the narrow opening in the door. Then she looked around and seemed to be motioning to someone with her head.

"This is ridiculous—" I said, but Betty closed the door on me, and then after what seemed like an inordinate amount of time, she removed the chain and opened the door again. But she still didn't seem willing to let me in.

"What brings you out on a night like this, boss lady?" she asked with a strange look on her face.

"Look, may I please come in? I need to talk to you."

I heard a door slam inside the apartment, and then she opened the front door wider and stepped aside. "Why didn't you say so? Yeah, come on in."

And there on the other side of the door stood Arthur, the doll doctor, with a silly grin on his face and his white hair even more disheveled than usual. He'd always reminded me a little of Albert Einstein, but now he looked like Albert Einstein on a *really* bad hair day—or maybe a good one, depending on what kind of spin you put on it.

His shirt was buttoned wrong and the tail wasn't tucked into his pants on one side. Oh, dear God, I must have interrupted them while they were having sex. It was something I didn't even want to contemplate.

"Geez," I said, suddenly embarrassed. "I hope this isn't a bad time."

Betty was innocence itself. "Nope, we weren't doing nothin'."

In the background Arthur's face turned red, but he still

managed to keep his polite demeanor. "No, not a thing, Ms. Dyer. Won't you have a seat." He motioned me to the sofa, which had a rumpled blanket at one end.

I took a chair instead and looked over at the food on the kitchen table. If I didn't know better, I would have thought I'd interrupted their dinner, but why would they act so guilty if I had? Unless of course their libidos had gotten out of control midway through the meal.

They both came over and sat down side-by-side on the couch.

Never one to mince words, Betty said, "So what was so all-fired important that you kept banging on the door?"

"I wanted to ask you about that painting we saw at the art gallery the other day," I said. "What did the little horse look like down at the bottom of the picture? Do you remember?"

"Sure I remember. It looked like a horse."

"Did it look as if it might be rearing up on its hind legs?"

"Not to me, it didn't."

"Was it white?"

"Yeah, white and mean-looking." Betty pinched up her face in a mean-looking expression.

Just then there was a noise that seemed to come from beyond her bedroom door. "What was that?"

Betty put her hand up to her ear. "I didn't hear nothin'. Did you, Artie?"

Arthur shook his head, but he didn't seem able to make eye contact with me.

I heard the noise again, followed by "Damn." A male voice, no less.

"There," I said. "You must have heard that."

"Not me," Betty said.

"Perhaps it was the neighbors in the apartment next door," Arthur suggested.

Betty nodded. "Oh, yeah, they're a rowdy bunch."

I hoped so, because if that wasn't where the sounds were coming from, there might be a *ménage à trois* going on here, which would totally blow my mind.

I didn't hear any more noises from what I hoped was the apartment next door, so I continued. "You said the little horse was peeking out from under some red leaves—"

"Yeah, scared me half to death." She turned to Arthur. "You should have seen it, Artie."

"How many leaves were there?"

"Oh, for criminy's sake, how am I supposed to remember that?"

"Just approximately."

Betty seemed really disgusted with me now, but willing to play along just to get rid of me. "Okay, let's say three. How's that?"

"Could it possibly have been an orange mane on the horse—not three red leaves?"

Betty looked at me as if I needed a few more holes punched in my belt, which is an expression my uncle Chet used to say when he thought someone was strange. "Who ever heard of a horse with an orange mane?" she asked.

"Just think about it? Forget about the color. Could it have been the horse's mane?"

She considered it for a few seconds. "Okay, but if it was a mane, it was about the dumbest one I've ever seen. It hung down over the horse's head like he had bangs."

"Thanks," I said, and started to get up.

Betty and Arthur popped up in unison, seemingly more overjoyed to see me depart than I was myself.

"I'll walk you out to the front stoop," Betty said when I got to the door.

"You don't have to do that." I took one final look at the bedroom door. "I know the way out."

"No, I'll tag along." Betty was in the hallway and had the door closed before I could stop her. Good. At least I wouldn't be tempted to hang around out in the hallway for a while to see what else I might hear from inside her apartment.

Since it wasn't like Betty to play the perfect hostess, I was suspicious about her sudden concern to escort me to the front door. I thought maybe she wanted to explain what was going on in her apartment, but apparently she wanted to make sure I left.

"So why'd you want to know about the picture, boss lady?" she asked.

"I think the painting might have something to do with the murder of that man in the alley where your friend lived."

She came to a complete stop on the first-floor landing. "So did what I tell you help?"

"I don't know. I think I'm just going to have to go to the gallery and take a look for myself."

Betty continued with me toward the front door. "Do you think that's a good idea this time of night? The lady who ran the place was pretty nasty."

"Oh, it'll be fine." I glanced at my watch. "But I'd better hurry before the gallery closes."

"Want me and Artie to come with you?" Even as she said that, she edged me toward the front door.

"No." I probably didn't need to sound quite so emphatic, but the last thing I needed was for Betty to go with me on another little covert visit to the gallery. She's the one who'd called attention to us and nearly got us ejected the first time.

"Well, be careful," she said as she pushed me out the door.

It wasn't like Betty to worry about me, and I was getting mixed messages here. Still I tried to reassure her. "Don't worry. I'll make sure there are other people around when I go inside."

"Good," she said, "you do that. Anything so old Honest Abe can go home." The door slammed shut in my face.

So much for her concern, but maybe she was right. Maybe I should wait until morning. I rejected the idea even as I thought of it. Now that I was on to something, I couldn't wait to see if my theory was right or not.

The Broncos had changed their logo a few years ago, along with the complete design of their uniforms. If Jeremiah had used a modified version of the logo as his "signature," might he have also changed his horse when the Broncos did?

It was Betty's description of the horse that made me think he had. The Broncos' new logo had a horse with an orange mane that flowed out behind it in three different parts. Could Betty have mistaken the mane for red leaves, especially if Jeremiah didn't copy it exactly? I had to find out.

CHAPTER 25

The sign on the front door said the gallery would be closing in half an hour. Unfortunately there was no one inside right then, so I hung around on the street for a while hoping some art lovers would decide to wander in.

I even considered asking some passerby if he would like to accompany me into the gallery, and in retrospect that's probably what I should have done. There was a lot of foot traffic out tonight, not to mention cars passing by all the time, but unfortunately there didn't seem to be anyone but me who wanted to browse through the gallery.

I stood outside, like a runner waiting for the starting gun in a footrace. It was only a few short yards to that second room where Jeremiah's painting hung just out of my line of vision, but I couldn't seem to get off the starting line.

I checked my watch. The place would be closing in ten minutes. No one had come out of the back room in the time I'd been waiting. I could have been in and out of there a dozen times if I'd just had the nerve to make a run for it in the intervening minutes.

At that moment a couple stopped to look in the window. This was probably the best chance I was going to have, and since the coast appeared to be clear inside, I rushed the place.

Damn. A little bell tinkled above the door as I opened it, and I stretched up on tiptoe to silence the clapper. The door banged shut behind me. Maybe whoever was in the back room would think the customer had started in and then gone back out again.

With a bit of luck the salesperson could even be a part-time employee who had never seen me before. I hurried across the main gallery, heading for the spot where I'd seen the painting. I rounded the divider that separated the two rooms and came face-to-face with a blank wall. I turned around to retreat and came face-to-face with Kevin. He'd apparently been lurking in an alcove off the main room at the front of the store.

"Mom," he said in a loud voice, "there's someone here to see you."

Before I had a chance to consider that Kevin was her son and bound to be on her side, Laura Deverell emerged from the back of the building. She was every bit as glamorous-looking as she had been on that earlier occasion when Betty and I had been here, but now she was wearing a mauve pants suit with stiletto-heeled shoes to match. Could anyone this well turned out be evil?

"Oh, you're the woman who was here the other day, aren't you?" she said, "I bet you've come back about the Atkins painting. I could tell you were interested in it the last time you were here."

What did I say now? Maybe I could just play along that I was a wealthy art lover with an unlimited bank account. "Well, yes, I would like to have another look at the paint-ing."

"It's in my office. Would you like to come back there

with me?" She motioned for me to join her out of sight of the front window.

"Maybe you could bring it out here. I'd like to see it in museum-type light and"—I probably shouldn't have paused so long—"and I'm waiting for a friend who was going to meet me here to take a look at it."

Laura and I both glanced toward the front door. Regrettably the window shoppers who'd been staring inside the gallery only minutes before had disappeared.

"Kevin," Laura said. "Will you lock up now? If Miss Dyer's *friend* shows up, you can let her in." The way she made that last remark indicated that she thought I was running a bluff.

Before I could even move, Kevin turned the sign on the door to CLOSED and flipped a couple of locks. He then turned, arms folded, like a bouncer ready to see that no one else got in or out.

I gulped, but I hoped they didn't notice. "If this is a bad time, I can come back tomorrow." Hadn't I just said something similar to Betty and Arthur?

"No," Laura continued pleasantly. "I just wanted to be able to give my full attention to you if you're really interested in acquiring the painting."

Something suddenly occurred to me. "How did you know my name?"

Laura smoothed back the blond tendrils of hair at the side of her beautifully coiffed chignon. "Well, I saw it on your uniform, dear, and I made a few discreet inquiries around the neighborhood to see if you might be a sincere devotee of the arts."

Maybe Mack was right, after all, about the reason for Kevin coming over to the cleaners, but somehow I didn't think so. Still, I had to play along.

"So if I could just see the painting one more time, I

think I might buy it." Actually what I wanted to do was get out of there with or without seeing the horse.

Suddenly Laura's face turned mean—a whole lot meaner than Betty's when she'd tried to show me how the horse looked. "You don't really expect me to believe that, do you?"

"Well"—I glanced at the front door, and Kevin was still standing there, looking for all the world like an exterminator instead of a blond surfer guy—"uh, yes, I do."

"Maxine warned me about you," Laura said, her voice still smooth as silk.

"Excuse me?"

"She called me from work Monday night and told me that you and Jeremiah's widow were down in Trinidad asking a lot of questions."

I was standing where anyone from the street could see me, but how would they know that I was in urgent need of help. I finally decided my only choice was to make a break for the back room, where I already knew there was an exit. After all, Kevin had mentioned it when Betty and I were here. He'd said there was a hysterical woman at the door demanding to see Laura.

I started to take a step in that direction.

"Where do you think you're going?" Laura said. "Stop right where you are."

I stopped. The gun in her hand convinced me. Unfortunately the divider between the two sections of the gallery shielded the gun and Laura from the view of any passersby.

I was still in the line of sight from the street, and I stood as still as the statue of the wire unicorn that Betty had thought looked like bent clothes hangers. It had been moved from the front of the gallery and was right beside me on a waist-high pedestal.

"How did you know Maxine?" I asked.

"I became acquainted with her when her son would bring me the paintings Jeremiah did in Mexico. She seemed like a nice woman, but she eventually became a liability, even before that afternoon you were here with your aunt."

Laura's candor was not exactly a good omen that I was going to get out of here alive, and I felt as if I had a glob of plaster of Paris in my mouth when I tried to speak. "So you killed her?"

Laura shrugged her shoulders. "I didn't have any choice. She tried to blackmail me because Jeremiah called her after he got to Denver. Seems he thought I'd been ripping him off all these years, and he made the mistake of telling her we were going to meet on Friday night two weeks ago to settle things."

I really regretted that she'd told me all this. The only thing I could think of in response was to tell her something that might rattle her composure enough that I could somehow set off a burglar alarm. Surely an art gallery had a burglar alarm.

"What did Jeremiah do, drop by the gallery after he sold you his latest painting," I asked, "and find out that you'd put a fifty-thousand-dollar price tag on it?"

Her mascara-rimmed eyes closed until they were little black slits. "How do you know it's a new painting?"

"Oh, that's simple, and everyone's going to know you bought it from him after he came back. He'd changed his 'signature' on the bottom of the painting."

I saw her tense. "What do you mean?"

"Surely you knew he used a little horse as his trademark—kind of symbolic of the West and the Denver Broncos. He was a big Broncos fan."

Her nostrils flared, like a bucking horse as it came out

of the chute. "I don't know what you're talking about. You aren't making any sense."

"Well, why don't you take another look at the painting? He changed the horse so that it has a little orange mane—similar to the Broncos' new logo."

Of course I had no way of knowing if that was true or not, but I could see that the news had shaken her. The gun wavered for just a second, and I pressed whatever small advantage I had.

"So the painting couldn't have been from before he disappeared, now, could it?"

She seemed to recover nicely after the initial shock. The gun steadied in her hands, and she smiled at me. "Sadly," she said, "the painting has been taken off the market. But enough about me. Please move over here out of view of the door." She motioned toward the back room.

I was sure I'd be dead the moment I moved. I glanced to the front of the gallery one last time in hopes of seeing someone looking in from the other side. All I saw was that Kevin was no longer guarding the door. He was coming toward me in a menacing fashion.

"Get going," Laura said. She edged forward until she was finally in the line of sight of any passersby, but what good did it do if there was no one there to see her?

I took one more look at Kevin. Behind him and beyond the glass front of the gallery, I saw a faint movement. I must be going crazy. It was the silhouette of a man in an extra-tall top hat. Either it was a Fred Astaire look-alike on his way to a fancy-dress ball or it was Honest Abe.

Right then all hell broke loose. Something hit the windows and the door at the same time. Glass shattered, and an alarm started going off.

Kevin turned, ran to the door, and threw it open to chase the vandals away. Someone hit him on the head, and he dropped like a rock. Laura rushed forward when she saw him fall. I grabbed the only thing available, the wire unicorn, and brought it down on her gun hand.

The gun crashed to the floor, but not before going off and sending a ricocheting bullet through the already broken window. She was running toward Kevin, or maybe she was just trying to escape. Four people blocked her path.

They were probably the most unlikely assortment of people she'd ever seen: a tall skinny guy in a stovepipe hat, a guy who was about half his size and looked like Albert Einstein, and a woman in a bilious green pants suit. Behind them was a tall black man with a cell phone. Mack was calling the police.

I went over and picked up the gun just in case Laura had any ideas about turning and trying to escape through the back door.

Honest Abe and Arthur had her pretty well subdued by the time I got to them.

"Told you Artie and me should have come with you," Betty said, giving me her gap-toothed smile, only it wasn't gap-toothed anymore. I noticed that she'd had a false tooth put in the vacant space, and her grin would never be the same again.

"I was very concerned when Betty told me what you were planning to do," Arthur said. "You should never have come here alone."

"Good thing he talked Betty into calling me," Mack said. "You never will learn to stay out of trouble, will you?"

Honest Abe, who actually had a little of Abraham Lincoln's craggy look, didn't say a thing—but what did I expect from a mime? It was kind of nice. At least there was one person who wasn't chewing me out.

CHAPTER 26

This was D day. The Date. Dinner. Decision time. Take your pick. In fact it might even be triple D day. The day the Detective Dumps the Dry Cleaner.

I had to find out what was on Stan's mind, and besides, I was itching—sorry, just a figure of speech—to find out what had been happening with Laura Deverell in the two weeks since her arrest.

"I hear you're going out tonight with *that cop,*" Betty said when I went to the break room to get a cup of coffee.

"Where'd you hear that?"

"It don't matter, but if you want my opinion, you could do better than him."

She was right about one thing. I didn't want her opinion.

But I sat down with her anyway. "So tell me, is Honest Abe still staying at your place?" Unfortunately he'd slipped away from the gallery in all the confusion of Laura's arrest and Kevin's departure in an ambulance, and I hadn't had a chance to see what it would be like to have a conversation with a guy who doesn't talk.

Betty was speechless for a moment herself. "So you knew what was going on that night at my apartment, huh?"

"I figured it out."

"Well, I didn't want you to find out he was hidin' there and call the cops."

"So is he still there?"

"Nope, he's gone, and I've gotta tell you, I was kind of glad when we caught the killers so he could go back home." She leaned over toward me and winked. "It was kind of puttin' a crimp in things with Artie and me, if you know what I mean."

Okay, I'd heard enough, but I hoped maybe this whole experience had made her realize how she'd overstayed her welcome at my place a couple of times herself.

Stan took me to a seafood restaurant that night, and before we even ordered, a waiter came over and put bibs around our necks. If all restaurants did that, it could hurt the dry-cleaning business, but at least it protected my only good dress. And I certainly hadn't wanted to buy a new one if I was about to be dumped.

"So what's going on with Laura Deverell?" I asked after the waiter brought us a couple of glasses of wine.

"The D.A. filed two counts of first-degree murder against her, but her son has already pleaded guilty as an accessory and agreed to testify against his mother."

"What about the missing paintings from Rosalie's cabin? Did they ever turn up?"

"We found them in a storage locker that Laura rented, and they *were* part of that burglary seven years ago. Kevin said his mother was furious that Jeremiah hadn't handed them over to her at the time, but she paid him for them anyway. She just hadn't managed to dispose of them by the time she was arrested."

I'd already identified Jeremiah's painting that I'd seen in the gallery that day with Betty. The horse at the bottom was definitely different from the "signature" on his earlier paintings, but whether it had an orange mane was open to debate.

"I have to tell you, it looked to me like the horse was peeking out from under some red leaves," Stan said, then took a sip of wine.

So what did a detective know about art? He'd thought the people in my mural about the history of fashion didn't look real either.

I'd already found out that Juanita wasn't involved in the murder. She had a legitimate reason for knowing that Jeremiah had grown a beard. She'd come all the way across town on the bus the night before the funeral for a viewing of the body. Her name was the only one in a book that visitors signed that day.

As for Susan Quigley, she denied that she'd sent the list of dormant account holders to Jeremiah, but she was apparently the only person who knew where he was. Besides, she was awfully upset when the money—fourteen thousand dollars and change—was turned over to Rosalie as Jeremiah's widow. She said half of it should have belonged to her because Joey's name had been on the account and he and Jeremiah had agreed to share the money that Laura paid them for Jeremiah's paintings from Mexico. However, Rosalie gave half the money to Juanita as Joey's next of kin.

"Did you ever find out about Juanita's husband, Carlos?" I asked, partially as a delaying tactic to avoid getting into the personal stuff. And in fact I'd even wondered if Stan was being so forthcoming with me for the same reason.

"No, and there are some things we'll probably never

know," he said, "but we did find some of Jeremiah's things in a hotel room downtown."

"What kind of things?"

"Most of the four thousand dollars that Laura had paid him for his latest painting and the two stolen canvases that were in the storage locker."

No wonder Jeremiah had been angry when he saw the fifty-thousand-dollar price tag on his painting the next day when he stopped by the gallery.

"But we never did find his wallet or any ID," Stan added.

I wondered if Honest Abe had stolen them when he went through Jeremiah's pockets. No, surely not *Honest* Abe.

The waiter came to take our order, but Stan told him we wouldn't be ready for a while.

"Look," he said when the man left, "I've had something on my mind for a long time, and it's something you need to know."

Okay, here it came.

"When I went up in the mountains that time, and Erin pulled my shift at work—" He stopped and took a gulp of wine. "The reason I wanted to get away was that I needed to think about our upcoming marriage. While I was up there, I finally decided to break off the engagement, but when I came back to Denver and found out she'd been killed, I felt so damned guilty that I've never told anyone else about it."

"Oh." I didn't know what else to say, but then I'm not as good as Mack when it comes to playing psychiatrist. "I'm sorry."

"So when I thought I was falling in love with you, it scared the hell out of me."

He thought he'd been falling in love with me. Wow.

"Anyway I realized I was scared shitless about getting married. My dad was a drunk and a wife beater, and I don't ever want to get into something like that."

"Wait," I said. "Back up a minute. Are you insinuating that I'm looking for a husband?"

He looked embarrassed, but I was too irritated to care.

"Please, you've met my mother. She's on her sixth husband, and the jury is still out on whether this marriage will last or not. I don't want to be like her any more than you want to be like your dad. I've been married once, and that was enough for me. Now, can we just relax, order dinner, and see what develops?" I sounded like Nat with his smart-aleck comment about my photographic ability, but I couldn't resist a final comment. "So you thought you were falling in love with me, huh?"

Things moved along fairly well after that. I even invited him up to my apartment after our date a few nights later. He kissed me with enough passion to light up the room. Who needs a 120-watt bulb when rockets are going off all over the place?

We moved urgently through the darkness to my couch, and that's when the real fireworks began. There was a bloodcurdling yowl, and Spot went clawing and scratching his way up Stan's back and off the sofa, hell bent for the closet.

I turned on the lights after-the-fact and removed Stan's torn shirt to look at his wounds. They were deep and ugly-looking, and although the cat was up-to-date on his shots, Stan was due for a tetanus booster. I gave him an old sweatshirt to wear to the hospital and took him to the emergency room.

So much for our romantic evening. But wounds heal, and we have plenty of time ahead to see what develops.

P.S. I bought Stan a new shirt, which I'm going to give him on our next date. He's fixing dinner for me at his apartment, and he swears his dog Sidecar may bark but he won't do me bodily harm.

MANDY'S FAVORITE CLEANING TIP

To remove grape juice from your shrink-proof cotton garments (Chapter 11), stretch the stained area over a bowl and pour boiling water from a height of several feet through the stain. This also works with red wine.

For grape juice or wine spills on carpets (also Chapter 11), blot, sprinkle with table salt to absorb the stain, then brush out and vacuum. Repeat until the stain is gone. Other methods of removing red wine include club soda, white wine, or if the carpet is colorfast, spraying shaving cream from an aerosol can on the stain, then sponging with water. Always blot first and keep blotting until all moisture is gone.

Available wherever books are sold November 9, 1999

"A series that accomplishes the task of being satisfyingly different"

–Mystery News

❑ Dancing Made Easy
by Phillip DePoy
22618-x $5.99/$8.99

Also Available

❑	Easy	22494-2	$5.99/$7.99
	Easy as One, Two, Three	22617-1	$5.99/$8.99
❑	Too Easy	22495-0	$5.99/$7.99